D0948246

MURDER
IN THE
READING ROOM

Center Point
Large Print

Also by Ellery Adams and available from
Center Point Large Print:

Murder in the Locked Library

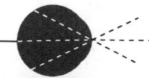

**This Large Print Book carries the
Seal of Approval of N.A.V.H.**

MURDER
IN THE
READING ROOM

A Book Retreat Mystery

ELLERY ADAMS

CENTER POINT LARGE PRINT
THORNDIKE, MAINE

They were going to look at war, the red animal—war, the blood-swollen god.
                                —Stephen Crane

I am sure that if the mothers of various nations could meet, there would be no more wars.
                                —E. M. Forster

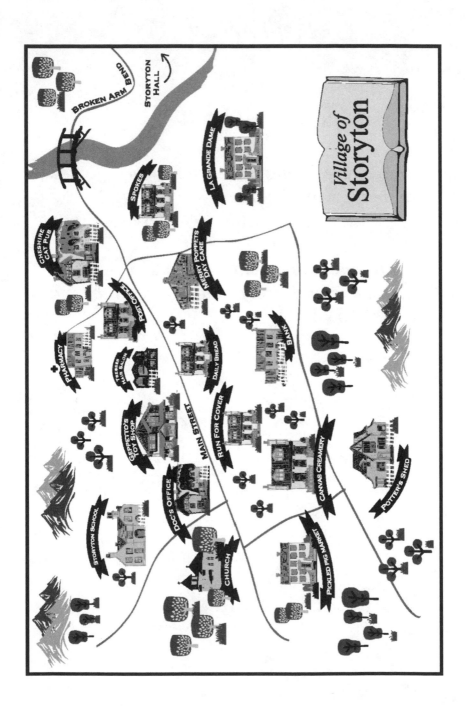

Welcome to
STORYTON HALL

OUR STAFF IS HERE TO SERVE YOU

Resort Manager—Jane Steward
Butler—Mr. Butterworth
Head Librarian—Mr. Sinclair
Head Chauffeur—Mr. Sterling
Head of Recreation—Mr. Lachlan
Head of Housekeeping—Mrs. Pimpernel
Head Cook—Mrs. Hubbard

SELECT MERCHANTS OF
STORYTON VILLAGE

Run for Cover Bookshop—Eloise Alcott
Daily Bread Café—Edwin Alcott
Cheshire Cat Pub—Bob and Betty Carmichael
The Canvas Creamery—Phoebe Doyle
La Grande Dame Clothing Boutique—
    Mabel Wimberly
Tresses Hair Salon—Violet Osborne
The Pickled Pig Market—the Hogg brothers
Geppetto's Toy Shop—Barnaby Nicholas
Hilltop Stables—Sam Nolan
The Potter's Shed—Tom Green
Storyton Outfitters—Phil and Sandi Hughes

BILTMORE ESTATE PERSONNEL
Manager—Ramsey Parrish
Former Manager—Julian Douglas
Head Gardener—Gerald Tucker

BACKSTORY CLUB OFFICERS
Clarence Kelley
Michael Murphy
Archibald Banks

CHAPTER ONE

Jane Steward was heading straight into the storm.

At least I can see the storm in front of me, she thought as she turned on her windshield wipers. *The other storm I'm racing toward is invisible.*

The rain struck the pickup truck with timidity, but Jane knew that it was only a matter of moments before the drops changed from hesitant taps to a machine-gun hammer.

Ahead, the sky was smudged with gray. Soot-colored thunderclouds hovered over the ridges of the Appalachian Mountains. In some places, the clouds had descended low enough to cover the valleys in mist. There were farmhouses and fields in those valleys, but Jane couldn't see them. Her world consisted of a dark road and a darker sky.

And noise.

One of the windshield blades squeaked with every pass, and as the rain picked up its pace, Jane had to turn the wipers to a higher speed setting. This made the squeak sound like the whine of a petulant child.

Between the rain, the wiper blade, and the groan of tractor-trailer engines adjusting to the winding road, Jane was glad for her taciturn passenger. Landon Lachlan, head of Storyton Hall's Recreation Department, rarely spoke. He'd spent most of the trip from Virginia staring out the window in contemplative silence.

Jane could guess his thoughts. Or more accurately, she could guess which questions were whirling inside his head. The same questions whipped around in hers, echoing the wind that threatened to push their vehicle into the next lane.

Gripping the steering wheel harder, Jane focused on what awaited them once they were clear of the storm.

Ahead, in Asheville, there would be new hazards. If Jane's theory that her lover was being held captive at Biltmore Estate was correct, there would be danger.

If she was wrong, then Edwin Alcott was beyond her reach. She was certain he would die if she and Lachlan didn't rescue him, so here they were.

Edwin had been gone for nearly two months. During that time, his sister, the manager of his restaurant, and Jane had all received postcards written in Edwin's hand. Jane didn't think the words were his. However, she'd had no way to prove this until her twin sons, Fitzgerald and Hemingway, were kidnapped. It was at the abductor's house that she discovered a clue to Edwin's whereabouts.

The clue had been a Templar cross pinned to a map. The location was Asheville, North Carolina.

Jane was positive that the pin marked Biltmore, and she was equally sure that the Templars were responsible for Edwin's disappearance.

How I wish I had that map, she thought mournfully. But the map was gone. It had burned, along with the rest of the kidnapper's house. That despicable man had taken Jane's sons. He'd threatened what she held most dear. He'd taunted her, deceived her, and laughed at her. He'd also provided invaluable hints about Edwin. And while it seemed like madness to take a madman at his word, Jane was doing just that.

Her sons had come out of the ordeal unscathed. As for Edwin's welfare, Jane couldn't say. She needed to see him, face-to-face, before she'd believe that he was okay.

Not too long ago, she would have laughed over the absurdity of her mission. If someone had told her that she came from a long line of Stewards who vowed to guard a secret library filled with rare and potentially dangerous books, she would have called them crazy. If she'd had an inkling that the Knights Templar was still a functioning society, and that it had split into multiple brotherhoods, one of which was determined to locate Storyton Hall's hidden library at any cost, she would have gone elsewhere following her husband's death.

"We're not making very good time," she said to Lachlan as lightning rippled over the dark sky.

11

Seconds later, there was another brilliant fracture. And a third.

"I have a feeling caution won't be a priority once we get to Biltmore," Lachlan said.

Lachlan was part of an elite group called the Fins. These former military men had specialized combat training and had pledged to protect the members of the Steward family with their lives. Despite this, they managed to pull off their Storyton Hall staff member personas with conviction.

Jane glanced at him and shrugged. "I'm just a resort manager attending the Luxury Lodging Symposium, and I plan to use that cover to my full advantage. We have three days to find Edwin. We don't have time for caution."

"If Biltmore is a secret Templar hideout, their people will monitor everyone who passes through their doors. Just as we do," Lachlan said. "We might be able to count on one employee. When I met Master Gardener Gerald Tucker at a lecture on rehabilitating raptors, I knew he was a really decent person. After researching Mr. Tucker, Mr. Sterling agrees that the veteran gardener could be helpful. But he's very devoted to Biltmore. He won't tell us a thing unless we gain his trust."

"Mr. Tucker is Army Retired? Like you?" Jane asked.

A curtain fell over Lachlan's features. He didn't like to discuss his time as an Army Ranger. The atrocities he'd witnessed during his tours still haunted him. These ghosts from the past appeared without warning, paralyzing his emotions and causing him to withdraw deep inside himself. Jane had witnessed this sad transformation, but Lachlan always came through for her and her family when called upon. Jane just hoped that his PTSD would remain dormant over the next few days. Lachlan was the only person she had to rely on, and Jane needed his fighting and tracking skills. In addition to these talents, women of all ages found Lachlan irresistible. If Jane could exploit his roguish good looks and quiet charm to save Edwin's life, she would.

"What about your Biltmore manager friend?"

"Julian Douglas." Jane repeated the name for Lachlan's benefit. "He's a former manager. He doesn't have the level of responsibility he once did, but he can access restricted areas of the estate. Mr. Douglas still has the keys to open all those doors closed to the public."

Lachlan glanced out the window. "From what I've read, that's a ton of doors."

Jane lapsed into a reflective silence. Lachlan was right. There were lots of doors. And rooms. And outbuildings. The French-style chateau had 250 rooms and over four acres of floor space. Storyton Hall was an impressive manor house, but Biltmore was colossal in comparison.

One of the things that separated the two estates

was money. Biltmore's coffers never seemed to run dry. The gardens and lawns were impeccably manicured, there were multiple inns, shops, and eateries on the grounds, and an army of staff kept everything in tip-top order.

During the past week, Jane and Sinclair, Storyton Hall's head librarian, had read everything they could about Biltmore. They began their research by familiarizing themselves with its construction. They studied blueprints, photographs, newspaper articles, letters, and archived materials referring to the chateau.

Jane felt that she knew George Vanderbilt and his incredible house after reading so much material. However, she was sure there were plenty of details left unwritten concerning Biltmore and its occupants throughout history. She still had much to learn.

"The house features multiple secret passages," Jane had said to Sinclair a few nights ago. "Most of the books state that Vanderbilt requested these because he wanted his rooms to have a seamless look." Jane had pointed at two photos. One showed a door in the billiard room that was noticeable only because it was ajar. Otherwise, it would have been camouflaged by its wood paneling and framed art. The second photo was of a similar door. This one was in the breakfast room. Jane imagined that other doors were better concealed than these and had shared her theory with Sinclair.

"I have no doubt there are more hidden doors, passageways, and rooms than we'll read about in books," Sinclair had said. "There is another resource to consider, Miss Jane."

Jane had met her mentor's kind, intelligent gaze and known what he was implying. He was suggesting she enter Storyton Hall's secret library to search for material on both Vanderbilt and his famous house.

Immediately following this discussion, Jane and Sinclair had taken the staff stairs to the only private apartments in Storyton Hall. After greeting the residents of these apartments, Uncle Aloysius and Aunt Octavia, Jane had entered her great-aunt's closet and removed the tiny key once kept inside a locket around her neck. The key was now hidden in a compartment on the back of her oval wristwatch. Uncle Aloysius did the work himself, astonishing Jane with his cleverness.

"I can be quite handy," he'd said, touching the brim of his ratty old fishing cap. "I've made my entire collection of flies and hooks, you know."

"Your tinkering is most charming, Aloysius," Jane's great-aunt had said. "We all need hobbies. They prevent us from becoming dull."

As Jane had slid the key into the keyhole behind the air vent in her great-aunt's closet, she thought about George Vanderbilt's hobbies. Like the Stewards, he was a devoted reader and collector. His personal library contained over twenty-two thousand books, and he kept a record of all the titles he read. He was also friends with famous authors like Edith Wharton and Henry James.

Jane hadn't wanted to unearth dark secrets about George Vanderbilt—a bibliophile, an art lover, and a conservationist. Luckily, there was nothing nefarious to discover. She and Sinclair had ascended the narrow spiral staircase to the secret library, where they'd searched a document drawer filled with letters. They'd found a single missive written by George Vanderbilt to Uncle Aloysius's father. The letter was congenial and polite—written to an acquaintance, not a close friend. Vanderbilt praised Storyton Hall and its reading rooms and went on to mention the books he'd recently read. He finished by inviting Cyril Steward to visit Biltmore.

"I'm not sure why this letter is here," Jane had said to Sinclair. "It's completely innocuous."

Sinclair had looked pensive. "There must be a reason it was stored here and not with the rest of Mr. Steward's personal papers."

"I'll take a photo with my phone. We can study it later."

Jane and Sinclair had returned to the Henry James Library and resumed their reading on the Vanderbilts and Biltmore.

The blare of a car horn snapped Jane out of her reverie. She checked her rearview mirror and glared at the minivan behind her. It was within inches of her bumper, and she was already driving over the speed limit.

"You okay?" Lachlan asked.

"I just want to get to our hotel," she said.

A green road sign ahead indicated that their journey was nearly over. Jane relaxed her grip on the steering wheel.

Most of the drive had taken them up and down mountain roads. These curving, fog-covered rises and descents were unpredictable. It had been a harrowing trip, and Jane was ready for it to be over.

Lachlan helped her navigate around Asheville. She took the Biltmore exit, and he directed her to Village Lane.

"I still don't understand why we didn't book rooms on the estate grounds," Lachlan said as Jane pulled into a gravel lot facing a four-story Tudor Revival structure made of pale brick.

"I don't want to use Biltmore's Wi-Fi or have Templar eyes on us."

Lachlan grunted in approval. Any remaining doubt dissipated when he realized that the hotel was a series of apartments lacking a front desk or any visible staff.

After checking her text messages for the access codes, Jane opened the outside door. She and Lachlan ascended to the second floor, and Jane used the second code to unlock the apartment door. Inside, there was a living room, a dining

17

area, a full kitchen, and two bedrooms with en-suite bathrooms.

Jane's bedroom overlooked a small patio garden, but she ignored the rain-soaked café tables, the lush greenery, and the bubbling fountain. Instead, her eyes traveled to where she knew the chateau sat, perched like a king on a high throne, atop a rise in the distance.

"I'm coming, Edwin," she whispered.

Though Jane had been to Biltmore as a young girl, the sight of the magnificent building still took her breath away.

Lachlan was also gazing over the main lawn toward the house. He frowned and said, "It'll be a challenge to find a human needle in that massive haystack."

"Ernest Hemingway warned that we should never confuse movement with action. We don't have time to waste moving around the estate without purpose."

Jane took out her phone and reread the text message Julian Douglas had sent ten minutes ago. "Mr. Douglas promised us a behind-the-scenes tour. Now is when your interest in roof pitches and drainage comes into play. You get to the attic, and I'll work on the basements."

"Got it."

After handing their tickets to a Biltmore employee stationed at the front doors, Jane and

Lachlan entered the house along with dozens of tourists.

It had been years since Jane had last seen Julian Douglas, but there was no mistaking the round-cheeked, round-bellied gentleman with the silver hair standing in the Winter Garden Room. Julian watched the passersby with friendly interest, but when he saw Jane, his mouth curved into a broad smile.

"Ms. Steward! It's an honor to have you grace these halls." He pumped her hand enthusiastically. "I understand you're interested in a peek behind the scenes."

After introducing Lachlan, Jane said, "That would be lovely. It'll be fascinating to compare notes between Biltmore and Storyton Hall. We have secret passages and rooms, though not as many as this house, I'm sure."

"Those hidden doors and corridors never fail to intrigue," Julian said. "I can't tell you how many guests have ducked under our velvet ropes or dashed through closed doors clearly marked with STAFF ONLY signs to search for a secret hideaway they read about in a book or on the Internet, which can be as wildly fantastical as any novel."

"Personally, I like the informal spaces," Jane said. "The butler's pantries, laundry rooms, root cellars. These places aren't pretty, but they hold so much energy. I can imagine teams of servants bustling around the kitchen, hanging sheets up to dry, or rushing to answer a bell."

Julian beamed at her. "I also enjoy the inner workings of large houses. What about you, Mr. Lachlan?"

Lachlan pretended to hedge. It was only after Julian assured him that another guide could be called should his interests depart from Jane's that Lachlan said that he'd like to visit Biltmore's tallest points.

"Ah, a man who wants to conspire with the grotesques!" Julian exclaimed cheerfully and pulled a small walkie-talkie from the breast pocket of his suit coat.

He called for another tour guide, and a slender man with a ginger-colored beard arrived a few minutes later. After introducing himself to Lachlan, the two men ascended the stairs.

Julian's private tour took Jane through Vanderbilt's library, den, and the tapestry room. As they began their descent to the basement, Jane asked questions about the arrangement of the lower rooms. Julian supplied her with many facts and figures, but since he steered clear of rumor and supposition, it was impossible to ferret out Biltmore's best-kept secrets.

Of course, Julian might be unaware of a Templar presence. The secret society hardly advertised itself, and its members wouldn't betray themselves to anyone. In light of this, Jane tried to use her own powers of observation to search for clues. She had to keep reminding herself that she wasn't a tourist. She was the manager of Storyton Hall, a single mother of two, and Guardian of the secret library and its treasures. Her role as Edwin Alcott's lover had been last on her list. Until now. Now, Jane was putting the other parts of her life on hold until she found Edwin.

Julian showed her the kitchens, the laundry and drying rooms, the vegetable pantry, and the servants' bedrooms. As he led Jane down to the sub-basement, she wondered what the house had been like without guests—back when George Vanderbilt was a bachelor. Had he wandered through his empty rooms, wishing for more intimate company than his books could provide? Or had he built his home in the middle of nowhere because he craved solitude? Or was it secrecy he wanted?

Again, Jane wondered if there was a connection between Vanderbilt's love of books and his zeal to acquire fine and rare objects that indicated a link to the Templars. If not the Templars, perhaps he was affiliated with another secret society. Jane believed Vanderbilt had been a good man, but people were multifaceted, and she knew there was far more to George Washington Vanderbilt than what appeared in books.

She suddenly realized that Julian had spoken and was waiting for her to respond.

Jane realized they were in The Dynamo Room. She said, "I read about this machine in a book called *Seraphina and the Black Cloak.*"

Recalling how Seraphina, the main character, had found hiding places throughout the house, Jane felt a tingle of hope. Perhaps her request to view the lowest level of the house would bear fruit.

After examining the walls surrounding the massive furnace and coal bins, Jane could sense that their tour was coming to an end. She had to coax Julian into showing her the storerooms along the length of the house. These were most likely to have a secret entrance to a hidden room or to a staircase or tunnel leading deeper underground.

However, Julian assured her that there wasn't anything of note in the storage rooms. He even offered to take her to one as proof. When she saw a long, shadow-filled room with a bare floor, exposed pipes, and whitewashed brick walls, she was dejected. It was difficult to create a hidden door in a brick wall, and if all the storerooms looked like this, then Jane's belief that the sub-basement would lead her to Edwin was unjustified.

"Let's go back up," Julian said, casting a glance at Jane's face.

They climbed stairs until they reemerged on the ground floor. On the landing, they were instantly surrounded by a cluster of people wearing identical blue T-shirts. The members of a group tour were snapping pictures as their guide spoke about the Vanderbilt family. Unfortunately, the group was so large that they took up most of the standing room near the stairs, so Jane suggested she wait for Lachlan outside.

"I'll have him meet you at one of the lion statues. It's a good place to reconvene." As they headed for the main doors, Julian took out his walkie-talkie and contacted Lachlan's guide. "They'll be along shortly," he told Jane.

Jane thanked him effusively for being such a knowledgeable and gracious guide. Julian flashed her one last smile and merged with the crowd entering the house.

Jane made her way down to the pair of lions perched on blocks on the wide front steps. Standing close to one of the regal felines, she gazed over the long lawn to the esplanade in the distance, and finally, at the surrounding mountains. They were similar to Storyton's mountains, and as Jane swept her eyes over the brilliant autumn foliage, she felt a pang of despair.

This place was beautiful. It was impressive. And big. Too big. Storyton Hall, despite its large size, was warm and inviting. It was home. Biltmore was more than a little intimidating, especially considering the urgency of Jane's task.

"We'll never be able to search it from attic to basement," she complained to Lachlan when he appeared at her side. "Even if we could gain free and unlimited access, which we can't, there's too much ground for us to cover. What kind of security devices did you spot?"

"Tons of cameras," said Lachlan. "There are eyes on the house at all times. It'll be a challenge to get into restricted spaces undetected. We can cross off the roof as a connector to a holding cell, though. After comparing the blueprints with what I saw in person, there's no place to keep a man prisoner."

As Jane digested Lachlan's news, she put a hand on the top of the lion's head. The marble was sun-warmed and smooth, and she drew comfort from its solidity.

Until she looked at its face.

"He seems sad," she said. "Like he's waiting for his master to come home and—" She suddenly grabbed Lachlan's arm. "Look. There's a piece of paper sticking out of his mouth."

Lachlan leaned closer to the lion. "The paper's from Storyton Hall."

Jane felt a prickle of dread but shoved the sensation aside and plucked the paper from the lion's mouth. Lachlan was right. The paper was from one of the notepads found in every Storyton Hall guest room.

"What does it say?" Lachlan asked. He wasn't

looking at Jane but scanning the nearby faces as if one of them could explain the sudden and bizarre appearance of the note. His gaze roved over people standing on the steps, milling about the driveway, taking selfies on the great lawn, and lingering by the garden and stable entrances.

Jane's vision blurred. She had to blink back tears to reread the words written by an anonymous hand.

She handed Lachlan the paper and turned around to face the house.

Touching the lion again, she repeated the words aloud.

"He's here."

CHAPTER TWO

Lachlan dropped Jane at the Deerpark Inn to attend the opening reception of the Luxury Lodging Symposium. Jane would have preferred to track down Julian Douglas and ask if he knew anything about the note in the lion's mouth, but she had to go to the reception to maintain her cover.

"I know that note rattled you," Lachlan said. "But we'll have to focus on it later."

"I get it," Jane said. "It's time for me to play hotel manager. I just hope you have more success with Mr. Tucker than we had with our tour guides. Ask him about the outbuildings. Find out if he knows rumors about the house's initial construction."

With a nod, Lachlan drove off to meet Gerald Tucker, the master gardener.

Jane made her way to the lodge. The spacious room had exposed brick walls and a vaulted timber ceiling, giving it a mountain cabin feel.

Jane had no desire to exchange small talk with her fellow hotel managers. She wanted to find a quiet corner and study the note in her pocket. However, there were no quiet corners. And since she was hungry, she took her place in the buffet line.

As Jane savored her food, the symposium organizer gave his welcome speech. When he was done, he invited the group to tour the mansion.

"This tour has been on my bucket list for ages!" cried the woman sitting next to Jane. She grabbed her purse and hurried toward the exit.

The hotel managers boarded small buses while Jane sent a text to Lachlan. He replied that he and Mr. Tucker were still at the cottage and that she should proceed on her own.

Left with a large chunk of free time, Jane caught a bus to Antler Village. Some of the managers had mentioned private tasting rooms in the winery cellars, so Jane decided to check them out.

On the way, she called Julian Douglas to find out if he knew about the note in the lion's mouth. He didn't answer, and Jane opted not to leave a voicemail.

It must have been him, Jane reasoned. *He told me to meet Lachlan by the lion. He knew I'd be standing there. There's no other explanation. But if he knows about Edwin, why the cloak-and-dagger act?*

The more she thought about it, the more Jane realized that Julian couldn't have placed the note. He'd never left her side. This meant someone else wedged it in the lion's mouth, perhaps at Julian's request. It couldn't have been there long. Visitors posed for pictures with the lions all the time. Jane had seen several people do this when she'd first entered the house.

As the bus drove through Biltmore's grounds, Jane tried to remember if she'd seen a staff member near the lion while she'd been waiting for Lachlan on the front steps. She didn't think anyone wearing an official Biltmore shirt had come close, but she'd been gazing at the mountains and missing the comforts of Storyton, so she couldn't be sure.

When the bus came to a stop at Antler Village, Jane was no closer to having an answer about the mysterious note. All she knew was that its author wrote in an elegant script.

Seeing as Edwin would hardly be kept a prisoner in a gift shop stockroom or the freezer of the ice cream parlor, Jane bypassed the Antler Village directory and headed straight for the winery. The entrance took her into a tunnel whose walls were lined with placards detailing the winery's history. The building, which was once a dairy, but had been renovated in the 1980s to serve as the estate's winery. Despite the fact that it looked and felt like the interior of a European castle, Jane doubted the cellar held any secrets. It was just too new.

Still, she thoroughly scrutinized the nooks containing stacked barrels and poked her head into the champagne cellar. Like the brick walls in the basement of the main house, the rough stone walls of the cellar couldn't easily conceal a hidden opening. The feature could be covered up by a piece of furniture or a collection of wine barrels, but Jane didn't think Edwin was being held in this cellar.

Having finished her inspection, she ascended a flight of stairs to the tasting area and gift shop. As she meandered near the tasting bar, a female bartender offered her a small glass of Biltmore's brut. The sparkling wine was bright and airy and carried notes of apricot and honey.

"It tastes like summer," Jane said to the woman.

She smiled. "If you enjoy light and fruity notes, try the Moscato."

The bartender poured Jane's sample and moved away to serve another customer. Though it was still afternoon, the tasting bar was busy, and the lines to purchase wine or other Biltmore-related gifts stretched far back into the store.

"You should come back for the wine and cheese hour," the bartender said when she returned to check on Jane. "It starts at six."

Jane pulled a face. "I'd like to, but I have another conference commitment. I wish there were a secret room around here where I could hide for an hour or two."

The bartender laughed. "The closest you'll get to privacy in Antler Village is in one of the cellar rooms. I guess that's why our manager likes to hold meetings down there every now and then. His important guests get lots of privacy and lots of wine."

Jane wondered if the woman was talking about Ramsey Parrish, the current manager of Biltmore. "I don't know Mr. Parrish," Jane said. "I'm friends with Julian Douglas, the former manager."

"Never met him. Mr. Parrish has been in charge since before I was hired." The woman removed Jane's empty tasting glasses. "He came over from England to work here, and I think he takes his job super serious. Hardly anyone sees him out and about the estate."

Jane thanked the bartender for her time and lined up to purchase a case of the Moscato to be picked up later on.

It was only half past three, but Jane felt tired. After the harrowing drive from Storyton to Asheville, the tour with Julian, lunch with her fellow conference goers, and her exploration of the winery, Jane was ready to call it a day.

Unfortunately, there was another Luxury Lodging event to attend that evening. Jane needed information from Sinclair before then, so she decided to have a cup of tea and a cookie. She was used to her tea breaks at Storyton Hall. She needed them to recharge and felt a pang of longing for Mrs. Hubbard's afternoon spread.

Taking out her Biltmore map, Jane decided to try the bakery located in the stables and boarded another shuttle bus.

Like most Biltmore venues, the bakeshop was crowded. Jane had to wait in another long line for her tea and cranberry oatmeal cookie. However, the tea was brewed to perfection, and the cookie was divine, so she didn't mind. She sat at a table near the door and people-watched while she sipped her tea.

When her cup was empty, she called Sinclair.

"Searching this place is a gargantuan task," she told him, trying not to let fatigue or disappointment come through in her voice. "Could you do some digging on Ramsey Parrish, the current manager?"

"I already gathered a dossier on Mr. Parrish," Sinclair said. "Due to its size and number of departments, Biltmore has multiple managers. Mr. Parrish oversees them all. He's known for being a reserved man. He rarely engages with visitors, regardless of their stature. Like Mr. Vanderbilt, Mr. Parrish is a collector. He has a penchant for signed first editions by authors who served in the military. John Dos Passos and his contemporaries, in particular."

"Signed first editions? Sounds expensive," Jane said. "He must earn a sweet salary."

"Mr. Parrish comes from money. Like many unfortunate members of England's peerage, Parrish's family couldn't keep up with their estate and lost their ancestral land. Though Mr. Parrish wasn't in line to inherit this bounty, he was still raised in posh circles."

"He's certainly in America's poshest setting," Jane said. "Can you text me his photo? I want to know him when I see him." Sinclair promised to send a photo as soon as possible. "I have one more thing to tell you. I received a note."

Sinclair listened carefully as Jane shared the details of her tour, Julian's suggestion that she meet Lachlan by the lion statue, and the discovery of the Storyton Hall paper.

"As people say, this is a good news/bad news situation," Sinclair said when she was done. "The good news is that you're in the right place. Mr. Alcott is being held somewhere on the estate. The bad news is that your mission is already known. The question is, by whom?"

Jane scanned the faces of the people in the bakeshop. "Friend or foe?"

"Precisely."

After checking her watch, Jane told Sinclair that she needed to return to the hotel and get a recap of Lachlan's afternoon before they had to prepare for the evening's event.

Lachlan was unusually animated while recounting his time with Mr. Tucker.

"He's invited us to a picnic breakfast in his garden tomorrow morning," Lachlan said. "You'll like him. He's a sweet old man who's devoted his whole life to Biltmore."

"So he knows it well."

Lachlan took one hand from the wheel and gestured at the surrounding grounds. "Every plant, tree, and animal burrow on this estate. He lives on in a small cottage within sight of the manor house and has been here long enough to witness all kinds of changes. One thing that's never changed has been the strict rules and regulations. The staff keeps to their own departments. The winery employees aren't meant to be in unrestored parts of the house while the staff of the inn shouldn't be poking around in the subbasement or wandering in the gardens. The place is like a small city-state. There are borders."

"Rules keep the estate more secure," Jane said. "I don't view that as suspicious."

"Rules do increase security, which is important in a place holding as many valuables as Biltmore," Lachlan agreed. "But it also means that the few people holding keys to the restricted areas—"

"Can come and go unobserved," Jane finished for him.

Lachlan exited the Biltmore property and continued on to their hotel. Back in their suite, he said, "Tell me about tonight's event."

"It's all about food," said Jane. "There's a talk on culinary trends for luxury travelers followed by a meal of small plates where we get to try some of these choice delights."

"I wish my job came with more perks," Lachlan grumbled.

He was teasing, but Jane tossed an embroidered sofa pillow at him anyway. "Stuffing our faces isn't our goal. If Ramsey Parrish makes an appearance, I need to cozy up to him. And though you're my official plus one, your job is to charm any female staff members who might be able to tell us how the top-tier employees come and go from the estate."

"Got it. Just don't let Eloise know that I flirted with other women to elicit information. I'm already on thin ice with her."

Jane wanted to shower and get dressed now so she'd have plenty of time to call the twins. She felt incredibly guilty for leaving them after their recent trauma. Their memories of their kidnapping were fragmented and fuzzy, and neither boy seemed fazed by the experience. But they were only in grade school, and in Jane's mind, they were still her babies. She was still plagued by doubts over their welfare.

She sensed that guilt was weighing Lachlan down as well. Not only had he seen terrible things during his military service, but he'd also witnessed his brother's murder. This guilt had been eating at Lachlan for years, and Jane wasn't sure how to help him exorcise it.

"Things have happened to you," she told him now. "Frightening and horrible things. Incredibly sad things. These experiences wounded you. Not in the way your brothers in arms were wounded. Your pain isn't physical. It's in here." She pointed at her chest. "You've built walls around yourself because you're trying to avoid being hurt again. But Lachlan, if you shut out the bad, you also shut out the good. Joy and pain. Love and heartache. They're all rolled together. Like a big

34

ball of rainbow-colored yarn. Allowing yourself to be vulnerable with Eloise will scare you more than your most dangerous Army mission, but it'll be worth it. I promise."

Lachlan nodded to show that he'd taken in all she'd said. "I need to get ready." Turning away, he added, "And to call Eloise."

Satisfied by this outcome, Jane went to her own room to prepare for the evening.

An hour later, she emerged to find Lachlan waiting for her. He looked like a male model in his tux. Judging from his expression, he thought she looked pretty good as well.

Jane's favorite colors for formal gowns were blue, champagne, or deep crimson. She thought those hues complemented her strawberry-blond hair and freckled skin. However, Mabel Wimberly, Jane's friend and the owner of Le Grande Dame boutique, had convinced Jane to try a taupe dress with cap sleeves, a lace bodice, and a floor-length satin skirt. Jane felt classy and elegant. Better yet, she could actually partake of tonight's fare without worrying about busting any seams. Once again, Mabel had made her the perfect dress.

"I've never seen your hair like that," Lachlan said as they walked to the car. "It's nice."

Jane touched the coiled braid at the base of her head. "The last time I wore my hair like this, Edwin cooked dinner for me at his restaurant. I thought—I don't know—that I should wear it like this because he's close by. He can't see me, but it makes me feel connected to him." She shook her head in embarrassment. "It's stupid."

Lachlan shot her a surprised glance. "No, it isn't." After navigating through Biltmore's entrance for the second time that day, he murmured, "We'll find him, Miss Jane."

Jane carried Lachlan's conviction with her as she entered Biltmore's conservatory. The space was warm and fragrant with the scent of flowers. Everywhere Jane looked, there was greenery. Potted plants lined the walls, and stunning floral arrangements sat on every table. Jane could see stars through the glass roof.

The speaker, one of Biltmore's celebrated chefs, began his talk on cuisine. His descriptions of food made Jane's mouth water.

Jane and her fellow conference attendees were treated to an array of edible works of art. These included duck consommé, pigeon with truffle soufflé, lobster ravioli, Iberian pork ribs, saffron potatoes, Madagascar chocolate topped with a caramelized letter B, and more.

As the coffee service began, a distinguished-looking gentleman in a smart-fitting tux stepped behind the lectern. His commanding presence immediately coaxed the room into silence. Jane recognized him at once and sat a bit straighter in her chair.

"Good evening, ladies and gentlemen." The man's voice was as smooth as the chocolate they'd had for dessert. Jane had always been a sucker for British accents, especially when spoken by a man who could have stepped out of an Ian Fleming novel. "Welcome to Biltmore. I'm Ramsey Parrish. I'll be hosting this evening's discussion on trends in luxury dining. I've invited groundbreaking chefs who've earned at least one Michelin star to speak on this topic. We will continue our food journey with aperitifs and a fruit and cheese course in the walled garden." He smiled graciously at his guests.

"I'm fond of classic literature," Ramsey continued. "Ernest Hemingway, one of my favorite authors, lived life to the fullest. Like many of us, he enjoyed his wine. He once said, 'Wine is one of the most civilized things in the world.' He believed everyone should experience its sensory pleasures. So sip and savor, ladies and gentlemen."

Ramsey stepped away from the lectern, and Jane tried to weave her way through the crowd to reach him before he could disappear through a side door in the garden wall.

By the time she opened the small, wooden door that looked like it belonged in Middle Earth and peered out, Ramsey was gone.

Like one of Tolkien's wraiths, Ramsey Parrish had melted into the shadows.

CHAPTER THREE

Early the next morning, Jane and Lachlan drove to Gerald Tucker's cottage. The quaint little house, with its stone walls and low-slanting roof, looked like the picture on a jigsaw-puzzle box.

Gerald met them at his garden gate with a cheerful "Good morning!" Shaking hands with Jane, he said, "Thanks for letting Lachlan hang out with me yesterday. He's the best company I've had in ages."

"He's at your disposal," Jane replied with a smile. "Not many people share his passion for birds of prey, so he's lucky to have you to talk to while I'm at my conference."

Waving for his guests to follow him into the garden, Gerald proudly watched as they admired the colorful flowerbeds and the manicured bushes and trees.

"I could imagine spending hours out here with a thick book," said Jane. "It's lovely."

"My favorite outdoor reading spot is right there." Gerald pointed at a garden bench shaded by a Japanese maple. "Please call me Tuck. I might work at a fancy place, but there's nothing fancy about me."

Tuck removed items from a straw hamper and placed them on the checkered cloth he'd spread out over the surface of a metal café table. There was egg and breakfast pie, fruit kebobs, and Mason jars filled with yogurt and granola.

While they ate, Tuck shared stories of what he loved most about Biltmore.

Jane understood his devotion. She felt the same about Storyton Hall. However, she inherited the responsibility. Storyton Hall had always been lived in and cared for by Stewards. How had Tuck become so attached to someone else's estate?

She decided to ask him, apologizing ahead of time for being nosy.

"Not to worry," he assured her. "Without a little backstory, it's hard to understand why I've given my heart and soul to this place. I'll try to keep a long tale short by saying that William Amherst Vanderbilt Cecil, grandson of the man who built Biltmore, gave me a job when I was down on my luck. Decades ago, I was a young man with a hot temper. One night, I got in a bar fight and ended up in jail. When I was released, I couldn't land a job because I had a record. Potential bosses saw me as a violent man. An unreliable man."

Jane glanced at Lachlan and saw empathy in his gaze.

"My folks taught me everything they knew about the plants in these parts. They were real nature lovers. I thought of us as three hobbits, walking everywhere in our bare feet. We were all as round-bellied and flat-footed as hobbits too."

This made Jane laugh. Tuck *did* look like a hobbit. With his short stature, curly white hair, and thick arms and legs, he could have been Bilbo Baggins in his golden years.

Tuck grinned and continued his story. "One day, I went out looking for work again. This time was a bit different because I had my dog with me. He always fell asleep at my feet while I stood on a street corner, holding up a sign." He smiled at the memory. "That day, I'd scrapped the usual messages about how skilled I was and wrote this on my sign, IF YOU DON'T WANT TO HELP ME, HELP MY DOG—THE HEARTBEAT AT MY FEET."

Jane's brows creased. "Where have I heard that before?"

"Edith Wharton," Tuck said. "I had no idea she was a friend of Mr. Vanderbilt's, but Mr. Cecil rode by on his horse and saw my sign. He dismounted then and there and asked about my dog and my situation. By the time we were done talking, I had a job. I'd be given a second chance to live my life right. And I took it."

An idea came to Jane, and she made a mental note to call Sinclair the moment she was back in the truck. She had a book in her collection that she wanted to give to Tuck.

"My tenure at Storyton Hall became my second chance too," Jane said and went on to tell Tuck how her husband, William, had been killed in a car accident. "He never had the chance to meet his sons, but he'd be happy knowing that they're surrounded by nature, loving family, loyal friends, and an endless supply of books."

Tuck gave Jane's hand a paternal pat. "It's rare to meet folks who like the simpler things in this complicated world. Would you like to see my book collection? I could make tea while you look."

Jane said that she'd like nothing better, and Tuck led them inside. The cottage had four rooms in total. Tuck showed them the cozy kitchen and the entrance to the bedroom and bathroom before inviting them into his reading room.

The moment Jane entered the reading room, she was filled with a deep sense of calm. There were books everywhere. Shelves hugged every wall, and each shelf was stuffed with books. Every table or stand held a stack of books. A row of books marched across the mantel. The only objects not covered in books were a pair of upholstered chairs with faded floral cushions. Embroidered stools were tucked under each chair. A round side table holding a coaster and a candle sat within easy reach. The candle's label read *Sherlock's Library*, and Jane couldn't resist giving it a sniff. She smelled vanilla, sandalwood, and a hint of citrus.

After inviting Jane to sit in his favorite chair, Tuck headed back to the kitchen. Lachlan wandered over to the window and gazed out.

It was pleasant to hear Tuck moving around in the next room. To Jane, the mundane sounds of opening and shutting cupboards, the rattle of silverware, or the ping of tap water striking the bottom of a kettle were as soothing as a bubble bath. She thought of the spacious kitchens at Storyton Hall and wondered if Mrs. Hubbard had started baking the Victoria sandwich for the afternoon tea. Jane could imagine her bustling about, her apple-round cheeks flushed as she barked orders at her staff. Later, when the twins popped in for a treat, her voice would turn sugary sweet, and she'd hug Fitz and Hem before plying them with fresh-baked cookies or bowls of marshmallow fruit salad.

Jane's pleasant reverie was disrupted by a knock on the front door.

"Coming!" Tuck called. The door creaked on its hinges and Jane heard Tuck say, "Come in, Mr. Parrish. I was just making tea. Would you like a cup?"

"Very much, thank you. And it's Ramsey. This is your home, after all."

"Yes, sir," Tuck said, sounding more than a little nervous. "Just so you know, I have two guests in my reading room. Ms. Steward and Mr. Lachlan are visiting from Storyton Hall. They're here for the managers' conference. I'll carry in some chairs from the kitchen, and we can all sit together."

"Allow me," Ramsey said. He appeared in the reading room with a ladder-back chair in each hand. After placing them near the fireplace, he turned to Jane with a welcoming smile and introduced himself.

Jane held out her hand. "Jane Steward."

Ramsey gave her hand a businesslike shake. "Gerald tells me that you're from Storyton Hall," he said, taking the other upholstered chair. He had a real lord-of-the-manor air about him, and Jane remembered Sinclair telling her that Ramsey Parrish descended from British aristocracy.

"Yes, we drove down yesterday," said Jane.

Tuck appeared carrying a heavy metal tray. He seemed at a loss as to where to place it.

Jane moved some books and Ramsey jumped up to relieve Tuck of his burden. After putting the tray on the coffee table, Ramsey offered to serve everyone, starting with Jane. As he handed her a cup, he said, "Sadly, I've never been to Storyton Hall, I hear it's quite the paradise for bibliophiles."

"It is." Jane looked at Tuck. "This room would fit right in with our other reading rooms."

Tuck was clearly pleased by the compliment. "Mr. Lachlan says that you have thousands and thousands of books on all kinds of subjects. Mine are mostly about nature."

Jane described a few of Storyton Hall's rooms like the Daphne du Maurier Morning Room, the Isak Dinesen Safari Room, and the Henry James Library. "We have loads of children's books too. We keep them in the Beatrix Potter Playroom." She turned to Ramsey. "Last night, you mentioned your love of literature. Who are your favorite authors?"

"I'm a fan of the Lost Generation. Dos Passos, Fitzgerald, Hemingway, Eliot." Light danced in his dark eyes. It was a look Jane knew all too well—the look of a book lover describing exactly what he loved about his favorite books. "To me, those men were heroes. Not only did some authors, like Hemingway, serve their countries in the Great War, but others wrote about wartime experiences with a level of honesty most of us are incapable of. I admire them to no end."

"Me too," Jane said, warming to Ramsey. "I was so enamored with Hemingway and Fitzgerald's work that I named my sons after them. They're twins, so I was able to use both names."

Ramsey finished his tea and set the cup aside. "Hopefully, they won't become as Bacchian as their namesakes. Poor Bacchus. He'd been reduced to a symbol of wild parties and drunkenness, but his cult originally celebrated the arts, especially literature and theater. He was revered as an outsider because those who worshipped him thought it was better to be an outcast than a mindless sheep. They made their own rules."

"Is that why you're so fond of the Bacchus fountain? Because you're from another country?" Tuck asked Ramsey. When Ramsey didn't reply, Tuck went on. "The fountain with the face. At the esplanade. Isn't it a Bacchus face? I've come upon you standing in front of it many times, especially after our visitors have left for the day, and the estate has gone quiet."

For a split second, Ramsey's mask of congeniality slipped. Something like anger flared in his eyes. By the time he reached for the teapot, however, he was once again the picture of amiability. "I like the Bacchus. Or satyr. I'm not sure which it's meant to be. But what I most enjoy is the view across the lawn. Such a sight keeps me humble." He looked at Tuck. "It also reminds me to be grateful to be where I am. Could I pour you more tea, Gerald?"

Tuck declined and shrank a little in his chair. Jane felt protective of the old gardener. Had Ramsey just issued a veiled threat? Had he not-so-subtly reminded Tuck to be humble and grateful? Was this a warning not to divulge additional details about Ramsey or the estate to strangers? Jane believed that it was, and she didn't like it one bit. She didn't like to see Tuck, a kind and sensitive man, treated like a disobedient dog.

Directing a steely gaze at Ramsey, Jane said, "I don't mean to be rude, but I'm already late for my first event. We should go."

Ramsey stood up and smiled. "I intruded on your visit with Mr. Tucker, so I should be the one to leave. If there's anything I can do to improve your stay, please call me."

He gave Jane a business card and thanked Tuck for the tea.

With Ramsey gone, Jane longed to do something to erase the glumness enveloping their host. Wandering over to a bookcase, she asked, "Is there a favorite in this collection, Tuck?"

Her question did the trick. Tuck brightened and made a beeline for the bookshelf next to the window. "I keep my best books together—like they're all the closest of friends." He chuckled. "Well, they're *my* friends. How could a person not feel something when faced with a book like this?"

Pulling a book with a blue cover down from the shelf, he handed it to Jane. "It's just an old field guide to birds. But look at those drawings. They're almost ready to fly off the page."

The illustrations were marvelous, as were those in the next book Tuck pulled down from the shelf, which was all about Southern apple varieties. He showed her a few more books, and when Jane was confident that his good spirits had been restored, she told him that she needed to go.

"Do you mind if we stop by tomorrow?" she asked as Tuck led them outside. "There's something I'd like to show you."

Though he looked somewhat confused, Tuck agreed. "Tomorrow's Sunday, so I might go fishing. Just give me a call and I'll tell you what I'm up to."

Back in the truck, Jane released an audible sigh. "I do not want to spend three hours listening to a talk on Hotel Technology in the Year 2030, but I'll suffer through it. You and I are *not* attending the evening event, however. We're going to investigate the Bacchus fountain instead." Jane smiled. She felt genuinely hopeful for the first time since coming to Biltmore. "There's a reason Ramsey Parrish hangs out near that fountain, and I doubt it's because he's a fan of Greco-Roman mythology."

"We'll have to be very careful," Lachlan said solemnly. "If we weren't on Parrish's radar before, we're definitely on it now."

Jane tried to be attentive during the afternoon's discussion on advertising strategies, but all she could think about was finding Edwin.

As soon as the session was over, she returned to her hotel and ordered pizza from a local restaurant. Lachlan had already picked up the case of Biltmore wine Jane had purchased yesterday and, having nothing else on hand to drink, asked if he should open a bottle.

"Why not?" she said. "We can always get more."

Lachlan suggested they stick to one glass, seeing as they needed to keep their wits about them to sneak around Biltmore after dark.

"While you were at your conference, I made preparations for tonight's outing." Lachlan

47

unrolled a map of the grounds closest to the chateau. "We'll park here." He pointed at a shaded area indicating a group of trees. "It's in the woods. No one should be able to spot the truck, and there are no cameras in the vicinity. From here, it's a short walk to the esplanade. It won't be quick because we'll have to stick to the woods."

After dinner, Jane dressed in black jeans and a long-sleeved black top. Lachlan gave her a black baseball cap and glanced out the kitchen window. "It's not dark enough. We'll give it another thirty minutes."

Jane decided to spend the time talking to her sons. Eloise, who'd volunteered to watch the boys while Jane was away, answered the phone mid-laugh.

"Sorry!" she giggled. "The twins and I were battling a dish soap blob in the kitchen sink.

"Your boys are tons of fun, Jane. And they know a million Harry Potter facts. This afternoon, we made butterbeer and went on a hike to find the perfect sticks to transform into wands. That's on the docket for tomorrow."

"You're like the coolest of cool aunts," Jane said.

"I have big shoes to fill. Yours! Listen, Hem is tugging my arm. He really wants to say hello."

As soon as Hem came on the line, words poured out of his mouth. He told Jane about the butterbeer and the plans for his wand. He would have continued, undeterred, had Fitz not picked up the receiver in Jane's bedroom.

"Uncle Aloysius is taking us fishing after church!" he cried. "The biggest catfish in the world is in the Storyton River, and we're going to catch him! If we do, we'll eat him for supper."

"Fitz!" Hem shouted angrily. "*I* was talking first!"

Jane knew she had to stop the boys before an argument used up her phone time. "I have an idea for your wands," she said. "Ask Mrs. Templeton if she has gold or silver thread in her sewing box. That could be your unicorn hair."

"Ron Weasley's wand had unicorn hair," Fitz said. "I like Ron."

"I don't want unicorn stuff. That's for girls," said Hem. "I want a dragon heartstring."

Jane and her sons spoke of wands until Hem announced that it was movie time. Eloise had brought *Hocus Pocus* and a container of Jiffy Pop for the evening's entertainment. The twins had never seen this stovetop popcorn, and Jane guessed that Eloise would convince Fitz and Hem that they were witnessing a bit of kitchen magic.

After reminding her boys to be on their best behavior at Sunday School, Jane wished them sweet dreams and hung up.

Next, she put on her hiking boots and black baseball cap and examined herself in the mirror.

"I hope a little bit of magic comes my way tonight," she told her reflection. "Just enough to lead me to Edwin."

As Lachlan drove to the estate, Jane reflected on how the crisp, autumn night seemed especially dark for September. Spectral clouds scudded over the black sky, blotting out the light from a pale quarter moon.

Gaining entrance to Biltmore was easy. All Jane had to do was flash her conference I.D. at the gatekeeper. He examined it, wished her a pleasant evening, and told them to proceed. Lachlan drove past Antler Village, the venue for the Luxury Lodging event, and slowly progressed on the quiet, curving road leading to the chateau. As he grew closer, he switched off the headlights and slowed even more dramatically.

Jane didn't know how he drove without lights, but Lachlan was known for his keen eyesight. Like the hawks and falcons he trained, he could see better than most humans. Once, when Jane asked about this gift, he said that he used more than his sight alone when tracking. He also used his sense of hearing and the laser focus he'd honed as an Army Ranger.

Despite her faith in his eyesight, Jane went rigid when he pulled off the road and eased the truck into a copse of trees. Though he came within inches of several tree trunks, he never made contact. Just as Jane felt that his luck was on the verge of running out, he turned off the engine.

"I don't want to use flashlights, so step carefully," he said.

Together, they set off through the woods toward the house. It was hard to believe that the behemoth structure was close by. Jane couldn't glimpse a single light. There were only trees, leaves crunching underfoot, and shadows.

Every so often, Lachlan would stop. He'd put his hand out to keep her from plowing into him and would stand, still as stone, and listen.

"Owl," he'd whisper. Another time, he murmured, "Possum."

Jane didn't know whether to be comforted by the presence of wildlife or not. Every time a rope of vines or a thin branch brushed her ankle, she imagined an opossum's tail. Having a run-in with a marsupial in the dark wasn't her idea of fun.

Edwin, she thought. *I have to find you. I want to go back to the days when excitement meant curling up on the sofa with a book and a glass of wine.*

Lachlan put a hand on Jane's arm. "We're here. When we reach the Bacchus fountain, I'll shine my penlight on the face. Try not to talk. If that fountain is covering an opening, there could be motion detectors or cameras with listening devices. It might also be booby-trapped. I brought Sterling's jamming device to knock out the signal from any surveillance feed, but if we use it, someone's bound to notice. Which means we won't have much time once I turn it on."

"I understand," she said and gave his hand an affectionate squeeze. "No matter what happens, thank you for helping me. This mission goes above and beyond your oath."

"My oath is to keep you safe. No matter where you go," Lachlan said before moving to the strip of lawn behind the esplanade. Sticking close to the base of the massive stone wall, he crept toward the end of the structure. He turned the corner, with Jane on his heels, and faced the Bacchus wall fountain.

A sconce affixed to the pillar of the wrought-iron gates separating the chateau yard from the rest of the grounds cast just enough light to pull the Bacchus head out of the shadows.

The mythological creature was a sinister-looking thing. He wore a wreath of ivy leaves and grapes, and a pair of impressive ram horns curled from his temple to the bottom of his ear. His furrowed forehead and scowling eyes made him look unusually grumpy for a god representing festivities.

Lachlan plunged his hands into the fountain and felt around while Jane concentrated on the sculpted face. After several minutes of touching and scrutinizing, she decided that Bacchus had nothing to hide.

There were several doors leading into the esplanade's interior. Lachlan chose to test the one closest to the Bacchus fountain. Unsurprisingly, it was locked. Lachlan took out the signal-jamming device and entered a code. After passing the device to Jane, he removed a lockpick kit from the pocket of his cargo pants.

The door was made of thick wood and, judging by its iron keyhole, required a coordinating skeleton key. Having seen most of her Fins practicing their lockpick skills, Jane knew that opening a skeleton key lock wasn't much of a challenge.

Lachlan passed her a tiny penlight and pointed at the keyhole. Dropping to a catcher's stance, Jane shone the narrow beam of light in the center of the hole.

It took less than a minute for Lachlan to spring the lock. After reclaiming the penlight and pulling a knife with a black blade from the holster strapped to his belt, Lachlan opened the door. He and Jane slipped into the cold, damp space and quickly shut the door behind them.

She and Lachlan stood very still in the darkness and listened.

The blackness was thick, permeated only by the gurgle of the water in the Bacchus fountain as well as the fainter sound of running water. Jane assumed this murmur came from the trio of fish fountains in the center of the esplanade. For a brief moment, Jane was lulled by the sleepy, rhythmic sound of water.

Lachlan touched her elbow, and she jumped. He gave her a reassuring squeeze and the space was suddenly flooded with blue-tinted light. Lachlan held a small camping lantern in one hand while proffering a second to Jane. She took it and began sweeping the light over the walls and floor. She saw only rough stone.

Jane and Lachlan walked along the cold corridor, searching for the smallest irregularity that could represent a secret door. With the uneven stones and the variation of hues over the walls and ground, it seemed an impossible task.

Luckily, Jane had Landon Lachlan. Her Fin's greatest asset was his tracking ability. He could find a broken branch or a blade of trampled grass and know precisely which direction his quarry had taken. When he plucked something from the ground, Jane paused to look at his discovery. He raised a piece of gravel in front of the lantern before continuing forward at a snail's pace, his eyes locked on the ground.

Though Jane was dying to ask what he was searching for, she kept her mouth shut. Any noise would echo in this dank corridor, and she didn't want to be discovered because she hadn't stayed silent.

A few minutes passed before Lachlan picked up another pebble. And another. He said nothing, but Jane could sense his excitement. His body was practically quivering with energy.

Finally, he stopped and raised the lantern over his head. Shadows leaped over the walls as he studied each side of the passageway. Next, he moved the light over the floor.

Jane added her light to his. She had no idea what trail Lachlan was following, and she was about to move on when he seized her hand. Pulling her down into a crouch, Lachlan pointed at a crack in the stone.

It looked utterly unremarkable, and Jane shrugged to show Lachlan that she didn't understand why it was important.

Lachlan held his hand, palm side up, in front of her. He then let it drop as if it were an elevator cab cut loose from a cable.

Or a slab of stone that can fall away from the surrounding slabs, Jane thought, her eyes shining with hope.

She pointed to the ground. Lachlan nodded.

How? Jane mouthed, and Lachlan began tracing the uneven crack with his fingertip. As he did so, Jane noticed how the crack ran all the way around the stone.

A hidden entrance, Jane thought and examined the wall more closely. There had to be some sort of lever or button that would release the slab. But where?

Jane tried to imagine how a Templar would

55

construct a secret opening. She thought of the diary Edwin had let her read—of its descriptions of modern Templar practices. The contemporary Templars liked to blend centuries-old traditions with state-of-the-art technology. The rogue Templars, as Edwin called the faction that had split from his, were little more than criminals. They stole, kidnapped, blackmailed, and committed murder to acquire knowledge. To them, knowledge was power and was to be obtained at any cost.

This splinter cell also romanticized their roots. They no longer devoted themselves to the Church, gave away their possessions, or vowed to protect the weak and defenseless. However, they still conducted certain age-old rites and rituals established by the original Templars.

One of these traditions involved communicating in Latin. It was the language of their order, even more so than the French spoken by their founding father, Hugh de Payens.

Inspired by what she knew about contemporary Templars, Jane turned off the signal-jamming device. She then took out her cell phone and sent Sinclair a text. She prayed the message would go through and that Sinclair would send a hasty reply. The light from her phone screen caught Lachlan's attention, and he came over to see what she was doing. She pivoted the screen, allowing him to read the query she'd sent to Storyton Hall's head librarian.

"It fits their profile of arrogance and exclusivity," Sinclair wrote back without delay. "You might have to try more than one of the following phrases. If it's a voice-activated door, the first or second phrase should do the trick. If the lock requires voice recognition, I'm afraid you won't succeed, no matter how precise your Latin."

Jane had seen her sons cross their fingers when they wanted a wish to come true. Figuring it couldn't hurt, she crossed hers and said, "*Aperi!*"

Nothing happened.

"Maybe it only recognizes male voices," she whispered to Lachlan.

Lachlan repeated the word to no avail.

Jane read the second phrase on Sinclair's list. This phrase was referenced in the Book of Revelation. It meant, "to break the seal."

Jane believed the combination of Latin and Scripture might be exactly what was needed, but saying, "*Apero Sigillum!*" produced no results.

The tomb-like dark of the stone space gnawed at Jane's hope. She clung to the last of it, though, and signaled for Lachlan to give the phrase a try.

In a clear, commanding voice, he repeated the phrase.

From somewhere behind the wall, a mechanism rumbled. The slab with the jagged crack around its perimeter began to sink.

Lachlan held out his knife and tensed, ready to spring.

The rumbling stopped, and he peered down into the aperture.

"Turn the jamming device back on," he whispered. "And wait here."

Jane followed half of his instructions. She switched on the device, but when she noticed how small lights embedded in the top step blazed to life under Lachlan's weight, she descended right behind him.

The narrow staircase led them down to another dark and damp passage. The moment Jane cleared the last step, the slab over their heads slid into its original position with a thud. Jane and Lachlan were entombed in the subterranean corridor.

At least, Jane assumed it was a corridor. Her suspicion was immediately confirmed when a row of wall sconces bloomed into life, illuminating the length of the passageway with a surprisingly bright light.

Lachlan touched her arm and pointed at the ground. A crimson runner covered the stones. The runner led to a dead end. On that dead-end wall was an enormous, blood-red Templar cross.

Seeing the symbol, Jane had to clamp her hand over her mouth.

Edwin! The cry rose inside her throat, but she held it back.

Her eyes moved from the cross to the row of doors lining the corridor. Unlike the door leading inside the esplanade, these were made of metal and what looked to be speakeasy grilles. A small door covered every speakeasy grille, so there was no way to know for sure what was concealed in each room unless she opened the speakeasy doors.

Moving to the closest one, Jane cast a quick glance at Lachlan. He was coiled like a snake, his knife held in the ready position. Jane opened the door covering the speakeasy grille. The grille wasn't easy to see through, but Jane was able to view a spartan room containing a cot, a table and chair, and a primitive toilet.

She mouthed the word "empty" and headed for the next room.

Lachlan continued to watch the corridor while Jane opened the next speakeasy door. And the next.

The feeling that she was running out of doors, time, and hope slowed Jane's movements. She opened another door, expecting to see yet another vacant room.

This room, however, was occupied.

And its occupant was the man Jane had been searching for.

She'd found Edwin Alcott.

Edwin flew from the table where he'd been bent over a book and shoved his fingers through the grille.

"Jane." He spoke her name like a man, dying of thirst, who'd been given a glass of the purest, sweetest spring water.

She curled her fingers around his. As she did so, an involuntary sob escaped her lips.

"It's all right," Edwin said, his voice a dry rasp. "You're here. Everything is all right."

He waited for her to nod before squeezing her fingers a little tighter. "I don't know how many days I've closed my eyes and whispered that I'd trade my soul to see you again. My prayers have been answered. But Jane, you've walked into terrible danger. How many Fins are with you?"

Jane inched to one side, allowing Lachlan to approach the speakeasy.

He was already focused on the next task, which was breaking Edwin out. "Are these doors automated? There's a panel next to each one."

"To open the food slot, they use a numerical code," Edwin said. "To open the whole door requires a thumbprint."

Jane tried to fight a sinking feeling. Lachlan was clever, but she didn't think he could disable the door's security system. Still, she asked if he could hack the panel.

"It has a dual fail-safe system," Lachlan said, scrutinizing the panel. "If I tamper with it, it'll transmit a signal. Even if that signal was jammed by our RF device, there's a second fail-safe."

Edwin looked grave. "Poisonous gas. It'll be released into my room."

Jane was silent following this remark.

"Your best bet is to wait for my meal delivery," Edwin said. "I assume it's nighttime and the estate is closed to visitors?" At Jane's nod, Edwin gestured toward the stairs. "Which means they could be here any second."

Lachlan checked his watch. "How many men come at once?"

"Two," Edwin said. "You'll have to take them by surprise."

Jane wondered how they'd be able to overpower guards with nowhere to hide. "We should wait under the stairs."

While her mind played out scenarios, her eyes took in Edwin's appearance. His body was gaunt. His face was sunken. His skin was pallid. He was a shade of his former self.

"I'm okay," he whispered as if he'd read her thoughts. "You're here. Everything will be okay."

"We'd better move, Miss Jane," Lachlan warned. "If we don't get behind the stairs, we'll be discovered."

Suddenly, the sound of clapping hands reverberated through the corridor.

Jane turned to her right, toward the last door, and saw a man. He was the source of the slow, mocking applause.

Ramsey Parrish lowered his hands, flashed them a smug smile, and said, "Too late."

CHAPTER FOUR

Jane was too shocked to react. She stood, rooted in place, as Ramsey Parrish smiled at her.

Lachlan was trained to respond to any situation, no matter how unexpected, with alacrity. His years in the military had honed his instincts so that even as his brain was processing the dramatic turn of events, his body was already in motion.

"Parrish," he whispered, whipping out his knife. He leaped forward in the same breath. Neither his swiftness nor his weapon mattered, for Parrish produced a gun and aimed it at Lachlan's chest.

Jane no longer thought of him as Ramsey Parrish, manager of Biltmore, but as a Templar and a miscreant. He was only Parrish now.

"Don't come any closer," he warned. The mirth was gone from his eyes. "In fact, I'd be more comfortable if you'd return to your original position. We all need our personal space."

Jane should have trembled at the sight of the gun. She should have thought of her sons, her family, Edwin, her friends—of all she stood to lose—and she should have been afraid. Parrish could shoot her and Lachlan without fear of discovery and toss their bodies in a cell. Then, he could dust off his suit and go about his business. No one would ever be the wiser.

Despite this chilling fact, Jane wasn't frightened. The initial shock had given way to anger. The anger mixed with a fight-or-flight reaction, pumping her full of adrenaline. She could feel the heat of her fury moving through her veins, and she wished Parrish wasn't standing so far away. How dare he threaten them? How dare he imprison Edwin?

"Real men of power don't need firearms," she said to Parrish, injecting her voice with as much haughtiness as she was able to muster. "A man who hides behind a gun when facing an unarmed woman is a coward."

Parrish seemed delighted by Jane's caustic remarks. "I couldn't agree more, Ms. Steward. Upon my honor as a gentleman, I will holster my weapon. I'd ask your lackey to do the same."

"He's no lackey." Though the term fanned Jane's anger, she didn't want Parrish to know it. She turned to Lachlan. "Please sheath your knife."

After casting a hostile glare in Parrish's direction, Lachlan complied.

Without realizing it, Jane put her hands on her hips and stared Parrish down. This was the posture she adopted when the twins were misbehaving, and it felt like a natural thing for her to do. "You're clearly not surprised to find us here, so why don't you explain why you've been holding Edwin against his will?"

Parrish spread his hands. "I plan to tell you many things, Ms. Steward, but not in this setting. We all need something to warm our bones. A roaring fire and a glass of excellent Scotch are in order."

"Are you letting Edwin out?" Jane pointed at his cell door, sounding more desperate than she meant to.

Parrish shook his head in feigned regret. "That's not possible at this time. However, if you and I reach a mutual understanding, then Mr. Alcott will return to Storyton with you."

For the first time since Parrish's arrival, Edwin spoke. "Don't bargain with this snake. I don't care what he says he'll do to me, don't listen to him. I'll be okay. No matter what he says or how he tries to scare you, I'll get out of here in one piece."

When Jane didn't respond, Edwin's gaze moved to Lachlan. "Keeping your oath means not standing by while she makes a deal with the devil. If he tries to use me as leverage to force her into a vulnerable position, promise that you'll get her out of here. I don't care who you have to kill to do it."

To Jane's annoyance, Lachlan gave a brief nod.

"Hello, I'm standing right here," she snapped at Edwin. "I will make my own decisions, thank you very much. If you treat me like a little kid, I might just leave you in that cell."

Though she didn't mean that, she was tired of people manipulating her and pushing her about like a pawn on a chessboard. This was her fight. Parrish had become her enemy the second one of his colleagues had abducted her sons. She was here to rescue Edwin, but she was also here to let these people see that she would not be intimidated.

"I can practically see the sparks flying between you two," Parrish said in an amused tone.

"Shall we get on with this?" Jane asked. She was impatient to find out what he wanted, though she was sure it would involve the location of Storyton's secret library. It made the most sense. After all, another Templar had kidnapped her sons in hopes of gaining access to the library. Though that man had failed and had paid a horrible price for his failure, Jane didn't feel an iota of sympathy for him. If he hadn't taken his own life, she might have killed him herself.

If Ramsey Parrish was involved in the kidnapping, he will pay for messing with my boys, she silently seethed.

After agreeing that it was time to leave, Parrish spoke another Latin phrase and the slab hiding the staircase moved. Once their exit was revealed, Parrish beckoned for Jane to go first. As she saw no other alternative, she whispered to Edwin that she'd be back for him and ascended to the ground-level corridor.

Switching on a flashlight, Parrish took the lead. His unhurried gait and self-assurance annoyed Jane. She wished there was an obvious course of action for her to take, but she didn't think there was anything to do but follow along.

The opportunity will present itself, Miss Jane.

Sinclair's voice echoed in Jane's head as if he stood right beside her. She pictured his face, as well as those of Butterworth, the head butler, and Sterling, the head chauffeur. She realized that no matter what Parrish did to her, she need only hold out until the rest of her Fins came for her. Besides, she still had Lachlan. Her faith in him hadn't wavered because he hadn't overcome an armed opponent. Like Jane, he'd been taken by surprise. It had been a learning experience for them both. They had to be prepared for more surprises, which was why Jane steeled herself when Parrish opened the door to the outside, and she saw an idling car parked on the grass in front of the Bacchus fountain.

"Who's in the car?" she asked Parrish.

"My driver. He will transport us to the cottage on the estate. He will not speak, so please save your questions for our fireside tête-à-tête."

Parrish's arrogance was maddening, but Jane refused to let him goad her. She slid into the sedan's roomy back seat and said nothing.

Though it was nearly impossible to see through the car's tinted windows, Jane pretended to be riveted by the dark grounds. Lachlan sat beside her and stared at the back of Parrish's head, fantasizing about sticking his knife into it.

It was a short ride to their destination. The driver opened the front door and waved for Jane and Lachlan to enter. Despite the precariousness of her position, Jane found the cottage quite charming. The living room was small but cozy. The fire was already lit, and a brass tray with glasses, an ice bucket, and a bottle of Scotch had been placed on the coffee table.

Parrish invited Jane and Lachlan to sit on the sofa while he took one of the wing chairs facing the fire. Lachlan refused and moved to stand behind Jane. He also declined Parrish's offer of a drink.

When Jane said that she'd rather have a cup of tea, Parrish snapped his fingers. Seconds later, a very tall, very wide, and very formidable-looking man appeared in the doorway.

"A pot of Himalayan White, Bruno."

The enormous man dipped his chin and left.

"Bruno is a man of many skills," Parrish said. "Luckily, brewing the perfect pot of tea happens to be one of them."

Parrish prattled on about tea for several minutes, describing his favorite Chinese blends and his preference for Chinese tea ceremonies over the British high-tea service. He was still talking when Bruno returned carrying a bamboo tray with a clay teapot and two plain mugs without handles.

Bruno poured the tea and offered Jane a cup. She accepted it but didn't drink. The tea could be drugged. Bruno had prepared it in another room, which meant she didn't dare take a sip.

"Bruno, please pour a taste of Ms. Steward's tea into the empty cup and drink it," Parrish commanded with the nonchalance of a man giving an order to a waiter.

The silent man reclaimed Jane's mug, tipped it over the second mug, and drank a swallow. He then set her mug on the tray, refilled the amount he'd consumed, and moved to the door. After taking up a sentinel position, he stared blankly at the opposite wall.

"I believe you'll find the floral notes and subtly sweet aftertaste quite pleasant," Parrish said, gesturing at the teapot.

Jane picked up her cup and took a tentative sip. The tea was light and lovely. She took a second sip and could feel the dampness of the secret corridor under the esplanade begin to dissipate. After a third sip, Jane was ready to dispense with the small talk and get down to business.

"Thank you for the tea," she said. "Could we move on to the topic at hand? What did you hope to achieve from abducting and imprisoning Edwin Alcott?"

"Such a strident choice of words." Parrish

frowned at Jane over the rim of his crystal tumbler. "I want you to know that Mr. Alcott was given the opportunity to upgrade to nicer accommodations, but he was less than cooperative. I hope you and I don't reach a similar impasse. I'd prefer we come to a mutually beneficial understanding."

Jane said nothing. It was clear that Parrish liked the sound of his own voice. He'd probably been looking forward to this meeting for quite a while and had practiced his speech in the shower or while shaving in front of a very big mirror.

"Ms. Steward, my request is simple. I would like to accompany you when you return to Storyton Hall. You are in possession of a great treasure." He held up a finger. "Please don't insult me by denying the existence of your secret library. I know that it's somewhere on your estate. I know that it is filled with many rare and wonderful materials. It is not my intention to storm your castle and steal your collection. There are select items that I would like to claim, and I'd like your assistance in procuring these materials."

Jane wanted to laugh in his face. His request was so bold and so utterly absurd that she had to sip more tea to keep from blurting out a string of insults. It was paramount that she weigh each word. After all, a human life hung in the balance of this bargaining session.

Don't show him any emotion, she told herself.

No matter what he says or does. Don't let him bait you into losing your cool.

"In exchange for access to your materials, I will set Mr. Alcott free," Parrish continued. "After obtaining what I need, I will leave your home, your family, and your companions alone."

"If I reject your proposal?" Jane asked. "What happens then?"

Parrish sighed. "I'd rather not state the obvious. Suffice it to say, you and Mr. Alcott will never be reunited."

Jane focused on the warmth moving from her teacup to her palms. "You'd kill him?"

Parrish spread his hands. The gesture made it quite clear that he had no qualms about murdering his prisoner.

"How many henchmen will be accompanying you to my home?" she asked.

Parrish shook his head. "I don't require any assistance. We're making a simple trade. That's all. You know what's at stake should you cross me."

Jane didn't believe this for an instant. If Parrish traveled alone, it meant that he had already had cronies in place. But where? Were they Storyton Hall staff members? Employees in the village shops? The cashier at The Pickled Pig Market? One of the seasonal clerks at Storyton Outfitters? Or would they be among the group of historians arriving at Storyton Hall that afternoon?

As this wasn't the moment to dwell on such possibilities, Jane pushed this subject aside. She could revisit it later.

"Edwin must return to Storyton with me," she said flatly. "I'm not leaving Biltmore without him. If you don't give me what I want, then you stand no chance of getting what you want."

To her surprise, Parrish didn't refute her. Instead, he drained the rest of his Scotch, put his glass to the side, and tented his fingers under his chin.

"In this matter, I am at liberty to give you a choice. You may choose freedom for Mr. Alcott—though he will ride with me and remain a guest in my suite at Storyton Hall until I've procured the materials I seek—or you may choose the person occupying the cell next to Mr. Alcott's. I was visiting this person when you and Mr. Lachlan arrived."

Jane turned to look at Lachlan, which wasn't easy with him standing directly behind her. She frowned as if to say, *what is Parrish babbling about?*

Lachlan put a hand on her back and applied pressure. Though the contact was brief, Jane understood its meaning. Lachlan was telling her to hear out the madman and to maintain an air of detachment.

Jane couldn't understand Parrish's game. He was confident that she'd agree to trade certain materials for Edwin's release. She didn't plan on

71

giving Parrish a thing, of course. She wouldn't let him have so much as a Storyton Hall notepad or pen. Not even one of the collectible bookmarks the children received whenever they borrowed a book from the Henry James Library. No. Once she was back home, Parrish would be on her turf. He would be a known enemy. Jane would have the full might and protection of her Fins, her friends, and her family. As would Edwin. If Parrish had colleagues waiting to assist him, Jane would ferret them out.

Bring it on, she thought, gazing benignly at Parrish. *You'll be sorry you tangled with me and the man I love.*

"I don't understand why I'd substitute Edwin for another prisoner," she said. "Exactly how many people do have you locked up?"

"Two." Parrish refilled his tumbler with Scotch and poured two fingers' worth into a second glass. "My dear, I believe you'll need this in a few minutes, so I'll place it close at hand. Bruno? Would you bring in the laptop?"

Jane felt a prickle of dread. What horrors were stored on Parrish's laptop? Had he managed to position another Templar within reach of her family? Or within reach of the Cover Girls, her beloved book club friends? Is that why Parrish was giving her the glass of Scotch? Because she'd be so unsettled by whatever Parrish showed her that she'd need a stiff drink?

Stop it, she told the panicked voice inside her head.

Her sons were fine. She'd just spoken with them. Aunt Octavia and Uncle Aloysius were also fine. She'd chatted with them during her lunch break, and her great-uncle had talked about tomorrow's fishing excursion with Fitz and Hem. Aunt Octavia had told Jane how much she was enjoying her current read, *I Capture the Castle* by Dodie Smith.

"You really *must* borrow my book when I'm done," her great-aunt had exclaimed. "Eloise suggested it and, as usual, her recommendation was spot on. Jane, the characters' ruined castle of a home will make you feel worlds better about our cantankerous furnace or overgrown orchard. We're Buckingham Palace compared to the dilapidated pile inhabited by these poor people. The burgeoning authoress of a narrator, a young woman named Cassandra, alternates between making me laugh and wringing my hands with worry."

Jane had promised to move the book to the top of her TBR pile.

Bruno returned, interrupting Jane's vision of the book stack on her nightstand. He removed the tea tray and replaced it with a large laptop. He opened the screen, pivoted it so that it faced Jane, and withdrew to his position by the door. All of this was completed without a word. It was as if the man didn't even breathe.

"When you push the play button on this video feed, I think you'll understand why your choice won't be easy." Parrish wore that smug grin again. Before, that mocking upward curve of his lips had made Jane angry. Now, it made her nervous. Who was in this video?

She moved her right hand toward the space bar and paused, her index finger hovering a centimeter above the keyboard.

"Your instincts are correct. Pushing that button will change reality as you know it." Parrish shifted in his chair, making himself more comfortable. "But what choice do you have?"

Jane hated that he was right. She'd love nothing more than to walk out of this room without seeing the video. However, she couldn't leave Edwin. She also couldn't run from an enemy who was out in the open. He was exposed, and he was challenging her. She wouldn't back down from his challenge. She would meet it head-on with fire in her eyes.

"I always have a choice," she said and let her finger drop.

The image showed a cell just like Edwin's. It had the same cot, toilet, desk, and chair. There was a row of books lined up on the desk, and a man was hunched over an open book. He stood with his back to the camera, swaying from side to side, as he focused on the pages before him.

Suddenly, he swept the book off the desk. He

went after the tidy row of books next, violently swiping them to the ground. There was so much rage in his treatment of the books that Jane winced.

When the desk was clear, the man plunged his hands into a mass of sandy brown hair and dropped on to his bed. He rocked back and forth, his arms folded protectively over his chest, his mouth stretched into what looked like an anguished cry. The video had no sound, but the man's face told a story of agony. And perhaps, madness.

Jane couldn't get a clear look at his features because his gaze was lowered. His dark, scraggly beard hid the entire bottom half of his face. However, as she watched this miserable stranger, something stirred inside her. It was a faint and enigmatic feeling that came from deep in her memories. It was a feeling that the word "stranger" wasn't accurate. This thought released a cascade of other thoughts and feelings. Jane was flooded with questions, confusion, and, finally, a sense of familiarity.

Before this last feeling could finish rising to the surface, the rational part of her mind tried to shut it down.

Despite this, her body leaned closer to the screen. She willed the man to look at the camera. She was so intently focused on his face that everything else faded away. She no longer heard the crackle of the fire or felt Lachlan's presence behind her. Parrish and his mute henchman might as well be on another planet.

"Look up," she softly commanded, her eyes locked on the man's face.

Several seconds passed before the wild-haired, wild-eyed, bearded man stopped rocking. He passed his hands over his face and blew out a long, slow exhalation. This was the behavior of a man resigned to his fate. A man who became angry and had no place to channel that anger. He was trapped inside that room. And inside his mind.

Jane's heart ached for the poor soul. Since Parrish and his maniacal sect had imprisoned him, he was probably a decent person. He was also a survivor. Judging by his beard, he'd been locked in that room for quite a long time.

The man started collecting the books and lining them up in a neat row again. When he got to the last book, he immediately brought it to his chest and cradled it. Moving absently toward the corner of the room where the camera was positioned, he hugged the book as if it were the most precious thing in the world.

And then, he looked up.

When his eyes met Jane's, time and space twisted and bent. The present vanished, and Jane was thrust into the past.

It was just a glance. A lightning flash of a

76

moment when he'd raised his gaze. It had taken a single breath for Jane to feel like he'd seen straight into her soul. He'd flicked his eyes upward. That was all he'd done. That was all it took.

Every air molecule rushed out of Jane's lungs, and a prickly and powerful heat swept over her. Sweat beads popped across her forehead, and her hands went clammy. She couldn't draw in a fresh breath. She couldn't remember how to breathe. How to think. How to swallow. Her mouth hung open. Her lips moved. But nothing came out. She looked like a dying fish.

Blackness was falling like a theater curtain in front of her eyes. It was as fuzzy as the distorted image on a TV screen. She decided to surrender to it.

Then, as if from a great distance, someone touched her hand.

"Make a fist and squeeze!" the voice told her.

She tried to focus on the words, but she couldn't. The darkness was coming closer.

"Squeeze, Miss Jane!" She felt pressure on her fingers.

She was falling backward. Someone was guiding her down. The buzzing noise in her head abated a little, but the blackness was still falling all around her. It had slowed, but it hadn't stopped.

"Fight it, Miss Jane! Make a fist."

The voice permeated the buzz, and Jane managed to curl her fingers inward.

"Breathe in," the voice said. It was so calm. So patient and gentle.

Jane balled her fists and drew in a gulp of air. The buzzing abated a little and, a few seconds later, the blackness did too.

"That's it. Keep going."

Jane recognized the voice now. It was Lachlan's. He was keeping her from passing out by applying techniques Sterling had taught Jane and the rest of the Fins.

Sterling is the head chauffeur, Jane thought, coming back to herself more and more. *Butterworth is the head butler. Sinclair is the head librarian.*

As the faces of her beloved mentors and protectors floated through her mind, so did the face of the man from the video.

No! an inner voice screamed.

But there was no sense fighting what she'd seen.

Squeezing her eyes even tighter, she grasped Lachlan's hand, clinging to it like it was the only thing that could keep her from going under. From drowning. She parted her lips and, because her mouth was so dry, managed to whisper a single word. "William."

"William?" Lachlan asked in bewilderment. "As in, your husband?"

Jane couldn't speak. She could manage only the ghost of a nod.

"I thought . . ." Lachlan faltered. Jane heard him stop and begin again. "I thought he died before the twins were born."

Involuntarily, Jane traveled back in time to that terrible, terrible night. The worst night. She'd been in her late twenties. She and William had been married for two years and were expecting their first child. At the time, Jane hadn't known that she was carrying twins. She also hadn't realized that when she kissed her husband before his business trip, that it would be the last time she'd kiss him. Or see him. Or speak to him.

He would never return from that trip because his car would skid off the side of an icy bridge and plunge into freezing waters. That's what the authorities had told Jane. They'd had a hard time meeting her eyes. And it had been even harder for them to come back several days later and tell her that they'd failed to recover her husband's body.

Numb with shock, Jane had made arrangements for William's funeral. She'd stood by his grave and witnessed the lowering of his empty casket. She'd tossed a handful of dirt on its polished surface, followed by a single red rose, and walked away from the cemetery. She'd never returned. Instead, she'd moved home. To Storyton Hall. Where she'd found the love and support she needed.

She hated roses now. She hated high bridges and frozen lakes. She hated knocks on her door when she wasn't expecting visitors. She hated the nightmares that plagued her for years. In her sleep, she saw a blue-faced, glassy-eyed William tangled in a bed of underwater weeds. Eels slithered around his arms and legs.

William had died. She'd buried him. She'd welcomed her sons into the world without him. She'd learned to live without him. She was a widow and a single mother because William Wordsworth Heath was dead.

Except he wasn't.

Her husband was alive.

And he was here, at Biltmore.

CHAPTER FIVE

Emotions, swelling like a tsunami wave, threatened to overwhelm Jane. As if those weren't enough, there were questions too. They fluttered inside her head like a flock of birds trapped in a cage. The combination of emotions and questions nearly undid her.

Other than the night she'd learned of William's death, this was the greatest shock of her life.

Very slowly, Jane sat up. Without looking at anyone else in the room, she picked up the glass of Scotch. She drank down the contents and wiped her mouth with the back of her hand. The liquor didn't clear the fog in her brain, so she thrust the glass toward Parrish, wordlessly requesting a refill.

After the second glass of Scotch, she felt a bit better. Just a bit.

"How is this possible?" she asked Parrish in a leaden voice. She felt as empty as the grave she'd had dug for her husband.

Parrish gestured at the laptop. "We believed William would become the Guardian of Storyton Hall. We kept on eye on him. And you. From a respectful distance."

Parrish waited for Jane to react, but she just stared at him.

"We were following your husband the night of his accident. We believed he had already begun training for his role as Guardian. We thought his business trips had a secondary purpose." Parrish's shoulders moved in a ghost of a shrug. "He was too complex and clever a man to devote his life to insurance. We were certain that his travels were a cover—that his true mission was to collect materials for Storyton's secret library."

"That's ridiculous," Jane said. "*I* grew up at Storyton Hall. William didn't even visit until after we were engaged. Why would you leap to that conclusion?"

"Because the Guardianship has always been passed to a male."

Though she knew this to be true, the insinuation that she, as a woman, wouldn't be chosen for such an important responsibility made her bristle.

"Times do change," Parrish went on. "However, tradition called for a male Guardian, which is why we followed your husband. It was lucky for him that we did. We saved his life."

Jane shook her head in disbelief and muttered, "No."

"It does seem impossible. It was a frigid night. Everything was covered in ice. I was there, and I saw William's car skid. He couldn't control the slide." Parrish leaned toward Jane. "He fought for control, but momentum was against him. He crashed through the rail. Even if he'd survived the impact, we knew that he wouldn't survive the water. It was a stroke of good fortune that my colleague was used to swimming outdoors in extreme temperatures. He dove into the glacial water and pulled William out."

Jane could picture the lake. Black as ink, the water had swallowed her husband and their future together in a matter of seconds. She'd always wondered if he'd been conscious inside his sinking car—if he'd felt the icy water rushing over his feet and bubbling up his legs and chest. She'd been plagued by terrible thoughts of him trying to unfasten his seatbelt or opening the driver's door, only to find himself stuck. In other horrific fantasies, she'd pictured William escaping the car but drowning before he could reach the surface of the lake.

This horrendous scenario made the most sense. She'd always assumed that the lake currents had carried William's body to the river. And from there? That mystery had remained unsolved.

Until now.

"We couldn't let it be known that your husband survived, Ms. Steward," said Parrish "The price of his being rescued was that Mr. Heath's fate became forever intertwined with ours."

Jane looked at the computer screen. She'd been watching William while listening to Parrish, but William was no longer facing the camera. He'd turned to the rear wall of his cell and was scraping at the rough stone with a small rock.

"He's been in that cell for *nine* years?" Jane's anger gained fresh momentum. "That's barbaric!"

Parrish held up his hands as if to ward off a blow. "His tenure as Mr. Alcott's next-door neighbor is very recent, I promise you. He has spent most of those years in a facility. A quiet, peaceful place for individuals requiring special care."

Jane didn't understand his meaning. "Was he hospitalized?"

"In a manner of speaking," Parrish said. "Your husband had a private room. Some of the finest doctors in the field saw to his care."

This was almost too much for Jane to take. Minutes ago, she'd learned that her dead husband was alive. Following this mind-blowing discovery, she was being told that he was no longer whole.

"What was he being treated for? What's wrong with him?" she asked Parrish.

For once, Parrish seemed reluctant to speak. He held his empty glass to the firelight and studied the starry reflections on the cut crystal. "In a manner of speaking, William died in that lake. By the time my colleague pulled him out of the water, he showed no signs of life. We were able to revive him, but we couldn't reverse the effects of the hypothermia. He suffered damage to his brain, Ms. Steward. Specifically, to the parts that store memories or attach emotion to certain memories."

Jane looked at the screen. It was William in that cell. And yet it wasn't. What kind of treatment had he endured? What drugs had he been given? Had he been given shock treatment?

"Please don't despair, Ms. Steward," Parrish soothed. "Cutting-edge treatments have allowed your husband to make notable strides toward recovery. I've been told that his memories of his time with you could be restored by your proximity. I warned you that your choice would be difficult. Two men need saving, but you can save only one."

Parrish had just finished speaking when the fattest log in the fireplace broke apart. As it sagged, a spray of sparks burst upward, forming a beautiful, bird-like shape for a moment before it was sucked up the chimney flue.

Jane felt like that log. She felt like she was made of ashes—that a strong wind could blow away every piece of her. She was as fragile as a phoenix made of sparks.

A phoenix doesn't die, an inner voice said. *It burns. It suffers. But it is renewed. The pain grants it another life.*

If Jane focused on her pain, she would fail everyone. She knew this, but it was impossible to think logically and to make rational decisions when she was so overwhelmed by emotion.

William was alive.

Edwin was alive.

She could never choose between the two of them.

Then don't.

The thought was so forceful that it rose above the maelstrom of other thoughts. Jane clung to it, and it grew in force, burning with the intensity of a million fires.

"I choose both," she said with remarkable aplomb. "I won't leave this place without Edwin and William. Toss me in a cell, if you'd like, but I'm not budging on this point. And you will never get what you want unless you agree."

Parrish fell silent. He was quiet for such a long time that Jane wondered if he'd ever speak again. At first, she watched him, but as the seconds passed, her gaze flicked to the laptop screen. She was still trying to absorb the fact that the bearded man was William.

What if it wasn't?

The thought made Jane draw back in surprise. "You could be using this man as bait." Pointing at the computer, she gave Parrish a challenging stare. "A ruse to trick me into leaving Edwin behind. That man could be an imposter. Someone who looks like my husband. It wouldn't be difficult. People were always saying that he was a dead ringer for their brother or a close friend. How can you prove that he's my husband?"

Parrish seemed genuinely astonished. "I didn't think proof would be required. I've never been married, Ms. Steward, nor do I understand the desire for a spouse, partner, or significant other. However, I thought you'd see your husband and instantly know him. Is that not the case?"

"I've learned that some clichés are full of wisdom. 'Looks can be deceiving' is one of them." She tapped the screen. "If that man is William I'll know it. But I can't tell from this distance. I need you to bring me to him."

When Parrish began to protest, Jane cut him off by insisting that Bruno get William right now.

"I will have your husband brought here. Before I do, you might want to consider something." Parrish's smug smile was back. "If the man on that screen is William, how will Edwin handle his return from the dead? How will you?"

These questions had already occurred to Jane, but she couldn't deal with them right now. They were too complicated. She could focus only on getting William and Edwin to Storyton.

"I'll figure it out," she said tersely.

"I am impressed by your composure, Ms. Steward. I feared you might become overly emotional after seeing the husband you thought was lost so many years ago."

Jane was distracted by what was happening in the bearded man's cell. His head had whipped around to face the door. Suddenly, he was on his feet. He walked toward the door and vanished from view.

Jane knew that it would be easier if she could continue to think of him as the bearded man. She couldn't accept him as William. Not yet. She couldn't accept the fact that the man she'd married might enter this room in a matter of minutes.

Her belly roiled, and she wished she had a cracker or a piece of toast to soak up all the liquid she'd consumed. It felt like a lifetime ago that she and Lachlan had eaten pizza in their hotel.

"Are you all right?" Parrish asked.

"I was wishing for a piece of bread," Jane replied honestly. "Or something to help settle my stomach. I'll be all right in a moment."

Parrish looked to Bruno and a wordless message passed between them. Bruno cleared the crystal glasses and returned from the kitchen with another tray, which he set down in front of Jane. He'd brought her a thick slice of farmhouse bread covered with strawberry jam.

No longer concerned about poison, Jane bit into the bread. It was pillowy soft in the middle, and the fresh jam tasted like a summer day.

She was just wiping her mouth with a napkin when William entered the room.

It was William. It was not a doppelgänger with a beard. It was her husband.

He was the right height. The right build. His

eyes were the right shade of brown. His sandy hair was the right texture. Everything about him felt right. He was the right man.

And yet he wasn't.

He looked directly at Jane and didn't react. He didn't know her.

"Hello," he said to the room at large.

He spoke with William's voice. His pleasant alto.

Jane wanted to run to him. She wanted to throw her arms around him. She was so relieved that he was alive. There he was, as familiar as a best friend from childhood.

He's not a friend. He's your husband.

As William stood there, looking perplexed, time shifted. It folded and bent, turning Jane into a younger woman. She was in her twenties, not her thirties. She was a wife and an expectant mother. She hadn't given birth to twin boys. She hadn't become the manager or the Guardian of Storyton Hall. She hadn't fallen in love with another man.

She was William's Jane again.

"Hello," he said, flashing her a friendly smile.

The smile hurt. How many times had he smiled at her that way? How often had that smile made her melt?

Be brave, she told herself.

"Hi," she said in a soft voice. "I'm Jane."

"William," he said, making no move to shake

her hand. He glanced at Lachlan, but Lachlan didn't speak. He was still assessing William with an air of cold detachment.

Parrish gestured to the sofa. "Why don't you sit down, William? Bruno will bring you something to eat. I'm sure you're hungry."

"I am, thanks." William took a seat at the other end of the sofa, keeping his distance from Jane. His attention was fixed on Parrish. "I don't want to go back to that room."

He sounded like a little boy who, having been given a harsh punishment, begs for a reprieve.

"You don't need to go back," Parrish assured him, closing the laptop. "While you eat, we're going to talk about where you came from."

"The facility?"

Parrish shook his head. "Before that. We want to talk about your life before your accident. Do you remember your accident?"

"I remember the water. It was dark and so cold. That's all." William folded his arms over his chest in a protective gesture. He froze in that position, and Jane wondered if his body recalled more than his mind.

Bruno returned with a tray. When William saw the offerings, a sandwich and a mug of beer, he visibly relaxed.

The sight of the beer drew tears to Jane's eyes. She remembered pouring beer into William's pint glass at their favorite corner bar the night before his ill-fated trip. He'd been playing darts with one of the locals, and Jane had waited until the game was over to fill his glass. She didn't normally steal the bartender's job, but he'd been really busy that night, and Jane had told him to leave William's bottle of lager and she'd see to it.

Without realizing what she was doing, Jane pointed at the glass on his tray. "You used to like honey lager. Your favorite was called Midas Touch. You drank it at a local bar called William Penn's Pub. You loved that place."

William stared at her. "You knew me? From before?"

Jane's heart was hit by a fresh stab of pain. He was William, but he wasn't her husband. Not anymore. Unless the man she'd married was trapped somewhere inside *this* man's head. Had his brain been too badly damaged for him to return or could his memories be brought back?

Do I even want him to remember?

Though the question was an honest one, it was also selfish and cruel. Jane had fallen in love with another man, but that didn't mean that she shouldn't do everything in her power to make William whole again. He deserved to be rescued, and if Jane could find a way to rescue him, she would.

"Yes, I knew you from before the accident," she said. "I can also tell you that you liked mustard on your sandwiches. Not mayo."

William peeked under the top slice of sandwich bread before looking at Bruno. "May I have some mustard, please?"

Bruno whisked the plate away and left the room.

"How did we know each other?" William asked Jane.

Jane didn't think this was the time to tell William that she was his wife.

"I'm a friend," she said, shooting a warning glance at Parrish. He shrugged as if to say that he wasn't going to interfere with their reunion. "We went to college together."

At that moment, Bruno returned with a fresh sandwich.

William thanked him, took a bite, and chewed. He grinned at Jane. "I do like mustard better. What else can you tell me?"

Seeing that boyish grin on his familiar face—a face that was older, yes, but still the face of the man she'd once loved—brought Jane's grief to the forefront. She longed to touch William but sensed that such an act would alienate him. She was a stranger to him—a truth she'd have to strive to remember.

"I can tell you so much more, but I have to go home," she said to him. "My home is a beautiful place called Storyton Hall. Have you heard of it?"

William cast a nervous glance at Parrish. "I don't remember it. I swear."

It sounded as if he'd given this answer hundreds of times before.

Anger boiled inside Jane. The very mention of Storyton Hall upset William, which meant he'd been questioned about it by Parrish and his heinous cohorts.

Questioned? Or tortured?

"Well, it's a bit like Biltmore," she said, fighting to maintain a neutral tone. "It's big and old with lots of rooms. It also has walking paths and hiking trails. You used to enjoy hiking." She smiled at William, and he smiled back. "Storyton Hall is a paradise for readers. We have thousands of books and dozens of comfy places to read them."

"I love books," William said, reaching for his sandwich again. "Especially books about history."

Jane's husband had also loved this genre. He'd plowed through biographies, nonfiction works, and historical fiction. As long as it focused on the past, no book was without merit.

"This week, we're hosting an organization celebrating the centennial of World War One. This group has been touring the country for several years now, educating people on the Great War. This is their final year of reenactments and other events, and they've chosen Storyton as one of their last stops. I bet you'd love to hang out with these historians."

"I would," William said. His eyes were shining, but when he looked at Parrish, the light instantly dimmed. "Can I visit Storyton Hall?"

"Certainly. Stay as long as you'd like," Parrish said magnanimously. "We should take a look at your things and make sure that you have what you need for a lengthy visit. If not, we'll take you shopping in the village tomorrow. Ms. Steward won't be leaving until Monday morning, so you have plenty of time to prepare."

William nodded obediently, thanked Jane, and stood up to leave. He was about to pass from the living room into the vestibule when he paused to glance back at Jane. "Steward? I feel like I've heard that name before." His gaze went fuzzy as if he was trying very hard to remember. "I hope you can help me. Like you did with the mustard. I have so many holes in my memory. I wish I could fill them all in."

It was getting harder and harder for Jane to mask her emotions. She didn't want William to go. She wanted to grab him and take him to her hotel. What if she lost him again? She didn't trust Parrish. It was because of this distrust that she knew she had to hide her anguish.

"I'll help you any way that I can," she told William. "See you soon."

A wave of sorrow hit her as she realized that she'd just repeated the same words she'd said all those years ago. Her final words.

Once he was gone, Jane passed her hands over her face. She wouldn't cry in Parrish's presence. To force the tears back, she pushed her fingertips against her closed eyelids. After emptying the air in her chest through a slow exhalation, Jane felt calm enough to speak. "That man is my husband, Mr. Parrish, and he needs to be in my care. I'd like your word that he'll be well treated until he returns to Storyton with me. Are you planning to put him back in a cell?"

Parrish was unfazed by the steely edge to Jane's voice. "No. His tenure there was temporary. The setting was meant to elicit a certain reaction from you."

"As was the beard? A ruse to make me think he'd been imprisoned for years? Did you put the note in the lion's mouth too? I think you did. I think you've been leading me around like a dog on a leash." Jane's voice was tight with anger. When she received no answer, she got to her feet. She was desperate to get outside—to suck in lungfuls of fresh air—and to have some time to digest the enormity of her new reality. "What happens next?"

"You return to your conference. I will inform Mr. Alcott of his upcoming departure on Monday morning."

Jane shook her head. "We're leaving tomorrow night. We need to return to Storyton Hall with you, Edwin, and William after dark. Especially since you intend on keeping Edwin locked in a hotel suite."

"Where he'll surely be treated like a king," Parrish said. "I'll meet you at your hotel tomorrow following the afternoon conference session. I look forward to getting to know you better, Ms. Steward, and I am most excited about my stay at Storyton Hall."

Parrish walked them to the door and explained that Bruno would drive them to their truck.

Jane slid into the back seat and closed her eyes. She didn't speak as she and Lachlan headed back to their hotel. Lachlan gave her the space and silence she so desperately needed.

Back at their hotel, Jane grabbed a water glass and the bottle of wine Lachlan had opened for their supper and told Lachlan that she'd be in the garden.

"I'm here if you need me," he said.

Jane's hands shook too violently to pour the wine, so she set the bottle on the low garden wall and dropped into a metal chair. Now that she was alone, she thought the tears would come streaming out, but something held them in check. It was if a stopper blocked all of her emotions and she didn't know how to unplug it.

"I don't even know what I'm feeling," she whispered to the empty patio. The quiet night and shadowy sky were of some comfort. But not enough.

Whenever Jane felt completely lost and overwhelmed, she turned to one person. Eloise would know exactly what to say to make Jane feel better.

She took out her phone and stared at the screen. How would she explain this fantastical turn of events to her best friend? Jane needed to come up with a credible story for the unbelievable revelation she was about to share not only with Eloise but with everyone else in Storyton as well.

"William is alive," she practiced saying out loud.

Deciding to wing it, she dialed Eloise's number. Within seconds of hearing her best friend's cheerful "hello," Jane was crying.

"What is it?" Eloise was instantly worried. "Is it Edwin?"

"He's okay. We found him, and he's okay," Jane said through a choked sob. She might be hurting, but she wouldn't let Eloise suffer unnecessarily. "It's hard to get the words out. I came to Biltmore for Edwin. He was here, and I'm bringing him home." Another sob escaped. "I found someone else too. My God, it's so . . . unreal."

Eloise made a shushing noise. "You won't be able to tell me anything if you can't breathe. Listen. I'll distract you with a little anecdote about the twins. By the time I'm done, you'll be able to say what you need to say. Okay?"

Jane made a noise of assent.

"Before I start, I should warn you that this story involves Fitz and Hem, Sunday School, rubber cement, and a burning bush." She paused. "The burning bush was supposed to be a craft activity to go along with the day's Bible lesson. Emphasis on *supposed to be*."

Eloise's strategy worked. Jane's brain immediately switched into Mom mode. She stopped crying and muttered, "Just tell me they haven't been banned from church."

"Not quite, but the twins are scheduled to polish pews next Saturday. They received a sentence of community service."

Jane actually laughed. "Thank the stars for you, Eloise." She raised her face heavenward, but the stars were still missing from the night sky. "Whenever I think I'm losing my mind, you keep me sane. And though you're a rock, you should probably sit down before I drop this bomb on you. I almost blacked out. Luckily, Lachlan wouldn't let me."

"You're really worrying me," Eloise said. "Can you just spit it out?"

"William is alive."

Eloise said nothing. Silence echoed through the phone speaker, and Jane didn't break it. She had to give Eloise time to take in the news.

When the pause started to grate on Jane, she started talking. "He didn't die the night of the car accident. And he doesn't remember me. He doesn't remember anything about his life before that night."

"Okay, I'm sitting down now." Eloise released a pent-up breath. "Good Lord, Jane. I don't even know what to say. It's a miracle." After another brief silence, she asked, "Where has he been all these years?"

"In a medical facility," Jane said. "He doesn't need to be there anymore, so I'm bringing him home."

This news was met by a low whistle. "This is some *General Hospital*–sized drama," said Eloise. "I can't wrap my head around it. What will you tell the boys? What will you tell Edwin? And speaking of my brother, why did he fall off the face of the earth for two months?"

"I'll let him explain that to you in person. Just know that he's okay and he's coming home with me tomorrow. As for William, I'm not going to tell the boys that the stranger I brought back from Biltmore like he was a souvenir is their father," Jane said. "Which is why the rest of the Cover Girls can't know about him. If Mrs. Pratt gets wind of this, the whole village will know. Same goes for Mrs. Hubbard. She'll be tougher to fool because William will be staying on the property."

"In your house?"

Jane considered this for a moment. On the one hand, being near her might trigger William's memories. Then again, she didn't know him. Not this version of him, anyway. And she had Ramsey Parrish to deal with. "He'll bunk with Sterling or Lachlan. I'm sorry if that puts a damper on your romantic life, but it's temporary. Promise."

"You went to Biltmore in search of my brother, and you end up finding your long-lost husband. Only you could manage such a feat."

"Well, I wanted to call and tell you to stop worrying," Jane said, buoyed by Eloise's banter. Just listening to her familiar voice was a balm to Jane's anguished spirit. "I'm beat, though, and I should probably try to get some sleep."

Eloise grunted. "Like either of us is getting much of that tonight. My worrying is now focused on you. I hate to point this out, Jane, but you're not a widow anymore. You're a married woman. And you're in love with another man."

Jane thought of a line from a Rumi poem that roughly translated to "Love is fearless in the midst of the sea of fear."

But she didn't say it out loud because she didn't feel fearless. She felt like she was standing at the brink of an abyss, and if she didn't step carefully, she and everyone she cared about would be pitched into blackness.

"I'll figure it out," she told Eloise.

But even as she spoke, she was reaching for the bottle of wine.

CHAPTER SIX

Jane wondered how she would even pretend to pay attention during the morning conference session. Tonight, she'd be returning to Storyton with her husband *and* her lover. She'd also be inviting a known enemy into her home.

She began planning for the complications that would inevitably stem from these events at daybreak. After brewing a pot of strong coffee, she called Sinclair.

"Are you certain the man is William?" Sinclair asked. "Could he be an imposter? A man disguised by prosthetics or plastic surgery? Has he been brainwashed into obeying Parrish's commands?"

Jane had asked herself these same questions. "All I can say is that he looks like William. He sounds like William. But it's not like I examined him for telltale scars or marks."

"I suppose not," Sinclair said, sounding disappointed.

"I couldn't take the chance that he *isn't* William. Can you understand that? I couldn't leave him here," Jane said. "I'm not being naïve. Knowing he could be Parrish's agent, I won't reveal things to him—only harmless details from our past. Because if he is William, I have to help him, Sinclair. I have to do anything I can to restore him."

Though the head librarian of Storyton Hall and Jane's mentor murmured in agreement, Jane knew that he was troubled.

"When I left Storyton for Biltmore, I didn't expect to be reunited with William or to bring a snake into our midst," she added. "At least we can prepare for Parrish's visit. He made his demands quite clear. The question is, how will we get rid of him without putting Edwin in danger? Or others close to me? Parrish is bound to have an insurance policy. He'll expect us to rescue Edwin. He'll expect to be kicked to the curb without getting what he wants. So what provisions does he already have in place to prevent that from happening?"

"Thus far, Mr. Parrish has orchestrated his plans with the skill of a chess master. It is my opinion that he arranged for the Luxury Lodging Symposium to be held at Biltmore over a year ago. Booking the conference, abducting Mr. Alcott, and luring you to Biltmore must have been Mr. Parrish's backup plan when the attempt to discover the secret library by kidnapping the twins failed."

When Jane considered what Parrish and his Templars had done to gain access to the secret library, she knew they wouldn't stop trying. The faction was willing to cross any line to achieve their goal, and that filled Jane with fear.

"It'll never end," she lamented. "There will never be peace for me or my boys."

Sinclair didn't argue. "There will be moments of peace and moments of peril. This is the life we have all chosen."

I was born into it, Jane thought. *I didn't have a choice.*

Jane spent a moment wondering if she could spare the boys the same fate by donating the entire secret collection to a reputable museum. This was a thought she'd have to return to later.

"We know this group is patient," Jane said. "We know this group planted someone in the Storyton community, and that he lived and worked among us for years, waiting for the chance to infiltrate Storyton Hall. Kidnapping my sons led to his death, but what if there's another spy in our village? Or, heaven forbid, working as a Storyton Hall employee?"

"I have complete confidence in our staff, Miss Jane. They've been thoroughly vetted. We can never be sure about the villagers. There are too many to monitor."

Jane felt a growing sense of frustration. "What can we do, then? How do we defend ourselves against these fanatical Templars?"

"First, we place someone loyal to us among the visiting historians. We've already made those arrangements," Sinclair said. He sounded completely untroubled. "Secondly, we've booked

Mr. Parrish into the Mystery Suite. As you remember, we made changes to those rooms."

"Yes."

"The *updates* will grant you full access to Mr. Alcott, even if he's locked in the suite from sunrise to sunrise."

Several years ago, before Jane was told of the secret library or her family's role as Guardians, there'd been a murder in the Mystery Suite. Following a terrifying series of events, Jane's newly revealed Fins had met with her to discuss heightening the security of Storyton Hall. Jane's ancestor, Walter Steward, had designed his behemoth mansion to include numerous secret passages, hidey-holes, and if the rumors were true, secret rooms. Unfortunately, the blueprints disappeared after the Georgian manor house was disassembled in England, transported across the Atlantic, and reassembled in a serene valley in western Virginia. An architect had done his best to replicate the lost plans, but none of Storyton Hall's secrets were included in that drawing.

Ever since the murder in the Mystery Suite, Jane had been looking for these hidden places. Uncle Aloysius had shown her the ones he knew, but he was well into his eighties and preferred not to linger in damp corridors shining a flashlight over the roughhewn walls or the cold flagstone floors in search of concealed doors or cubbyholes.

Uncle Aloysius remembered his father, Cyril, showing him a few of Storyton Hall's secrets when he was a boy. However, his father died when Uncle Aloysius was still young, and the memories of these hidden places died with him. One thing Jane's great-uncle never forgot was a passage from the Mystery Suite to what was now a housekeeping closet. The Fins had recently restored this passage.

"As far as dealing with Mr. Parrish, I'm afraid we can't hit him with the wrench in the library," Sinclair continued.

Jane appreciated his reference to her favorite childhood board game, but she was in no mood for levity. "Because he's like a hydra? If we chop off one head, another will grow back in its place?"

"We're not murderers," Sinclair said. "Our mission is protection. We don't seek violence."

"Well, it certainly seeks us," Jane grumbled.

It was barely seven, and she was already tired. She hadn't slept well. Her dreams had been riddled with fragmented images of sinking cars, the face of the Bacchus fountain, and a man who looked like Edwin one moment and William the next. Having risen with the sun, she was now feeling completely out of sorts. The coffee helped a little, but it wasn't nearly enough to combat the seemingly insurmountable obstacles facing her the moment she left Biltmore.

Reaching for her mug, she thought of all the wine she'd had the night before. No wonder she'd had such vivid dreams.

"Let's focus on what we have going for us," she said after a fortifying sip of coffee. "And by that, I mean Edwin."

"Yes," said Sinclair. "Presuming he's of sound mind and body. Have you spoken to him?"

Jane recounted the details of the previous night, omitting the conflicting emotions she'd experienced over William.

"If Mr. Alcott's weight loss is the only negative consequence of his incarceration, that can be easily remedied. Mrs. Hubbard would love to fatten him up."

At this, Jane barked out a laugh. "I can totally imagine her wheeling a cart with a six-course meal through the secret passageway. She'd sit in a chair and chat away as he ate, scolding him if he left so much as a crouton on his plate."

"I believe Mr. Parrish will try to control Mr. Alcott's environment in any way that he can. Undermining that control would be in our best interest."

They spoke a little longer about which questions Jane should ask Edwin on the drive from Asheville to Storyton. They also decided the best place for William to stay and what could be done to keep him busy and out of harm's way.

"What about our undercover historians?

Shouldn't I know more about them? They'll be arriving tomorrow morning."

"I'll fill you in when you're back," Sinclair said. "You have enough to focus on today. Including taking receipt of the book you requested for Mr. Tucker. A courier should be at your hotel within the hour."

Checking her watch, Jane saw that it was time to get ready for the morning meeting. She thanked Sinclair and hung up.

The courier arrived when Jane was in the shower. Lachlan showed her the package when she appeared in the kitchen.

"This came for you."

"It's for Tuck," Jane said. "I asked Sinclair to send me a book—by way of a truck driver passing through Asheville—from my personal collection."

"What kind of book?"

Jane cut the padded envelope and pulled out a bubble-wrapped object. She severed the bubble wrap and carefully unfolded the layers of white paper protecting a large book in green cloth with decorative gilt.

"*Italian Villas and Their Gardens,*" Lachlan read the title. He looked unimpressed. "I'm sure Mr. Tucker will like it. It's about gardens, and he's a gardener."

"It's more than a simple gardening book." Jane turned several pages. "This was written by Edith

Wharton and illustrated by Maxfield Parrish. Edith Wharton stayed at Biltmore. She and George Vanderbilt were friends. Tuck loves this estate and any connection to it, and I'm sure that he'll love this book. It's full of what Wharton called 'garden-magic,' and she writes about the unique harmony between house, grounds, and the surrounding countryside. It'll be the perfect addition to Tuck's collection."

Lachlan nodded absently. His mind was not on books. "When should we take it to him?"

"At the lunch break following my morning session," Jane said.

Though Jane sat in the conference room with her fellow hotel managers, the notes she took had nothing to do with catering to today's luxury traveler and everything to do with besting Parrish.

As soon as the session was over, she hurried outside and told Lachlan to drive to the bakery in Biltmore village. Here, she bought three curry chicken croissants, a jug of iced tea, and a selection of treats including baklava, pot de crème, chocolate fudge cake, and peanut butter pie.

"Are you hoping Mr. Tucker will share?" Lachlan asked as Jane loaded the goodies into the truck.

"Maybe," Jane said. She'd gladly sample any of the desserts.

Lachlan held out his phone. "I haven't heard back from him yet, but he told us that he might go fishing."

"Let's wait for him at his place," Jane said. "We can eat our sandwiches on his garden bench."

She expected Tuck to respond to Lachlan's text fairly quickly. However, when they finished their lunches, they still hadn't heard from Tuck.

"He might be fishing in a place with little or no reception," Lachlan said.

Jane moved around Tuck's garden. Even though it was autumn, the garden was a riot of color. A variety of bushes grew in the dappled light under weeping cherry and Japanese maple trees. Butterflies flitted from bloom to bloom and birds rustled in the leaves. It was such a serene place.

After slowly circling the garden, Jane returned to Lachlan to see if there'd been any word from Tuck. Lachlan shook his head.

Jane felt a keen sense of disappointment. She wanted to give Tuck the book in person—to see his face break into a smile of childish delight. In addition to her own desires, she was also worried about him. She kept wondering if Tuck would pay some kind of penalty for consorting with Lachlan. And with her.

I wonder if he has room for this book on his shelves, she thought, looking for a distraction.

Recalling how pleasantly stuffed the reading-room shelves had been, Jane decided to peek in the window to see if Tuck would be able to display his new prize on the shelf holding his favorite books.

As there was a bush with small thorns right below the window, Jane had to approach from the side and stand on her tiptoes to look inside. However, the sun was shining at her back, and her reflection blocked her view. Edging closer, she put her hand to her forehead and moved right up to the glass.

She drew back as if she'd been stung. In her haste to get away from the window, she dragged her right arm across a row of prickly thorns. The pain barely penetrated her shock. She called for Lachlan.

He was at her side in seconds. She didn't need to tell him to look in the window. He figured that out on his own.

"Is he dead?" Jane whispered.

"I think so." Lachlan peered into the reading room for a long moment before meeting Jane's horrified gaze. "I'm going in. You—"

"Don't tell me to wait here, because that's not happening," Jane said.

There was no need for Lachlan to take out his lock-pick tools because the door leading from the patio to the kitchen was open. Lachlan pushed it inward, coaxing a soft creak from the hinges. When he and Jane stepped into the room, the delicious aroma of freshly baked bread greeted them. Two loaves sat a cooling rack next to the stovetop. Tuck had also left an oven mitt and a green mug on the counter. The sink held a mixing bowl, two measuring cups, a pair of loaf pans, and measuring spoons. Though all the items were dirty, Tuck had managed to fill the bowl with water in an attempt to soften the dried bread dough encrusting its sides.

Jane and Lachlan proceeded to the reading room in silence.

Tuck was sitting in his favorite chair. There was a book on his lap and a teacup on the stand next to his chair. Tuck's book was closed, but his eyes were open. They stared, unseeing, at the fireplace. Tuck's lips were parted, and his hands curled around the edges of his book as if he'd held onto it with the last of his strength. Jane wondered if the feel of it had given him comfort in his final moments.

"What happened?" she whispered to Lachlan. "Was he worn out after a morning of fishing and baking? Leaving the dishes in the sink, he decided to rest with a cup of tea and a book. And he just drifted away in his chair?"

Lachlan surveyed the room before his gaze settled on Tuck's face again. "He looks peaceful enough. Still . . . things are out of place."

"The second mug in the kitchen?" Jane guessed. "It's not a teacup. It's a mug."

"As if Tuck planned to pour coffee for a guest."

Lachlan plucked a tissue from a dispenser on the bookshelf and used it to pick up Tuck's teacup. There was an inch of liquid left on the bottom. He gave it a good sniff.

"Anything?" Jane asked.

Lachlan swirled the liquid around in search of residue. "No. Let's go back to the kitchen."

In the bright and cheerful room, Jane put her hand on the bread to see if was still warm, but both loaves had thoroughly cooled.

Lachlan pointed at the coffee carafe. "It was paused in the middle of a brew session. See the flashing light?"

"The clock is flashing too. Mine does that whenever we lose power, or if I unplug it and plug it back in."

Jane scanned the kitchen. It was a cozy, well-used space. Jane could only imagine how many meals Tuck had prepared in this sunlit room over the years.

"He was in perfect health yesterday," Jane mused aloud. "Today, he got up, did whatever he did in the morning, and decided to bake some bread. He probably planned to eat it this afternoon, at teatime." She pointed at a jar of jam on the counter. "I bet that's the same jam Parrish gave me last night. It's warm in here. That jar should be in the refrigerator."

Lachlan grabbed a paper towel and handed

it to Jane. "I want to check his bathroom for medication. Use this to open cabinets. See if you come across any pill bottles."

Jane did as she was instructed. She examined the contents of cabinets, drawers, and the inside of the refrigerator and found nothing out of the ordinary. In fact, the room's ordinariness was one of the things that made it so appealing. She liked that Tuck kept a chipped plate because it was part of a set and that he had magnets on his fridge. He had a wall calendar marked with Biltmore events and a single unpaid bill in the drawer closest to the phone.

It doesn't have to be foul play, she told herself. *He wasn't a young man. He could have died of natural causes.*

But she didn't believe that. Tuck worked hard every day. He pruned, dug, planted, weeded, fertilized, and more. He was spry and incredibly fit for a man of any age.

The truth was that Jane didn't want Tuck to be dead. But since he was, and there was nothing she could do to change that, she wanted his ending to have been peaceful. What could be more peaceful than sitting in one's favorite chair, in one's favorite room, with a book and a cup of tea? To Jane, it was the ending she'd wish for those she loved. As long as they'd reached their golden years, that is.

Lachlan returned from the bathroom wearing

a grim expression. "He took medication for high cholesterol. That's all I could find."

"He might have had a heart attack," Jane said without conviction. There was something ominous about the unplugged coffee maker and the empty mug on Tuck's kitchen counter. Someone had stopped the coffee from brewing. Someone hadn't tarried long enough to wait for that empty mug to be filled.

"We need to go back to the reading room and call Butterworth. He or Sterling might be able to tell us what to look for on Tuck's body."

Lachlan placed the call as he walked. He quickly explained the situation and waited for a reply.

"There are no signs of a struggle. His hands are curled around his book, but otherwise, he looks, well, staged."

Jane realized this was an apt description. Even if Tuck had suffered a heart attack, it was unlikely that he'd be sitting perfectly upright in his chair with his book on his lap. At the very least, he would probably have fallen forward or slumped to one side. He wasn't slumped, though. He was sitting as most people would sit to read and drink tea.

The book was also closed, making Jane question if he'd ever opened it.

Could the book be a clue?

As it had no dust jacket, Jane squatted beside

Tuck's chair to read the title on the spine. *Arundel* wasn't familiar to her, so she looked it up on her phone. She knew the author, Kenneth Roberts, and had read *Lydia Bailey* and *Northwest Passage*. She'd never heard of *Arundel*, though.

Lachlan was watching her expectantly, the phone still pressed to his ear.

Jane pointed at the book. "This is the story of a man who marches with Benedict Arnold. Essentially, it's about a traitor who joins the British during the American Revolution. He defects. He aids the enemy. Just like Tuck helped us. We're the enemy he befriended."

Seeing the stricken look on Lachlan's face, Jane almost regretted having shared this with him. Lachlan had spent hours with Tuck, and the weight of culpability fell heavily on his shoulders.

Jane felt the weight too. Between the empty coffee mug, the positioning of Tuck's body, and the book title, she believed the old gardener had been murdered. Because of them.

Because of her.

She ordered Lachlan to get close to Tuck—to see if he could worm information out of him. The result of that prying was right in front of them. Tuck was dead. Here, in his book-lined sanctuary. His wonderful reading room.

"I think it was the reference to Bacchus," Lachlan said in a leaden voice. He then spoke

115

into the phone. "Mr. Butterworth, I'll call you back."

Jane turned away from Tuck to stare at Lachlan. "The fountain?" She considered this. "You're right. Parrish was unhappy about Tuck mentioning his partiality for the sculpture, especially that tidbit about coming across Parrish near the Bacchus fountain at all hours."

"I think that detail got him killed," said Lachlan. "I don't know how it was done, but there was probably an injection of some kind."

Jane fought to stop her brain from forming an image of Bruno pinning Tuck to the ground and pressing the point of a needle into his neck.

"We have to call the police," she said.

"We will, but it won't change anything. Even if you hint at foul play, they're unlikely to order extra lab work or perform an autopsy. Whatever drug he was given was undoubtedly meant to mimic a heart attack. Given his age and preexisting condition, the ME is bound to rule this a death by natural causes."

"Even so, I'm not going to leave him like this!" Jane said heatedly. She realized she was cradling the book she'd meant to give Tuck as a gift and eased her vise-like grip on its cover. "Parrish knew we'd try to get close to Tuck. In fact, I think he wanted Tuck to work the Bacchus fountain into a conversation. How else would we have discovered that underground passage in three days' time? How else would Parrish have suddenly found himself in a position to bargain with me?"

Lachlan put his hand on Jane's back and coaxed her out of the reading room. "I wouldn't put it past him. And if all of that's true, Parrish will expect us to call the police. I have no doubt that he's made provisions to ensure that the authorities will view this as a death by natural causes. Parrish has been several moves ahead of us all along."

"So how do we level the field?"

When Lachlan didn't answer, Jane took out her phone. "Even if Parrish planned it, I still need to report Tuck's death. The man deserves that small decency. I won't leave him to be found hours or days from now."

Jane called the emergency dispatch operator and was irked by the man's lack of urgency. With nothing else to do, she and Lachlan returned to the garden to wait for the police. Fifteen minutes later, a single cruiser pulled into the parking nook next to Tuck's cottage, followed closely by a coroner's van.

The two cops, both males, greeted Jane and Lachlan with stiff courtesy. After Jane told them who they were and why they'd come to Tuck's, Lachlan explained that they'd entered the gardener's house through the unlocked door.

"We wanted to help Mr. Tucker," Jane added.

"When we looked through the window, we could see that he wasn't okay."

"Next time, call for help first," one of the cops advised. "We're trained to handle this type of situation."

Jane bristled. She probably had more crime-scene experience than this baby-faced cop. Lachlan shot her a warning look, and she bit back her retort.

After a few more follow-up questions, in which the policemen established that she and Lachlan were visitors and didn't really know Tuck, the interview came to an abrupt halt.

"We have your contact information," the younger cop said. "We'll be in touch if we need anything."

Jane gaped at him. "That's it? You don't want to ask us anything else?"

"Not right now. We'll talk to the HR folks at Biltmore and contact the next of kin."

This is exactly how Jane would want a death at Storyton Hall to be handled, but she wasn't ready to be cut out of the equation. "You should know that Mr. Tucker was hale and hardy yesterday. He showed no signs of heart trouble and does strenuous physical work on a daily basis."

The policeman spread his hands. "Ma'am, you can't always tell that something's wrong until it's too late." He touched the brim of his hat in dismissal.

Jane almost begged him to test Tuck's blood for traces of a foreign element when she stopped herself. She had to trust in the local law. She had to believe they'd notice Tuck's peaceful posture and the presence of the coffee cup and be savvy enough to question the cause of death. Then again, they could be too busy with other matters to pay much attention to the sudden passing of an old man.

"I didn't think people died like that," she added, as the policeman was walking away. His partner was already inside the house. "You'll see. He's sitting in his reading chair with a book on his lap. It looks like he was posed by another person."

Without turning all the way around, the cop glanced over his shoulder and said, "Sitting in a chair with a book? That's not a bad way to go."

Making it clear that the conversation was over, he followed his partner into the house.

CHAPTER SEVEN

When Jane saw Edwin alight from Parrish's dark sedan, all the emotions she'd felt during his absence boiled over. Smiling through her tears, she rushed into his open arms.

They clung to each other without speaking. They didn't need words. The strength of their embrace said it all.

After a time, someone coughed, and the couple reluctantly separated. They held hands and stared at each other.

"You're so thin," Jane whispered to Edwin. "Are you okay?"

"I am now, you brave and foolish woman."

Jane smiled again. It was just like Edwin to be relieved and angered over being rescued.

"You can scold me later," she said and turned to Parrish. "I'd like to see William, please. We're not leaving until I do."

Parrish issued a mocking bow and knocked on the passenger window. William rolled it down and waved at Jane. "Hello."

There he was. Her husband. With his friendly smile and animated eyes. Jane wondered if she'd ever be able to look at him without feeling a knife-twist of loss in the center of her chest.

"Hi," she said with remarkable composure.

"I'm glad you're coming back to Storyton with us."

"Me too. Mr. Parrish thinks I stand a chance of recovering some of my memories." The light in his eyes dimmed a little. "I really hope so, because it feels like part of me is missing. I've felt this way for years."

Jane nodded in understanding before focusing on Parrish once more. "Mr. Lachlan will ride with you and William. Mr. Alcott will be with me." She quickly held up her hands. "I don't plan on spiriting him away when we reach Storyton Hall. I just want to reconnect with him on the ride home. I'll release him to your care as soon as we arrive."

"That will be satisfactory," Parrish said, undaunted as always.

Jane wished there was something she could do to wipe that arrogant grin off the man's face, but she had to settle for the fact that he was leaving his sanctuary and heading toward hers.

In the truck, she leaned over the console and pressed her forehead to Edwin's. They didn't kiss, but Edwin took her hands in his and held them flat against his chest. In the rhythmic beat of his heart, Jane felt all the love and tenderness she'd been missing.

Parrish revved his engine, and Jane reluctantly pulled away from Edwin.

"I had a bag stuffed with food for you," she

121

said. "We have so much to talk about, but you need to eat first."

Edwin made no move to pick up the bag. "If I hadn't kept so many secrets from you, Parrish wouldn't be following us back to Storyton Hall. It's all my fault that you're in such a vulnerable position."

"Eat," Jane commanded. "I put myself in this position when I fell in love with you, and we're sitting here because this is what people who love each other do. Crazy things. Illogical things. Love means doing what it takes to *be* together. After that, it means doing what it takes to *stay* together."

When she saw the stricken look on Edwin's face, she knew exactly what was running through his mind.

"Did you know about William?" she asked as she merged on to the highway.

Instead of answering, Edwin took out the sandwich Jane had bought at the bakery. After leaving Tuck's house, she'd almost tossed the entire bag in the trash, but Lachlan had pointed out that Edwin needed food.

After eating a few bites of his sandwich, Edwin replied to Jane's question. "I just learned about him. I had no company until William was put in the next cell. I asked the man who delivered my meal for the identity of my new neighbor, but he didn't answer. You've met Bruno. He's not exactly chatty."

At this, Jane couldn't help but laugh. There was no humor in it, but the sound helped defuse a tiny bit of stress.

"Did Parrish tell you about William?"

"Yes. He tried to use your husband to get to me," Edwin said. "Parrish hoped that I'd weaken after learning that the man you married was still alive. He taunted and taunted, expecting me to fall apart and tell him about Storyton Hall's secret library. I didn't say a word."

Jane shot a quick glance at Edwin. "But did it upset you? Hearing about . . . William?"

"Of course," Edwin said. "I don't want anything coming between us, Jane. Not ever. But I wasn't going to let Parrish know he'd gotten to me. I wouldn't give him the satisfaction."

They rode in silence for a minute. Jane looked in her rearview mirror and saw that the black sedan was right behind them.

"Things are about to get complicated in so many ways," Edwin said. He searched for Parrish's car in the side mirror, and Jane didn't know if his frown was meant for Parrish, William, or both. "If you choose to be with William when this is over, I'll understand. He's your husband. You're bound to have powerful feelings for him, even if you aren't sure what those feelings are. Your loyalty is one of the things I admire most about you. But be careful, sweetheart. This whole scheme could be a ploy to gain access to the secret library. Or worse."

This was such a chilling statement that Jane didn't respond for some time. Eventually, she said, "I won't tell William a thing. Parrish is a cunning bastard, which is why I need to know everything about him and his sect. By the time we reach Storyton, we have to come up with a plan to stop him. For good."

Edwin finished his sandwich, popped off the fruit cup lid, and speared a piece of apple with his plastic fork. " 'Hang there like the fruit, my soul, Till the tree die!' "

"I have no idea who said that."

Edwin smiled. "It's Tennyson's favorite line from Shakespeare. It's from *Cymbeline*, a play full of trickery, treachery, and rumormongering. I thought of it because you're about to encounter treachery from multiple directions. Also, my soul, I am with you. As your lover, ex-lover, or friend, I will be the fruit that lasts beyond the life of the tree."

He glanced in the side mirror again before adding, "Now that you know what's in my heart, let's focus on the complete annihilation of the man who dared to lock me in a cage."

By the time Jane passed through the massive iron gates marking the entrance to Storyton Hall, dark was falling. She drove up the winding driveway and felt a rush of pride when the Georgian brick manor appeared on the hilltop, glowing like a lighthouse beacon in the night.

Heading around back to the loading dock, Jane was relieved to see the rest of the Fins waiting to meet her. Butterworth, the head butler, had his hands clasped at his waist. Sterling, the head chauffeur, stood stiff as a soldier. And Sinclair, the head librarian, scanned the surrounding area. When his gaze met Jane's, he smiled affectionately.

Jane felt encouraged. The men she admired and trusted more than any others were ready to face this new challenge.

"Home," she said to Edwin.

Butterworth came forward and opened the passenger door for Edwin. The butler then bent at the waist, his bow a sign of respect. Edwin responded in kind.

"It's good to have you back, Mr. Alcott," said Butterworth. "It would be my honor to escort you and Mr. Parrish to the Mystery Suite."

Edwin thanked him and, turning to Jane, briefly laid his palm against her cheek.

"'Goodbyes are only for those who love with their eyes,'" he said. "Rumi expresses what I can't."

Jane watched Edwin and Parrish enter Storyton Hall but made no move to follow. Butterworth would get them settled in the Mystery Suite and see to their needs.

Tomorrow, Jane would play hostess to Ramsey Parrish and to dozens of historians as well.

Parrish's spies would undoubtedly be among the incoming guests, as would two people loyal to Storyton Hall. However, Jane still had no idea who these people were.

Sinclair will tell me tomorrow, she told herself. *Everything can wait until then.*

Sterling came forward to welcome William and to walk him to Lachlan's cottage near the mews. Jane watched her husband glance up at Storyton Hall, his face filled with wonder. Wonder, but not recognition.

At that moment, he looked so much like his sons that Jane had to turn away. She needed the pleasure and distraction of being with her boys. She needed to squeeze them, ruffle their hair, and listen to their prattle. Her sons were her true home. And they were waiting for her.

The next morning, Jane cooked eggs and bacon for Fitz and Hem. She shaped the food into smiley faces and listened to their chatter. After breakfast, she walked them around the corner to the garages where Sterling waited to drive them to school.

"Why can't we ride the bus?" Fitz complained for the second time that morning.

"Yeah, it's fun! If you sit in the back, you get bounced around," Hem added.

Jane gestured at the vintage Rolls-Royce sedan, which was idling in the driveway. "A few weeks ago, we talked about times when you'd have to be on your guard. We have new guests arriving today for a conference, so this is one of those times."

The boys exchanged excited glances.

"Okay," Fitz said. "But when the conference is over, can we ride the bus?

Jane glanced at her watch. "We'll see. You'd better get going or you'll be late."

"Grown-ups always say, 'We'll see' when they really mean no," Hem muttered as he climbed into the back seat.

Jane returned home to put on makeup and arrange her strawberry-blond hair in a low chignon. She wanted to look as polished as possible when her new guests arrived. When they entered Storyton Hall, she wanted these visitors to be dazzled by its beauty and grandeur, but she also wanted them to see that the manager was a poised and confident woman.

As Jane selected a string of pearls from her jewelry box, she let her fingertips brush over the owl pin Edwin had given her. Then, she opened a small velvet box nestled at the bottom of the box. Inside was her wedding ring. As she stroked the band of rose gold, she felt nothing. She'd buried William many years ago. She'd let him go. She'd finally stopped thinking of herself as a widow and had begun to view herself as a single mom and working professional. She was no longer the naïve girl William had married. Even if he suddenly remembered her, the woman he once knew was gone.

As she strode across the great lawn, her thoughts turned from William to another man. Tuck's death still weighed heavily on her. Last night, she'd dreamed of bringing him the Edith Wharton book. He hadn't been in his reading room when she arrived, but hard at work in his garden. Upon seeing her, he'd smiled. But his smile had turned to a look of shock as he snatched his hand out of a clump of ornamental grass. Jane saw twin drops of blood. He'd been bitten by a snake. In the dream, Jane had been frightened for Tuck. And for herself. The snake was nowhere in sight. It was lying in wait, a shadow among the shadows.

Jane didn't need a degree in psychology to know that she was upset over Tuck's death, concerned over the influx of new guests, and anxious about Ramsey Parrish's presence.

She decided not to dwell on obstacles, but to keep in mind that two of the historians were on her side.

Entering Storyton Hall by the terrace door, Jane found the main lobby, with its plush seating areas, glittering chandeliers, and stately grandfather clock, filled with an early morning hush.

Butterworth was instructing a member of the housekeeping staff on the proper way to polish brass, but he abandoned his lecture to follow Jane to the table bearing the large coffee urns.

"When will the first guests show up?" she asked.

"Mr. Sterling will go directly from the twins' school to the train station. The officers of the BackStory Club wanted to arrive before the rest of the attendees by several hours. It is my understanding that these gentleman plan to greet the other historians dressed in military uniforms from the Great War."

Jane hadn't had the opportunity to study the names, ages, faces, and occupations of these men. "Are any of these BackStory folks in our corner?"

Butterworth knew what she meant. Glancing at his customary place by the door, he decided he could leave it unguarded for a few minutes and told Jane to accompany him to the Henry James Library.

Sinclair was seated at his desk when they entered but sprang to his feet when he saw Jane.

"You've been missed," he said with such warmth that Jane wanted to hug him. Sinclair looked at Butterworth. "Shall we continue this discussion in my office?"

The walls of Sinclair's small office were lined with enlargements of driver's license or passport photos. Sinclair had affixed a sticky note containing relevant information to each photo.

"Let's begin with the BackStory Club officers. These gentlemen from New York City have been meeting for over a decade. They're united by their love of history. The club members read and discuss books, watch films, attend lectures, reenactments, museum exhibits—anything relating to the first half of the twentieth century."

"Are any women in this club?" Jane asked.

"Not as officers. However, Mr. Kelley's wife, Isabel, shares his passion for history. She has been most instrumental in the success of the centennial tour." Sinclair showed Jane the photo of Clarence Kelley, who bore a close resemblance to former President Eisenhower, before putting his finger on Isabel Kelley's photo. Isabel was a handsome woman with a gray bob and a pair of cat's-eye glasses with lilac frames.

"Who are the other officers of the boys' club?" Jane wanted to know.

"This gentleman with the red hair and beard is Michael Murphy. This gentleman"—Sinclair pointed at another photograph—"is Archibald Banks."

Having noticed a slight change in Sinclair's tone at the mention of Mr. Banks, Jane studied his image more intently. He was a bald man with a sharp chin covered in dark bristle and an intelligent gaze. Jane guessed him to be in his mid-forties. "Is he one of ours?"

"Mr. Banks is my first cousin on my mother's

side," Butterworth said. "I knew him as Archie when we were children. Like myself, Archibald has been in America for many years now. He is the custodian of a very large house in New York known for its collection of twentieth-century art."

Jane was intrigued by Archibald Banks. She'd never met a member of Butterworth's family, let alone had one stay at Storyton Hall.

"It's fitting that we're hosting a group of historians celebrating the centennial of the First World War because I feel like we're on the brink of war," she said, examining the faces on Sinclair's wall. Who was in league with Parrish? The man with the cold stare? The woman with the pronounced widow's peak? How would they know? Sinclair had already run background checks on every guest without finding a single red flag.

"We need more allies," Jane said. "I could recruit the Cover Girls."

Butterworth grunted. "To do what, exactly?"

"Keep their eyes open for shady behavior. Follow people who've entered staff-only areas. Get to know certain guests more intimately. That sort of thing."

Sinclair glanced at Butterworth. "It couldn't hurt." He turned back to Jane. "How will you explain the need for their help?"

"Well, one of the things Edwin and I talked

about on the way home was whether it was time to reveal his secret to Eloise."

The men stared at her with expressions of incredulity.

"That would be foolish," Sinclair said. "Mr. Alcott would only put his sister in danger."

"Ignorance is far more dangerous," Jane countered. "Are my sons safe because they know nothing of the secret library? No, they aren't. Are my friends safe because they have no idea that I'm a Guardian? No. I'm not telling them my secret, but Edwin had time to think during his imprisonment, and he no longer wants to keep his double life from his sister."

Sinclair spread his hands. "If this is Mr. Alcott's choice, so be it. Eloise Alcott is a clever woman. She could prove to be invaluable during this event. But mind this, Jane. The larger we make our circle of trust, the easier it will be to break."

His words echoed in Jane's mind for the rest of the day. She pushed them aside to greet guests and to oversee the erection of the Art and Poetry of the Great War exhibit in the Great Gatsby Ballroom. This was to be the setting for tonight's cocktail party and the unveiling of the war memorial that would later be given a permanent home in the community park.

Tonight, Jane would mingle with the historians and get a feel for their personalities. She'd invited the Cover Girls to join her, and they'd all accepted except for Betty and Anna. Betty had to tend bar at the Cheshire Cat, and Anna was bogged down with homework. Following the violent death of the previous pharmacist, Anna had been working with his replacement while taking online classes toward a doctorate in pharmacy.

"I warned you ladies that I might miss some book-club meetings, but I didn't think I'd be giving up any possibility of a social life when I enrolled in this program!" Anna lamented over the phone. "Do me a favor, will you? If you get another millionaire bachelor with a heart of gold like you had at the last conference, call me!"

"I thought you had a thing for Sam?" Jane had asked, referring to the hunky proprietor of Hilltop Stables.

Anna sighed. "He's been in love with Eloise since the fourth grade. It's impossible to compete with that. Can you imagine falling so deeply that you can't let go? No matter how much time passes?"

Jane thought of William. Theirs had been a true love, but seven years after his car had gone into that lake, she'd had him legally declared dead. She remembered signing the documents. She remembered feeling like she'd sealed up her heart. She hadn't wanted to feel anymore, and she would never love again. And then Edwin Alcott had come along. Against her will, Jane had fallen for him.

Edwin.

She wouldn't see him tonight. It was too risky. Butterworth would keep an eye on him, just as Lachlan would look after William.

Jane was having afternoon tea with Fitz and Hem in the kitchen when Lachlan asked to speak with her in private.

"Mr. Heath is a natural with our raptors," he said. "After teaching him how to feed them and clean their aviaries, I left him at my place with a book on training birds of prey. I told him to stay in the cottage and to eat supper and watch whatever he wants on TV. He was thrilled to have these small freedoms, Miss Jane. I don't think he's had many."

"No," Jane said sadly. "But you can't be responsible for him all the time, which means I have to tell Aunt Octavia and Uncle Aloysius about him. I'm just worried that the revelation will kill them."

Lachlan shook his head. "If you could handle it, so can they."

Jane finished her tea and sent the boys upstairs to do their homework under Aunt Octavia's watchful eye. Because Jane didn't want to take any chances with their safety, the boys were to stay in the apartment until bedtime.

Jane ate a light supper before changing into a burgundy cocktail dress. Over Great War era cocktails like the Sidecar, French 75, Gin Rickey, and Bee's Knees, Jane told the Cover Girls that the man who'd abducted the twins hadn't been working alone and that there were likely villains at the conference.

"Here and now? These bearded, pipe-smoking professor types?" asked Phoebe, the owner of Canvas Creamery. "Why would they mess with your sons? I don't get it."

Having anticipated this question, Jane had an answer ready. "People who don't know any better think I'm rich. I'm not sure how this rumor began. Does it have something to do with the construction of the Walt Whitman spa? Is it a result of all the media attention Storyton Hall has received the past two years? I have no clue. But I need your help."

"We'll do anything," said Violet. She owned a beauty salon called Tresses and always looked chic. Tonight, she'd styled her hair in a bun with rolled sides, replicating a 1915 hairdo. "Tell us what you need."

Jane asked them to cozy up to anyone who seemed unusually aloof or reserved. "If the guests feel like they're being watched, they might think twice before doing something illegal or immoral. Ours is a kill-them-with-kindness campaign. We'll get to know their names, their interests, and their movements. This should help prevent shenanigans."

"What if I like a man who misbehaves?" Mrs.

135

Eugenia Pratt teased. She was the most senior member of the Cover Girls and the group's most devoted fan of romance novels. She was also a notorious gossip, second only to Mrs. Hubbard.

"Seduce any man you want," Jane said. "That'll make my job easier. And I should point out that the male-to-female ratio at every event will be four-to-one."

Eloise slid an arm around Phoebe's waist. "Don't share that statistic with Anna. She'll be even more disappointed to miss out on the excitement."

"I doubt that very much," said Mrs. Pratt knowingly. "Have you seen the new pharmacist? He's a dead ringer for Clark Gable without the mustache."

As her friends launched into a discussion on male facial hair, Jane's eye was drawn to a tall man with a neatly trimmed, dark beard and a shiny pate. Jane told her friends to enjoy the art and poetry and drifted off.

The exhibit pieces were either mounted on folding display panels of rose-colored fabric or projected on large white screens. To bolster the effect of the screens, the room had minimal lighting.

Even in the dimness, Archibald Banks stood out. Though Jane saw no resemblance to Butterworth, she wondered why the Fins had recruited someone who was unlikely to blend in with any crowd.

Jane studied the painting on the projection screen opposite Archibald. It was a futuristic image of a horse being attacked by bayonets.

"It's hard enough to see images of men fighting men, but it's even harder to look at an animal under attack," Jane said without turning to Archibald. "Especially by bayonet."

"It's a powerful piece," he said. "I believe Umberto Boccioni meant to upset the viewer. This piece is unlike his previous ones. Typically, the horses in his paintings represented labor and the working class. Not war."

"It's powerful, but I keep returning to the piece over there." Jane pointed at another projection screen.

Archibald followed her gaze. *"The Ypres Salient at Night.* What about the painting speaks to you?"

Jane thought for a moment. "It's full of contradictions. You have your soldiers in the trenches on the bottom half. Above, in the night sky, a shell is bursting. It looks like the Star of Bethlehem. The star has been painted that way in lots of nativity scenes. But in this piece, it's not a star. It's a weapon. It's announcing the death of countless men. It's horrible and beautiful."

Archibald nodded with approval. "You have a good eye for art, Ms. Steward. I'm Archibald Banks, but my friends call me Archie."

As Jane shook his hand, she noted that Archie

had the same piercing blue eyes as Butterworth.

Archie gestured at the Storyton Band and said, "I'd better go. They're playing my song."

Having sat in on the band's practice session, Jane recognized the patriotic strains of "Keep the Home Fires Burning." Just below the raised stage where the band members sat, two men stood at a podium, watching Archie's approach. Jane had already spoken with the men several times that day, as they were both officers of the BackStory Club. With his tweed coat, wool vest, and bow tie, Clarence Kelley looked every inch the college professor. Michael Murphy, the bearded redhead, had opted for monochromatic attire by pairing a black turtleneck with black jeans. Jane guessed both men to be in their fifties.

When Archie reached the podium, Clarence signaled to Butterworth, who was conducting the band. When the song was over, Clarence took the microphone and welcomed his fellow historians to Storyton. Next, he gestured at Michael Murphy. "My colleague and I have traveled across the United States for the past two years with this centennial celebration. There has never been a dull moment." He turned to his friend. "It has been an honor to work with you."

Michael's cheeks turned ruddy. He acknowledged the compliment with a smile.

"Though our third Musketeer, Archibald Banks, couldn't join us on the road as much as he would have liked, he had a noble reason for missing some of the tour. Mr. Banks had a masterpiece to create. That masterpiece, ladies and gentlemen, is here tonight."

A spotlight illuminated a large object positioned alongside the podium. It was covered by a white sheet and guarded by Sterling and Lachlan.

"The sculpture bound for Storyton's community park is called *Steadfast*," Clarence continued. "It shows us another kind of soldier. The hard-working, never-faltering horse of the Great War. These majestic animals carried men and equipment—surviving the harshest of conditions. The stables of Storyton and its environs produced many notable war horses. This monument is dedicated to them. Ladies and gentlemen, I give you Archibald Banks's *Steadfast*!"

Sterling whisked off the sheeting, and the crowd burst into applause.

Though Jane had already seen the sculpture, she clapped as loudly as her guests. The metal horse had a steampunk vibe. It was made of gears, wrenches, and what she later learned were scraps of metal from original Great War tanks and airplane debris. Archibald had melted bullets to form the eyes. Somehow, the act of transforming a potential weapon into art had brought a spark to those eyes. The polished metal orbs seemed to contain a glint of light. Of life.

"A monument for a beast of burden. Ridiculous,"

said someone behind Jane. The arrogant tone was unmistakable.

Jane turned around and raised her glass in greeting. "Good evening, Mr. Parrish."

"Good evening, Ms. Steward. I thought I was here to mingle with historians, not a group of bleeding hearts. Would you like my opinion on animals?"

Glancing at the horse, its skeletal ribs barely concealed by a piece of sheet metal, Jane knew that Archibald was conveying starvation and suffering. The entire body of the horse was a hodgepodge of hardship. And of courage.

Since she didn't want to hear Parrish's answer, Jane planned to walk away before he could speak. However, he grabbed her by the elbow and said, "I view animals as trophies. Because man is the king of the jungle. Man is the hunter, and animals are his prey." He paused and grinned at her. "I'm a hunter. Which one are you, Ms. Steward? Hunter? Or prey?"

CHAPTER EIGHT

By the second day of the event, the staff at Storyton Hall declared the historians their quietest and most courteous guests of all time.

"They're so tidy," a housekeeper remarked to a sous chef.

"Smart too," added a member of the waitstaff. "I delivered in-room meals to two of them last night, and their desks were piled with books and papers. They bring books everywhere they go. They even read while they eat. It's like having a resort full of librarians or college professors."

Jane heard this exchange as she was passing through the kitchens. Normally, she'd greet all the staff members, but she was too distracted to be cordial.

She'd dreamed of Tuck again the previous night and had woken with a burning need to know how the Asheville police were handling his death.

After several frustrating minutes explaining herself to the officer answering the non-emergency line, Jane was transferred from one officer to another. No one wanted to deal with her, and when she was finally put through to yet another person's voicemail, she hung up and started all over again.

This time, when she reached the desk officer,

she said that she wished to speak with Officer Reece. Reece was the baby-faced policeman she and Lachlan had met at Tuck's house.

"Reece, here," he said when Jane was put through.

When her name didn't ring a bell, Jane reminded him that she'd called in Tuck's death. "I'd like an update on Gerald Tucker's case. I haven't been able to get him off my mind. Did you reach his next of kin?"

There was a pause as Reece decided how to proceed. Opting for the I'm-too-busy-to-deal-with-you approach, he said, "He doesn't have any, ma'am. They've all passed on. The Biltmore estate has generously offered to cover his funeral expenses. Is that all?"

Jane could practically hear the unspoken "little lady," tacked on to the end of Reece's question. Though her ire was rising, she remained calm. "Have you ruled on his death?"

"Natural causes," was Reece's terse reply.

"Were medical or lab tests conducted, or was this ruling based on his advanced age?"

Jane knew she'd made a mistake before the words had left her mouth. Playing naïve or coy might have gotten her more information, but she couldn't stand condescending men like Reece.

"Ma'am, all I can say is that proper procedures were followed. If there's nothing else, I have a—"

"Yes, there damn well is something else!" Jane decided to let it all out. "Mr. Tucker's death is suspicious. How can you explain the extra coffee cup in his kitchen? Or that his coffeemaker had been unplugged mid-brew? Or his staged body posture? No one dies sitting upright with a book on their lap and their head resting on the chair back."

Reece expelled a long and exaggerated sigh. "Are you in the medical field, ma'am?"

"No, I'm not. But I have common sense, and common sense points to a suspicious death."

Reece had had enough. "Ma'am, if you'd like to discuss your theories with someone, you should contact Bruno Volkov of the Biltmore Company Police."

Jane was about to ask for a number and the definition of Company Police when the name suddenly struck her. *Bruno*. How many Brunos could there be in Biltmore? Was Ramsey Parrish's hired thug also a member of Biltmore's Company Police force?

She was unable to ask Officer Reece for clarification because he'd already disconnected the call.

Turning to her computer, Jane searched for Biltmore Company Police but found no information on their officers. She was just about to look up Bruno Volkov when Sterling knocked on her door.

"Biltmore has its own Company Police," she told him. "What does that mean?"

"It's basically a private police force. Instead of working for a town or city, the officers work for a private company. Though licensed and armed, they can only make arrests on company property."

Jane thought about this. "Which means they shouldn't have jurisdiction over a suspicious death."

"Are you referring to Gerald Tucker?"

"Yes."

Sterling took a seat in the guest chair facing Jane's desk. "Mr. Tucker's death doesn't look suspicious from the outside. With no witnesses crying foul play, the police are likely to make the least-controversial ruling. I can't really blame them. Is there concrete evidence indicating murder?"

"No," Jane admitted.

"And blaming Mr. Parrish would make you seem fanciful, if not downright crazy," Sterling went on. "I hate to play devil's advocate, Miss Jane, but is it possible that you're assuming murder without proof?"

Jane was about to spit out a hasty reply when she stopped to consider Sterling's question. What hard evidence was there to indicate that Tuck had been poisoned? None. The police didn't launch investigations based on hunches or gossip. They used hard evidence to build cases.

"Thanks, Sterling. After thinking about it, I see that my hatred for Ramsey Parrish has colored all of my experiences at Biltmore."

Sterling got to his feet. "Don't let Parrish pull you down to his level. You'll beat him because you're the better human being."

Filing this advice away, Jane busied herself with checking items off her to-do list. Work was coming along nicely on the Walt Whitman spa. The first phase should be complete in time for Jane to offer a Winter Rejuvenation package. After scheduling a meeting with the future spa manager to discuss putting her organic spa products in the hotel's boutique by the end of the month, Jane paid bills and reviewed several inventory request forms.

By the time she was done, she realized that the morning centennial events were over. The historians would now be enjoying a leisurely lunch in the Rudyard Kipling Café or in the Madame Bovary dining room.

Jane and Mrs. Pratt, the only Cover Girl without a job, were attending one of these. Examining the choices weeks ago, which included Political Cartoons of the First World War, Posters and Flags of the Great War, and Wartime Culinary Challenges, they'd opted for the culinary event.

Mrs. Hubbard was in charge of the hands-on cooking class. She started her lesson by passing out white aprons.

"I'm sorry that we're in the smaller kitchen, but we're prepping for dinner in the main kitchen," she explained to her students. "I hope you're ready for noise. Commercial kitchens aren't exactly quiet. Maybe you'll feel like you're in a military mess hall, eh?"

Mrs. Hubbard studied her class, which was predominantly male. "I'm sure that many of you gentlemen are skilled cooks. But today, we're pretending it's wartime and that you're the woman of the house. Your man has gone off to fight for his country, and life at home is no cakewalk. You have to learn how to balance the budget, make repairs, and feed your family. Items are disappearing from the shelves in the general store, but you have to learn to make do. You have to make the best of the situation."

A man raised his hand. "Are we pretending to be American women?"

"For this exercise, you're a British gal," Mrs. Hubbard said with a smile. "Those poor women had it harder than our ladies when it came to rationing."

The man nodded in agreement.

"Right. Now, that you've been paired off, we'll begin with fish sausages," Mrs. Hubbard continued.

Mrs. Pratt turned to her cooking partner, a man in his sixties with glasses and thick gray hair. "The combination of fish and sausage doesn't sound the least bit appealing to me."

"Nor me," he said. "But we must soldier on."

Jane's partner was Michael Murphy, the ginger-haired BackStory Club officer. He pointed at the teacup on the counter in front of him and frowned. "How much is a teacup of fish? Do we loosely fill the cup or cram the fish in?"

Seeing mass confusion in her kitchen, Mrs. Hubbard showed the group exactly how much haddock to put in their teacups.

"As for the dried herbs, the resourceful cook would have used whatever was available in the garden. We have parsley and thyme, harvested from our own herb garden."

Jane and Michael moved in sync to mix the fish, cooked rice, and a beaten egg. Next, they rolled their mixture into finger-sized sausages. Michael's looked more like tater tots than sausages.

He surveyed his creations with a helpless shrug. "I've had less-appetizing-looking food."

Because they were pretending to be out of flour, the students rolled their sausage in oatmeal before frying them in boiling fat.

Mrs. Hubbard waited until everyone had finished cooking their sausages and had set them aside to cool before praising her students for their excellent work. "For our second recipe, we'll be making parkin."

Jane had never heard of this dish. Her face must have reflected her puzzlement, for Michael leaned close and whispered, "It's a gingerbread cake from Northern England, usually made with oats and black treacle. Treacle is the British version of molasses."

"How do you know so much about British food?" Jane asked, hoping Michael would turn chatty.

"I have family in England and Ireland," he said.

As they began to assemble their ingredients for the wartime parkin—coarse oatmeal, butter, ground ginger, salt, treacle, and milk—Jane tried to learn more about her cooking partner.

"I'm a professor at NYU," he explained. "Currently on sabbatical. When the centennial tour is over, I'll have to stop puttering around and get back to work. My department has been very supportive of my involvement in this tour, though I'm sure they'll expect me to publish a few thousand pages about it."

While Michael tried to figure out what kind of measurement a breakfast cup was, Jane asked if it had been hard to spend a year on the road. "Your family must have missed you."

"My fiancée has been a great sport," he said before turning away to reread the recipe.

In the front of the room, Mrs. Hubbard banged on a pot with a wooden spoon. "Attention, my dears! There's no need to fret over the breakfast cup. Think of a nice mug of milky coffee. Or, in mathematical terms, fill a standard measuring cup once, and then add another smidgen."

"One point two cups?" Mrs. Pratt's partner asked.

"Precisely!" Mrs. Hubbard beamed at him, and he smiled with pleasure.

Jane and Michael mixed the ingredients for their parkin and stared at their bowl.

"It's supposed to look like a firm paste," Jane said, studying the recipe again.

"Ours looks like granola clusters." Michael laughed. "The recipe called for a little milk, but I guess we used too little."

While Michael stirred another splash of hot milk into the dough, Jane glanced to her left to see what Mrs. Pratt was up to.

She was clearly having a ball. Her partner, a debonair gentleman in a sky-blue dress shirt, a polka-dot tie, and silver spectacles almost identical to Sinclair's, was just her type. Of course, she preferred men in kilts, but Jane could see that Mrs. Pratt wasn't disappointed to be cooking with a dashing academic.

While the parkin baked, Mrs. Hubbard told her class to remove the white napkins covering the metal trays at each of their stations. "I'm a big fan of *The Great British Bake Off*. I particularly love the challenges without recipes, so I've made a Great War technical challenge for you. You'll be making apricot charlotte without the aid of a recipe. This will help you understand how women were forced to cook in wartime. They learned to improvise and become more creative with food. Let's see how you'd do in their shoes."

"Yikes," Jane said, removing the napkin. "I hope you know how to make an apricot charlotte."

Jane was pretending for Michael's sake. She'd watched Mrs. Hubbard bake dozens of charlottes over the years.

"I think we have to line the mold with cookies or sponge cake and then fill it with pudding." Michael's brow creased in thought. "However, we haven't been given cookies or cake. Just bread."

Picking up an apricot, Jane pressed the soft flesh. "Fortunately, we won't have to soak these. That's been done for us. I'll butter the mold, and you can line it with the bread."

Intent on her task, Jane didn't notice Aunt Octavia's arrival.

"May I have your attention?" Mrs. Hubbard's voice easily rose above everyone else's. "We have a celebrity judge for this recipe. It's my honor to present Octavia Steward, Mistress of Storyton Hall."

Jane looked up from her tin and saw her great-aunt preening. "Let's not stand on formality. I'm just the old lady who lives upstairs. Jane is the true mistress. Hi, love!" she wriggled her fingers.

After waving back, Jane turned to Michael. "She has a very discerning palate."

"Damn," Michael muttered. "Is she bribable?"

"You'd have to get your hands on a nineteenth-century children's book in excellent condition."

Michael pretended to be crestfallen. "We're out of luck, I'm afraid. I'm a college professor living in a shoebox in Manhattan, which means I don't have the funds or the room for nice books. My collection concentrates on my area of study, and most of my books are not-so-gently used. You'd probably cringe if you saw them."

Jane smiled. "I don't think so. I think a book is like a good climbing tree. They both yearn to be touched."

"I like that," Michael said with a grin. "Okay, the bread is in the tin. What's next?"

"We add the apricots and the brown sugar. I guess we still have the luxury of sugar at this point in our wartime cooking."

Michael topped their filled tin with a plate and put it in the oven for thirty minutes. The cooking time was a guess, but Jane and Michael decided that half an hour was a safe bet.

While the apricot charlottes were baking, Mrs. Hubbard passed out samples of the wartime fare she and her staff had cooked that morning. There was pea soup, Saturday pie—meat, potatoes, and onions—and 1918 Cake. Jane wasn't fond of the latter. It was similar to fruitcake, but denser and less moist. Mrs. Hubbard said that the consistency was due to the lack of eggs and the extremely thrifty amount of added fat.

Reviewing some of the recipes in the binder

Mrs. Hubbard had given to all of the participants, Jane ruminated over how portion sizes had changed since the Great War. What served a family of four in 1915 would now serve two.

The egg timer at their workstation went off, signaling the end of their thirty-minute bake. Jane pulled their apricot charlotte from the oven. After that, there was nothing to do except watch as Aunt Octavia went around the room, tasting any dish cool enough to eat.

When she reached Jane's station, she addressed the class.

"Don't worry, ladies and gentlemen, Jane isn't allowed to win the prize. And I suspect she'll be quite disappointed when she sees it." Looking at Michael, Aunt Octavia added, "You're still in the running, my dear. Let's see if your dessert is a winner."

Michael took in Aunt Octavia's purple and lime green housedress, her triple strand of pearls, and her Mary Janes, which were festooned with silver sequins. All of Aunt Octavia's dresses, which were handmade by Mabel, featured bold prints and multiple pockets. Jane had seen her great-aunt produce an astounding number of gadgets and goodies from these pockets. Having been diagnosed with diabetes, she'd stopped hiding sweets in her housedress and had made a Herculean effort to avoid sugar. Today was obviously an exception to this rule.

"Very nice," she told Michael. After daintily wiping her mouth with a napkin, Aunt Octavia returned to the front of the room.

"Do we have a winner?" Mrs. Hubbard asked in a theatrical whisper.

Aunt Octavia nodded. "The best apricot charlotte was made by Mrs. Eugenia Pratt and partner. Forgive me, sir. What is your name?"

Mrs. Pratt's partner, who was currently being enfolded in a congratulatory embrace, extricated himself and said, "Roger Bachman, ma'am."

"It is my pleasure to award each of you with a vintage First World War cookbook." Aunt Octavia held up two gift-wrapped books. "Mrs. Pratt, I present you with *Everyday Foods in Wartime*, publication date, 1918. Mr. Bachman, I present you with *The Conservation Cook Book*, publication date, 1917."

There was a round of applause as Mrs. Pratt and her partner accepted their prizes with unfettered delight. Jane was impressed when Roger offered Mrs. Pratt her pick of the books. Batting her eyes, she asked if he'd like to compare them over cocktails that evening. Roger hesitated until Mrs. Pratt added that Mr. Pratt was no longer in the picture. Hearing this, her partner readily agreed.

Is she sleuthing or does she genuinely like the man? Jane wondered.

Collecting the cups, bowls, and utensils she and Michael had used, Jane carried them to the

153

dishwashing area. When she turned to fetch the rest, Michael was right behind her, his hands loaded with dirty dishes.

"Oh, please don't," Jane protested. "You're a guest. We'll see to these."

"I've been well trained by my fiancée," Michael said. "When one of us cooks, the other washes up. And since you and I shared the cooking, we should share the cleaning."

Jane smiled. "That's a good system. Luckily for everyone, the kitchen staff will take care of the cleaning. I'm used to loading my things into the dishwasher, because I'm always sneaking treats back to my office, and I try to hide the evidence of my theft."

"Thefts are my area of expertise," Michael said as they returned to their cooking area.

Jane didn't have to pretend to be fascinated. "Really? What kind of theft?"

"Though art looted in World War II constantly makes headlines, a precedent for stealing art was set during the previous war. I teach a class on looting. It's pretty popular. More so than my Economy of the Great War class."

As a test, Jane said, "Crime is always interesting, especially if you're talking about the theft of a priceless or irreplaceable item."

"That's true," Michael agreed. "However, all the treasures discussed in my course have a price. Examining the value in 1917, per se, versus the current market value, is an excellent way to illustrate an item's worth. My students aren't impressed by much, but they'll look up from their smartphones if I mention a multimillion-dollar price."

Jane couldn't think of another way to lure her cooking partner into revealing that he was more than a history professor from New York. She'd already learned that he'd been a member of the BackStory Club for going on five years now and that he had a parrot named Doughboy in honor of American infantrymen. Michael's fiancée was a little afraid of Doughboy. Though Michael spoke of his fiancée with warmth and affection, he never mentioned her name.

Michael and the rest of the participants filed out of the kitchen, undoubtedly heading for the Agatha Christie Tearoom. Mrs. Hubbard had organized an array of Great War treats including a war cake flavored with raisins and brown sugar, butter tarts, almond paste cannoli, Genoa cake, orange jelly, boiled ham and biscuits, buttered graham rolls, and more.

The last historian had just left when Uncle Aloysius entered the room.

"Octavia." The name came out as a hoarse rasp.

Jane, who'd been gathering other soiled cooking implements, abruptly stopped what she was doing and looked at Uncle Aloysius.

His face was chalk-white. One arm was pressed

against the wall as if he'd drop straight to the floor without its support. His lips kept moving, but no sound came out. Something was very, very wrong.

"Aloysius!" Aunt Octavia rushed to her husband's side. "What is it? Are you ill?"

Jane sprang into action. She grabbed a chair and hurriedly placed it behind her great-uncle. As she coaxed him into it, Mrs. Hubbard appeared with a glass of water.

"I think he's had a shock," she said to Aunt Octavia.

Aunt Octavia waved off the water cup. "Black coffee. Not too hot."

Mrs. Hubbard dashed away, her eyes wide and panicked.

She probably thought Uncle Aloysius was having a heart attack. At his age, it was a possibility. But Jane didn't think his heart was the cause of his distress.

"Are you in pain, my love? Did you hurt yourself when you were visiting the mews?" Aunt Octavia asked, tears springing to her eyes. "Talk to me!"

Uncle Aloysius grabbed his wife's dress with a claw-like grasp. Though he clung to her, he gazed at Jane in horror. "I saw . . . Jane . . . it can't be. But he was there. At the mews. I saw a ghost."

A half hour later, with Uncle Aloysius resting on the sofa in his apartment, Jane finished telling her great-aunt and great-uncle all she knew about William.

Of course, Aunt Octavia had swooned upon hearing the news, and Jane was soon doling out shots of whiskey to her elderly relatives while they struggled to make sense of the incomprehensible.

Eventually, after answering the few questions she was able to answer, Jane made a time-out motion with her hands.

"I know this is hard to take in. I get that. But I have to go home and see the twins. The historians are watching a double feature of *War Horse* and *All Quiet on the Western Front*, so I should have time to talk to you both later, check on Edwin, and find out what William's been doing."

"It's too much!" Aunt Octavia cried. "How can you handle all of this at once? Oh, where is my beloved Muffet Cat when I need him?"

Jane knelt next to her great-aunt. "I *can't* handle it all. Not without help. Do you have any ideas?"

Uncle Aloysius, who'd recovered some of his natural color, and was no longer in danger of passing out, sat a bit straighter. When Jane started to fuss over him, he waved her off. "My body might be old, my dear, but my mind is still fit as a fiddle. And my Octavia could outwit the cleverest of men. Here's what I suggest. Let us spend time with William. Allow us to assess him. If nothing else, we'll keep him out of the public eye. We can't have the boys bumping into him."

"What will we do about Mrs. Hubbard? She heard your talk of ghosts." Aunt Octavia fanned herself with a magazine. "Oh, good Lord. No one can stop that woman's tongue. I love her dearly, but she is a force to be reckoned with."

"She can't hold a candle to you, my girl." Uncle Aloysius smiled at his wife.

Out of nowhere, Muffet Cat suddenly appeared in the doorway between the living room and the master bedroom. The portly tuxedo, who'd once been a bedraggled kitten lost in a storm, padded over to Aunt Octavia as if he wanted everyone in the room to admire his shiny fur and magnificent tail.

His display certainly worked on Aunt Octavia. Scooping him up, she covered his head with kisses and dumped a small pile of cat treats on her lap. Muffet Cat devoured them in seconds. He then curled into a circle of black and white fur and glanced around. His smug expression reminded Jane of Ramsey Parrish.

As if reading Jane's mind, Aunt Octavia said, "Let's focus on this Parrish person. How do you plan to convince him that he's found the secret library?"

"I'm going to lead him into the passageway between the two conference rooms. Sterling will accompany me. Without going into details, I can say that Mr. Parrish will eventually be relocated

158

to less-luxurious accommodations than the Mystery Suite."

"And you'll release Edwin," Uncle Aloysius said.

Jane nodded. "Though Parrish undoubtedly anticipates these maneuvers, I have no other choice but to execute them. It's the only way I can force him to show the ace he has up his sleeve."

"We'll see to William," said Uncle Aloysius. "If the man's an imposter, it will be made plain once Mr. Parrish disappears."

Aunt Octavia poured herself another splash of whiskey. "Exactly how long are you prepared to hold Mr. Parrish prisoner?"

Jane's expression instantly darkened. "Forever, if necessary. Who knows how many people he's held captive over the years? Who knows what ultimately became of them? Parrish orchestrated the plot to abduct my sons. For him, there'll be no mercy."

After the Fins had given her the all-clear, meaning that Parrish was attending the evening's film festival, Jane entered the secret passage leading to the Mystery Suite to visit Edwin.

They embraced for a long moment before Jane showed Edwin the bottle of wine she'd brought with her. "I think we deserve this, don't you?"

Edwin looked at the label. "Stag's Leap Cask 23. Nice."

"A gift from Butterworth," Jane said, handing Edwin a corkscrew. She watched him deftly remove the cork, her gaze fixed on his pianist's fingers. She remembered the last time those fingers had traced her jawline, the swell of her breast, the curve of her hip. It had been months since they'd touched each other that way, and she had no idea when, or if, they'd be together like that again.

After Edwin filled their glasses, Jane raised hers and said, "To not missing you anymore."

"I'll drink to that."

Jane wanted to savor her time with Edwin, but that was impossible. She'd have to soak up all she could and carry the memory around with her.

Trying to keep things lighthearted, she asked Edwin if he'd been given enough to eat and was told that he was being stuffed like a Christmas goose. Meals were being delivered five times a day, despite Edwin's protests. He explained that he was unused to so much food—rich food at that—and couldn't eat it all.

"I've gone from one extreme to the other," he said with a smile.

"Speaking of extremes . . ." Jane began and went on to tell Edwin her plans for removing Parrish from Storyton Hall.

"I wish you didn't have to take such a risk." Edwin looked down at his wineglass. "I haven't been able to discover Parrish's real intentions. I don't believe he's here to gain access to the secret library because he knows you'd never allow that. So if not the library, what *is* his goal?"

Jane wished she knew. "Have you been using the laptop I hid on your breakfast cart to research the historians?"

"Yes. I made a list of the men most likely to be working with Parrish." Edwin handed Jane a piece of paper. "They had to fit certain parameters to make this list. The ability to travel was first among the requirements. No serious romantic attachments. No children. All the attendees are smart and well-read, so I couldn't use that as a deciding factor. A lack of attachments is the key."

"That didn't work out so well for you, did it?" Jane teased.

He took her hand and planted a tender kiss on the inside of her wrist. "I'm glad it didn't."

Though Jane wanted to linger with Edwin, she couldn't. Above all else, she was a mother, and she needed to go home and be with her sons. She bid Edwin good night, knowing she'd see him soon enough. Just as soon as Parrish was taken hostage.

She didn't look at Edwin's list until after the boys were in their pajamas, quietly reading in bed. In the privacy of her room, she unfolded the paper and scanned the short list of names.

At the very top was Roger Bachman, Mrs. Pratt's cooking partner.

Mrs. Pratt's partner and the man she'd invited out for cocktails.

Please be in the Ian Fleming Lounge, Jane thought, dialing the bar's number.

But Mrs. Pratt wasn't in the lounge.

According to the Fins, she was nowhere to be found.

Because she was no longer at Storyton Hall.

CHAPTER NINE

Jane was wondering if she should change out of her beloved book-lovers pajamas and start searching for Mrs. Pratt when it suddenly occurred to her that Storyton Hall wasn't the only place to get a drink.

"Betty, it's me," Jane said when her friend answered the phone at the Cheshire Cat Pub. "Pleasc tell me Eugenia is there."

"She sure is," said Betty over the din in the background. "She's having the time of her life too. She even played darts! Claims it was her first time, but I don't believe her. The woman scored a double bull right off the bat."

Jane wasn't interested in discussing Mrs. Pratt's prowcss at bar games. "Don't let her leave with her date or walk home by hersclf. The man she's with is Roger Bachman. All we know about him is that he's a lone wolf."

"Do you think he'll harm Eugenia?" Betty was instantly concerned.

"My worry is that we don't know a thing about him," Jane said. "After what happened to the twins, we should all be cautious."

Betty covered the mouthpiece to tell a patron that she'd be right there and then returned to Jane. "It won't be easy to separate the two of them. Eugenia is acting like a barnacle on an oceanic pier. And Roger seems to be enjoying the attention. What if we're ruining a good thing?"

"I'll apologize later. Maybe you could ask Bob to step in," Jane said, referring to Betty's husband.

"Don't worry, I'll sort it out," Betty promised. "And we'll see you at the reenactment. Did you realize how rare it is for Bob to attend a Storyton Hall event with me? Our schedules usually make it impossible. I'll feel like we're on a date, and it's been a *long* time since that's happened."

Jane thanked Betty and hung up. She reached for her current read, Shobha Rao's *Girls Burn Brighter*. Luckily for Jane, it was exactly the book she needed right now—the kind of story that whisked her away from her own struggles. After a single page, she was transported to India to share in the trials and tribulations of Poornima and Savitha.

When the chapter was done, Jane closed the book. She looked at the bright flame filling a field of white and thought about the now-obsolete funeral practice in which some Hindi widows immolated themselves on their husband's funeral pyre.

There was a period of time before the twins were born when Jane might have considered *sati*. She'd read books about the practice and learned that not all widows were burned. Some were buried alive with their husband's remains. Some were drowned. Right after William's death, none of those things seemed as terrible to Jane as living without her husband.

In the worst stages of her grief, Jane felt like she woke each morning with water in her lungs. She felt like the weight of the air in her apartment would crush her. It took incredible energy to be near other people, to complete mundane tasks. But day after day, she got out of bed. She got out of bed because she had life growing inside her.

Ruminations on widowhood continued the following morning as Jane helped the grounds-keepers, the members of the BackStory Club, and a dozen other historians make the final preparations for the reenactment.

The fallow field behind the unkempt apple orchard was one of the many reasons the BackStory members had chosen Storyton Hall as a tour stop. This open area, which was surrounded by woods, was an ideal setting for a battle. After booking the resort, the historians had emailed their plans for the reenactment. Storyton Hall's groundskeepers had then dug trenches and erected parapets in the field. Damaged tents once used for weddings or other outdoor events were turned into mess tents or first-aid stations. A makeshift paddock had also been created for the horses Sam was bringing down from Hilltop Stables.

When Sterling drove Jane around the orchard to the reenactment site, Clarence Kelley, Isabel Kelley, Archie Banks, and Michael Murphy were already at the battlefield. Clarence and Isabel were overseeing the placement of sandbags while Archie and Michael were counting wooden crates marked with the words EGG GRENADES.

As Jane had been provided with a list of the simulated weapons used in the reenactment, she was familiar with the egg grenades. Wooden eggs, which could be found at certain crafts stores, were filled with black powder and baking soda. A fuse and a pair of strike matches were taped to the top of the egg. This allowed participants to light the grenade by striking the matches against their helmets. All participants, without exception, were required to wear helmets.

The egg grenades were meant for the Allies, while the German soldiers would use stick grenades. Jane had been forewarned that the reenactment was very, very noisy and she should expect a cacophony of air-gun shots, whistling mortars, exploding grenades, yelling, and, despite the organizers' desire to keep things clean, a generous amount of swearing.

The historians and participants from Storyton village and over the mountain—a term coined for anyone living in towns with strip malls and big-box stores—would be collecting their uniforms today from a rental company specializing in warfare reenactments. It was during this hubbub that Jane planned to relocate Ramsey Parrish to less-luxurious accommodations.

After the morning session—a mandatory review of the rules regarding tomorrow's reenactment—the participants were released in time for lunch. Jane and the Fins had eyes on Parrish, so she knew he was lunching in the Madame Bovary Dining Room. He ate alone, sitting at a two-top table near the windows. All around him, the historians sat at larger tables. They were clearly excited about tomorrow's event, and the dining room was buzzing with animated conversations.

Jane waited until Parrish had finished his meal and had been served a cappuccino before approaching his table. She put a hand on the empty chair across from him and asked, "May I join you?"

Parrish closed the book he was reading and pulled out Jane's chair. "I'd be delighted."

He waited until she was seated before gesturing at his coffee. "I judge establishments using two parameters: their coffee and their mattresses. The coffee should be strong. The mattress should be soft, but not too soft."

"How does Storyton Hall measure up?"

Parrish touched the handle of his coffee cup. "A perfect score on both counts. You have a lovely establishment, Ms. Steward. You're clearly an excellent manager."

"I'm glad to hear that you're pleased with Storyton Hall. I haven't seen you interacting with the group celebrating the Great War centennial. Is there a reason for that?"

Parrish put a hand on his book. The touch was possessive. Affectionate. "I'm celebrating by rereading *A Farewell to Arms*. Hemingway's novel is one of the finest and most honest pieces of wartime literature. Did you know that he was the first ambulance driver injured in the line of duty?"

Jane nodded. "He was struck by a mortar shell. He was only eighteen, and the injuries he sustained would bother him for the rest of his life."

"Though shell fragments were picked out of his legs, hand, and head, Hemingway never let pain hold him back. He hunted, flew planes, and fished. He documented wars and climbed mountains. He lived ten lifetimes in one."

Parrish was quite animated, and Jane wondered if Ernest Hemingway was the real reason Parrish had come to Storyton Hall. If so, he was to be disappointed. The secret library contained nothing by the famous author.

"I think Hemingway was a man who thrived in times of conflict," she said. "He seemed incapable of accepting times of peace. People tend to see him as this larger-than-life hero, but it's his use of plain language, honesty, and vulnerability that made me a lifelong fan."

Parrish smiled. "It's most refreshing to discuss literature with such a lovely woman. Hemingway would have found you very charming, Ms. Steward. However, I don't believe you joined me for an impromptu book discussion."

Jane scanned the dining room as if hoping to find one of Parrish's confederates watching them, but all the historians were focused on their tablemates. "You've kept your word, Mr. Parrish. Edwin and William are back where they belong. Now, it's time for me to keep mine. Let's address the real reason you came to Storyton Hall."

"Excellent," said Parrish. "When will this take place?"

"Immediately. The guests will be busy with uniform rentals, and we're headed to the opposite end of the manor house," Jane said. "However, there's one thing I'd like to know before we go. You never explained what would happen if I didn't fulfill my end of the bargain."

Parrish finished his coffee and put the cup down with a firm *clink*. "It would be very foolish of you to back out. That's all I can say. I am not a man who handles disappointment well. If you deceive me, you'll regret it."

Gazing blandly at Parrish, Jane said, "That's pretty vague. You won't even give me a hint? Will you try to abduct my sons again? Trip my great-aunt as she descends the main staircase? Plant bombs around our construction site?"

Parrish didn't respond. One of his most remarkable skills was his ability to keep quiet. He didn't care how she felt about his silence, and this disregard for others' feelings was a powerful weapon.

I have something more powerful, she thought, rising to her feet. *I have my family and my friends. I love these people. And they love me.*

Another voice chimed in. *Which means you have more to lose.*

Shoving these thoughts aside, Jane invited Parrish to follow her and led him through the lobby toward the wing housing the conference rooms.

"I know you have a plan," Jane said as they walked. "You'd hardly expect me to hand over priceless materials without a fight. I wouldn't expect that of you." When she reached the broom cupboard, which was positioned in the hallway directly between two conference rooms, she stopped. "What I don't understand is why we must be enemies. The information contained in the world's rarest books won't change our present or our future. No mystic tome will teach us how to live without sickness or strife. No ancient tablet contains the secrets to winning elections or to acquiring immense wealth."

Parrish smiled. "You are mistaken. Many of these artifacts reveal the location of invaluable treasures. But only if one knows how to read them. The Templars have already accumulated vast amounts of money and power. However, more wonders are waiting to be found. It is my duty to continue the search and to help my brotherhood shape the future of humankind."

Jane shook her head. "You talk like you're an omniscient group of Indiana Joneses. But he was a professor and an archaeologist. What does your order do for humanity?"

Parrish looked perplexed. "Why should we work toward a greater good? We're not Robin Hood and his Merry Men. We're scholar entrepreneurs. Visionaries."

"Why should you help people?" Jane spluttered. "Because your order was founded for precisely that reason. The Templar knights aided pilgrims journeying to Jerusalem. They made sure the pilgrims had food, water, and protection. What happened to that selflessness?"

"It's neither profitable nor prudent," said Parrish. "When our order was falsely accused of treason as an excuse to seize our lands and riches, we learned a valuable lesson."

Jane opened the cupboard door. "The Templars were mistreated, I agree, but people have been mistreated throughout history. The key is not to become like those who've abused you. The key is to rise above them."

"Spoken like a true bleeding heart," Parrish scoffed and gestured at the closet. "Am I supposed to be captivated by these cleaning supplies?"

"If you enjoy C. S. Lewis." Jane glanced both ways along the corridor, making sure there were no witnesses. When she looked back at Parrish, she saw that he'd recognized the literary reference. "After you," she said.

He stepped into the cupboard.

Following close on his heels, Jane shut the door and turned on her cell phone's flashlight. It was a tight squeeze in the cupboard, and she loathed being so close to Parrish. She could feel his breath and his eyes on her.

Shoving a regiment of mops and brooms to one side, Jane reached into a cavity in the back panel and twisted a hidden latch. A secret door swung away from her, revealing nothing but darkness.

Jane allowed Parrish to exit the cupboard before closing the door again. "This passageway runs between two conference rooms," she whispered. "They're empty right now, but a person could hear us through the air vent. See the octagonal shapes on the floor? That pattern is from the brass vent cover in the William Faulkner Conference Room. We'll pass by two of these before we reach the stairs. From that point, we go down."

"This corridor isn't on any of the blueprints I was able to acquire, and I purchased several at exorbitant prices," Parrish said. His voice held the faintest hint of excitement.

"Not everything is for sale, Mr. Parrish. Some secrets are meant to be kept."

Jane began to talk about Storyton Hall's architect. She wanted to distract Parrish with idle prattle until Butterworth could use a diminutive blowgun to shoot a tiny but potent dart into Parrish's calf. The butler was on his belly near the second air vent, awaiting their approach. If this attempt failed, Jane had a backup plan. Sterling was hiding at the end of the narrow passageway, dressed in black from head to toe. He was also armed with a dart dipped in a paralyzing toxin. Much like the batrachotoxin secreted by poison dart frogs, the toxin-dipped dart intended for Parrish's calf was tremendously fast-acting. It would render Parrish unconscious in seconds and keep him in a paralytic state for hours. The dose wouldn't be strong enough to stop his heart, but he wouldn't be sipping cappuccinos anytime soon.

Jane could envision Butterworth, stretched out on the conference-room floor, the mouthpiece of the blowgun pressed against his lips, as he listened for Parrish's approach. The blowgun was a nineteenth-century African weapon kept on display in a locked case in the Isak Dinesen Safari Room. It was painted red and black and a menacing mask was carved into the shaft. Sterling was armed with a twentieth-century blowgun. Cyril Steward collected these weapons, as well as the other treasures, on one of his many trips to Africa.

In some ways, Cyril was like Ernest Hemingway. He'd been a restless soul forever looking for adventure. At least, that's how Jane saw him until she learned the truth about her family history. She realized that many of Cyril's hunting trips were likely a front, and that he went abroad to take possession of materials destined for Storyton Hall's secret library.

"The hall is very narrow," Jane whispered to Parrish as they came to the second air vent. "You can touch the wall quite easily. If you just focus on my light, you'll see the door to the stairway. It will appear any moment now."

"I don't—" Parrish began.

Jane would never know what he planned to say.

She heard the ghost of a sigh, as if his words had been whisked away by a sudden wind.

And then he fell.

Jane made no move to break his fall. She simply pivoted and shone the feeble beam from her cell phone over his crumpled form. "Nicely done, Butterworth."

Sterling appeared behind her. "We'll take it from here, Miss Jane. Mr. Sinclair will inform Mr. Alcott that he's free to leave Mr. Parrish's room. We recommend that he makes his exit during tonight's film."

"Do you think *Sergeant York* will be as popular

as last night's double feature?" Jane asked. "I've never heard of it."

"It's a classic," Sterling said. "Gary Cooper plays the reluctant hero. I think it's his best role."

Jane knew some of her friends would attend just to watch Gary Cooper. Not Eloise, however. She'd been invited to join her older brother for coffee and dessert at Daily Bread, Edwin's restaurant. Tonight, Edwin would finally reveal his secret to his sister.

After leaving the broom cupboard, Jane visited the ladies' room to check her skin and clothes for dust bunnies. She then washed her hands and headed for the Shakespeare Theater to see how the uniform rental was going.

When she arrived, she was amazed by the number of people in the theater. It looked like half of the village had signed up to participate in the reenactment.

The uniform rental company had taken over the stage. Each participant was called up by name and given a bag containing a uniform and a helmet. The weapons would be distributed tomorrow after the Fins had inspected every gun to ensure they only fired blanks.

All the participants would be fighting with blank-fire weapons or, as was the case with the machine guns, modified weapons. The machine guns were gas guns. Fitted with spark plugs and hoses filled with oxygen and propane, they looked and sounded like the real thing. Though incapable of firing projectiles, these weapons appeared to do just that. Sterling had shown her a video of a gas machine gun and warned her that these "props" would significantly add to the battlefield noise.

"The twins are still furious over being too young to participate," Jane had said at the time. "Luckily for them, their teachers are as excited to watch the melee as their students. It's a good thing we bought those extra folding chairs."

After speaking with several visiting historians and an equal number of villagers, Jane was satisfied that every man and woman had a clear understanding of the rules.

With an hour left before teatime, Jane took one of the Gator vehicles and drove down to Storyton Mews. The mews were located close to the staff houses at the end of a long driveway. There was little else at the end of this lane other than the building housing the raptors and a small clearing where Lachlan worked with the birds.

The raptor training program had been a smashing success from the start. Jane remembered how dubious she'd been when Lachlan argued that rehabilitating injured hawks, falcons, and the occasional owl could turn a profit. But he'd been right. The resort guests enjoyed visiting the birds, stroking their feathers, and watching them fly. And they especially loved having one of the magnificent birds perch on their forearm.

There'd been a few complaints too. Some of the guests felt the birds should be hunting instead of eating frozen chicks. Some guests were repulsed by the chicks. Others declared that the birds should be set free, even though most of them had sustained some type of debilitating injury and weren't equipped to survive in the wild.

"You can't please everyone, so please the ones who matter," Uncle Aloysius had told Jane when she'd finished reading him a rather impassioned letter from a guest. In the letter, the guest vowed to leave a terrible review of Storyton Hall on as many online sources as possible due to the animal cruelty she'd witnessed.

"Against the raptors?" Jane's great-uncle had asked.

"Against the frozen chicks."

Uncle Aloysius had mumbled something like "what a nutter" and dropped the subject.

Jane parked at the mews and checked her watch. Feeding time had already passed, which meant the raptors were dozing in their aviary, being exercised by Lachlan, or delighting a small group of guests.

When Lachlan was especially busy, Billy the bellhop would assist with the birds. Uncle Aloysius was also drawn to the mews. The raptors were one of the few things that could divert Jane's great-uncle from his fishing pole, so she wasn't surprised to find him standing in the clearing, cooing to a peregrine falcon named Horus.

"Hello, Jane," he said as she approached. "This is a fine day. Horus has finally decided to trust me."

"That's wonderful." Jane was genuinely impressed. Considering the falcon had been the victim of a slingshot strike and that the injury had wounded him both physically and emotionally, Jane didn't think he'd ever allow anyone to handle him. It had taken Lachlan months to earn the bird's trust. And now, it looked like Horus had granted his trust to Uncle Aloysius as well.

Her great-uncle nodded. "He didn't try to bite me. I was able to stroke his head, and he ate right off of my glove."

The boyish pleasure on Uncle Aloysius's face made Jane smile. If only life could always be as simple as enjoying the company of a beautiful animal in a beautiful setting such as this.

"Is William with you?" she asked.

"He's cleaning Cillian's cage," her uncle said, referring to their resident merlin.

Jane moved a little closer to avoid being over-heard, but Horus didn't care for her proximity. He began to flap his wings and cry in an agitated manner.

"I'd better put you back now, old fellow." Uncle Aloysius soothed the bird with his gentle voice. Soon, Horus was glowering out at Jane from inside the security of his aviary.

"How's everything going with him?" Jane asked. "William, I mean. Not Horus."

Her uncle shrugged. "He's a nice enough fellow. Then again, he always was. Catches on quickly to anything he's shown. I remember him being a smart guy. But my dear girl, I see no glimmer of the man you married. He doesn't seem to recognize anything about Storyton Hall. That's not to say he won't in time," he quickly added.

"I'm a bit surprised by his interest in the birds. He wasn't an animal lover when we were together," Jane said. "At one point, I wanted to get a puppy or a kitten, but William was adamantly against it. He didn't want a pet. He used to be fastidiously tidy. It's strange to picture him cleaning up bird droppings."

Uncle Aloysius put a hand on Jane's shoulders. "He's had no choice but to become a new man."

But whose man is he? Jane silently wondered.

At that moment, William appeared from around the corner of the mews. He had a garbage bag slung over his shoulder and was whistling a tune Jane didn't recognize. Seeing her, his face broke into a friendly smile. "Hello," he said.

Jane had seen that look many times. It was the same look she used to see when he came home from work. It was a look that told her how glad he was to see her. How much she was loved. Though it hurt to see that familiar expression

179

on this stranger's face, Jane couldn't stop from smiling in return. "How are things going?"

"Great. I love it here," William said. "The birds are fascinating. I like being around them. The staff has been really nice to me too. Storyton Hall reminds me of Biltmore, except that it's quieter. I like the quiet."

"Well, it won't be quiet tomorrow," Jane said. "I have no idea what a Great War battle sounds like, but we're about to find out."

William pointed toward the orchard. "Mr. Lachlan drove me to the field. It's an excellent replication of the trenches. There's no barbed wire, of course, but with the sandbags and the wood supports, it looks pretty genuine. One of the historians said that even though the guns fire blanks, injuries can happen."

Jane studied William as he stared off past the clearing toward the orchard. Was he worried that someone might be hurt? He didn't look overly concerned, so Jane decided to drop the subject.

She was about to ask William to watch over the raptors while the reenactment took place when she heard a pair of familiar voices. Young, male voices.

"Oh no," she murmured, swinging around to see Fitz and Hem. The boys were running and shouting at the same time.

"Last one to Mom is a rotten egg!" Hem yelled.

"You're a rotten chicken even if you win!" Fitz called in response.

There was no time to keep the twins from reaching her. They were running too fast. And Uncle Aloysius was still fussing over Horus, so there was nothing Jane could do but hold out her hand like a traffic cop.

"Stop shouting!" she commanded. "You know the birds don't like it. Do you want me to tell Mr. Lachlan that you've been upsetting Horus?

The boys immediately slowed to a walk. "Sorry, Mom," they said in unison.

"We came to get you for tea," said Fitz.

Hem glanced around. "And Uncle Aloysius too."

This is it, Jane thought. *This is the moment where William meets his sons. This is the moment when Fitz and Hem meet their father. Except I can't tell any of them what's happening.*

Suddenly, Jane remembered the framed photograph in her bedroom. It was taken on her wedding day. William was wearing a borrowed tux, and Jane was wearing a bridal gown she'd found at a vintage clothing shop. The boys had seen that photo hundreds of times. Would they recognize William as the man inside the silver frame?

Before the silence could become awkward, Jane turned to William and said, "William, these are my sons, Fitzgerald and Hemingway."

"Nice to meet you." William shook hands with each of the boys.

"You too," said Fitz before pointing at the aviary behind William. "Who's your favorite? I like Tootsie the Owl. He's named after the owl in the Tootsie Pop commercial."

When William shot Jane a confused look, Hem elaborated on behalf of his brother. "In the commercial, a kid asks the owl how many licks it takes to get to the middle of the Tootsie Pop. The owl takes the Tootsie Pop and starts licking and counting. It's a *really* old commercial."

Fitz nodded. "I feel sorry for the kid. You know he'll never get his lollipop back from that owl."

"Unfortunately, I haven't seen the commercial," William said. "Or the lollipop."

Jane had been staring at William throughout this exchange, scrutinizing his face for the tiniest hint of emotion. She saw nothing but friendliness. He was as instantly likable as a golden retriever. He didn't recognize his sons any more than they recognized him.

Jane didn't know what to feel. Should she be relieved? Or should she feel sorry for the two boys who'd never known a father?

When she saw Fitz and Hem gazing at William in surprise, she felt a tug at her heart. The tug was sadness. And pity. William had missed so much— moments he shouldn't have missed. Tootsie Roll Pops were just one of many things in life he hadn't experienced. If not for one winter's night, his life would have been completely different.

"Would you like to have tea with us today?" she asked William.

"What a lovely idea," said Uncle Aloysius from behind Jane. "But I'm stealing your tea guest. William and I need to compare notes on Cillian's progress. Boys, you'd better get your mother to the terrace on the double. You know my lovely bride doesn't like to be kept waiting." He tapped his watch. "And if you leave her alone with the treats for too long, she might gobble them all up."

Fitz and Hem exchanged amused grins.

"You won't be smiling when all the cake is gone," Uncle Aloysius added. "I heard Mrs. Hubbard made your favorite chocolate sponge with the cherries on top."

Hearing this, the boys practically pulled Jane to the Gator and begged her to drive as fast as possible. Jane glanced over at their panicked faces and, seeing that they were truly worried about Aunt Octavia devouring the whole cake, burst into laughter.

The sound floated down the driveway, drifted over the mews, and dispersed in the sun-dappled woods beyond.

CHAPTER TEN

Jane expected to hear from Eloise before bedtime, but her best friend didn't knock on her door until the next morning.

"Come in." Jane led Eloise into the kitchen. "I'm going to pour you a strong cup of coffee. I'm sure you need it. The boys have left for school, so we can talk freely."

Eloise passed her hands over her face. "I feel like I've entered an alternate dimension. I can totally identify with the Time Traveller's wife now. How long have you known about Edwin?"

Jane gestured for Eloise to sit and poured two cups of coffee. She then plated one of Mrs. Hubbard's cinnamon apple scones and put it in front of Eloise. "A few months. He swore me to secrecy, Eloise. And even if he hadn't, I didn't think that it was my secret to tell."

"All these years, I thought he was jetting around the globe eating sautéed scorpions, bird's nest soup, or mangosteen while writing travel articles on culture and food. And yes, he did eat all that stuff, but he's also seen the inside of exotic palaces, museums, and prisons!"

Jane pushed the carton of half-and-half closer to Eloise. After doctoring her coffee, Eloise took a sip. She held her cup in both hands and sighed.

"I wanted him to tell you, but I'm not sure if it was the right decision. To be honest, I was selfish," Jane confessed. "I wanted you to share in this secret with me—to have someone to talk to about Edwin. Was that wrong of me? Would you have preferred not to know? To have kept your relationship with Edwin as it was?"

Eloise shook her head. "I feel like I've never known him. We were close as kids, but after college, he was always gone. Now, I know why. He was jetting off to foreign countries to steal other people's property." She loaded her fork with a piece of scone. "That's the hardest part for me to take. My brother is a book thief. I *sell* books for a living, for crying out loud. People should *buy* books or borrow them from the library. No one should steal them."

Jane wrestled with this aspect of Edwin's calling all the time. It was one of the main reasons she didn't want to fall in love with him. "He once said that his mission isn't about people. It's about the books. It's about preserving them at all costs. He would steal from the Pope if it meant restoring a broken book."

"He told me the same thing, but I'm struggling to accept it." Eloise chewed the scone, and for just a moment, she was distracted by the delicious flavors. Quickly reloading her fork, she said, "I love books as much as the next person. More than the next person. But what value does a book have without a reader? How can its words influence or shape a person if it isn't read? Edwin said that he and these other Templars—it sounds so absurd to say that out loud—collect knowledge for the greater good. They make broken books whole and rescue books from places where they might be damaged. When you put it that way, these Templars come off as book heroes. But are they? Who benefits from their *redistribution* of books?"

It was a question Jane had asked herself more than once. Not only did she take issue with the *modus operandi* of the Templars, but with the existence of Storyton Hall's secret library as well. How many times had she wondered if such secrecy was still necessary? Like Eloise, she believed words were meant to be read. Stories were supposed to be shared. But then, Jane would remember what had happened when she'd put a rare book on display. It had led to murder, and Jane now had conflicting feelings about the treasure trove housed in the highest turret.

"Book thief though he may be, Edwin is also my brother," Eloise said. She'd finished her scone and was gazing at the empty plate with longing. "He's all the family I have, so I'm going to do my best to accept his double life. However, I'll never accept any action that I think is criminal or hurtful. I'm going to call him out if I think he's doing something wrong."

Jane smiled warmly at her friend. She had such a big heart.

"What are Edwin's plans?" she asked.

"He's going to lie low. He said that you and I would be safer if certain people thought he was still being held prisoner." Eloise gave Jane a sharp look. "He told me about his rescue. My best friend and my boyfriend. Heroes of the hour. Am I the last person on earth to know the truth about my own brother?"

Jane promised that she wasn't. "I wish what he told you was an exaggeration, but I now know that robbery is the least of the crimes these sects will commit to own a piece of history," she said. "To these extremist Templars, the books represent power, wealth, and prestige. These people are not like you and me, Eloise. They don't love the books because they're book lovers. They want to own them as a means of amassing knowledge. Edwin's different, though. He loves the words on the pages as much as we do."

Eloise drank the rest of her coffee. "It'll take me a couple of days to adjust to having an anti-hero as a brother. Wouldn't he be a great comic-book character?" She let loose a humorless laugh. "Thank God for you, Jane. You're a perfect heroine—a blend of Jane Austen, Madeleine L'Engle, Louisa May Alcott, and Lucy Maud Montgomery women. You'd make an even better comic-book character. I can just see you in thigh-high, kick-ass latex boots."

"You know exactly what to say to make me feel good." Jane turned away, hiding the guilt that must be etched all over her face. What kind of heroine lied to her best friend? Jane was as much of an anti-hero as Edwin.

Eloise slipped off her stool and carried her plate and coffee mug to the sink. "I'm glad the Cover Girls are meeting tonight. I could use the distraction. And the cocktails. With book club and a Great War reenactment tomorrow, I have plenty of other things to think about other than Edwin. I'm going to open Run for Cover for a few hours, but I'll be here for the battle." She walked to the front door and stopped. Looking back at Jane, she said, "I almost forgot to thank you."

"For what?"

"For keeping Landon away from the battlefield. He told me how you asked him to hang out at the mews instead of helping with the reenactment. That man may have retired from the military, but the ghosts of his military past follow him everywhere."

Jane thought of William, and of how he was a ghost of the man he'd once been. "Landon Lachlan cares about you, Eloise. And because you care about him too, you might be able to chase away those shadows from the past with your sunny disposition."

Eloise smiled. "Speaking of sunshine, it looks

like the weather forecasters were wrong about us getting more rain. The clouds are breaking up and the sky is clearing. It's going to be a lovely day for a pretend war."

Having no experience with reenactments, Jane was unprepared for the amount of people, chaos, and noise that came into play before the first shot was ever fired. Villagers, guests, and members of the press milled about the field, waiting for instructions. These instructions, along with a brief reminder of the rules, were issued via bullhorn by members of the BackStory Club.

The spectators, who were sitting in folding chairs along one side of the field, included Jane and the Cover Girls, the children of the third, fourth, and fifth grades of Storyton's elementary school, and more than a hundred villagers. The rules for spectators were quite simple. Clarence Kelley patiently explained that they were to stay off the battlefield no matter what happened. It was paramount that the Great War and present-day worlds did not collide.

"What you're about to see and hear will *feel* quite real," he added with a touch of pride. "You will see men fighting. You will see them running for their lives. You will see them fall. Some may call for medical attention. Some may shout out for their mothers. This is all a part of the reenactment. Not every soldier will make it across the field. For one side to be victorious, the other must lose. That means you will see casualties. Men will die today. Fortunately, their death is temporary."

One of the fourth-grade boys raised his hand as if he was in class. He waved his arm back and forth like a flag blowing in the wind.

"Yes, son?" Clarence asked, amused by the boy's eagerness.

"How do the soldiers know if they should die?"

Clarence smiled. "An excellent question, young sir. There are several answers. If a soldier comes too close to an enemy, he'll realize that he's been shot and will fall on that spot. Sometimes, soldiers fall if they're too hot, too tired, or are just ready to be done with the battle. Quite a few enjoy the act of dying, especially if they have an audience." He winked. "Because we have many new recruits in today's battle, we decided to assign casualties. The soldiers who will fall in today's battle already know who they are."

A girl now raised her hand, and without waiting for Clarence to call on her, asked, "Are you using real bullets?"

"No, Miss. We use soft air weapons. They look and sound real, but nothing comes out of them. We call these blanks. Believe it or not, injuries can still occur with blanks. That's why it's important that all of you stay *far* away from the battlefield. Trust me, things are about to get very wild and very loud." He pointed toward the apple orchard. "The Allies will be at this end of the field, and the Central Powers will be at the opposite end. You will see horses, machine guns, mortar shells, and exploding grenades. We will begin with music. There will be two patriotic marches. This is when the soldiers will take the field. The battle is over when you see the white flag of surrender. Are you ready?"

Though most of the spectators shouted and clapped with excitement, others looked rather nervous. Jane was among the latter. Despite the autumnal sunshine, the golden hills rising around the field, and the looks of bright anticipation on the children's faces, she felt a sense of foreboding.

"There are so many people," she murmured to Eloise. "I hardly recognize any of them in their uniforms."

Eloise squinted across the field. "I saw Nandi earlier," she said, referring to Storyton's postmistress. "She looked pleased as punch to be fighting alongside the Hogg brothers."

"My Bob is in the trench closest to us," Betty said. "He wants to show me that he's still fleet-footed and nimble. Those are his words, mind you. Bob has never been either of those things, but I'll let him have his fantasies."

Phoebe nodded. "We all need those. My fantasy is that one of these dashing soldiers will trip over a root or step in a hole and find himself in need of a Great War Florence Nightingale. I'll rush out to the battlefield and offer him a cool drink of water. He'll gaze into my eyes and think—"

"That you're breaking the rules," Mabel interrupted. "You heard the man with the bullhorn. We need to keep our rumps in our chairs."

Betty turned to Mrs. Pratt, who was sitting between Violet and Eloise. "Have you spoken with Roger today?"

"Briefly," said Mrs. Pratt. "I know he's fighting under the British flag and has a reputation for his ability to break through enemy lines. He's quite famous among the reenactors."

Violet glanced around the peaceful field. "It's all so serious that I'm feeling pretty nervous. I don't know a thing about war or battles, and now that I'm about to get the smallest taste, I'm kind of scared."

Mrs. Pratt gave Violet's hand a maternal squeeze. "Just think of the insight we'll gain about the books we'll be discussing tonight. This whole experience will add a dimension of realism to our fiction."

"Indeed," Eloise said in an exaggerated British accent. "Keep calm and carry on."

Jane grinned at her friend. "Nice sentiment. Wrong war."

Eloise shrugged. "I've never been good at

history. I get details from the two wars mixed up all the time. There were so many battles. So many people fighting." She pointed at the soldiers amassing on the field before them. "I get what Vi means. When I look out there and see Rufus Hogg or Captain Phil, I think of what it must have been like when our village was nearly empty of men because they'd all gone off to fight."

"There would have been a helluva lot less laundry," Mrs. Pratt declared, clearly trying to break the tension building around them.

"I like that there are female soldiers in today's battle," said Phoebe. "It might not be historically accurate, but I bet those gals can fake shoot and fake die as well as any man. I just wish Anna could be here. She'll hate having to live vicariously through us."

Mabel was about to reply when music floated over the field. As Clarence Kelley had explained, this was the march signaling the start of the battle. A dozen horses burst from the cover of the overgrown orchard, and Eloise drew in a sharp breath.

"Is that Sam on the chestnut horse?" she asked.

"Oh, Anna will *really* be sorry she missed this! He looks dashing," Phoebe said.

She and Mrs. Pratt exchanged additional comments about the horses and their riders, but Jane tuned them out. She was trying to listen to the second piece of music. It was like the first, but with a stricter tempo and more percussion. This song came from the opposite end of the field.

"There's a German flag." Mabel pointed in the direction of the music. "What happens next? I wonder how one starts a battle."

This was the last calm remark any of the Cover Girls could utter for a long time.

At first, the noise wasn't overwhelming. A group of Germans edged around the right flank of an Allied-occupied trench and the two groups exchanged a wave of gunfire. The schoolchildren whooped and hollered with glee while the anxious spectators seemed to relax a little.

This isn't so bad, Jane thought, foolishly assuming that the rest of the battle would be more of the same.

She was wrong.

After several rounds of gunfire between small groups, the noise quickly escalated. Grenades were thrown. When these hit the ground, clumps of dirt and grass exploded in every direction.

Eloise jerked back in her chair, her eyes wide with surprise and fear. Glancing at her friends, Jane saw similar expressions on all of their faces. Even the twins, who'd been bouncing with uncontained excitement a few minutes ago, were shocked into stillness.

The clamor of detonating grenades was joined

by the staccato of artillery fire, the blasts of mortar shells, and a cacophony of shouts. Sinclair had said that reenactments typically lasted for hours, with many of the participants spending the whole day on the field. Though today's event was to be much shorter, Jane didn't know how anyone could tolerate this much noise hour after hour.

The real soldiers of the Great War had no choice, she reminded herself. *They were hungry, thirsty, dirty, exhausted, and they witnessed horrible things. But they kept going. For years. They knew the true meaning of hell on earth.*

It felt incredibly odd to sit comfortably on the sidelines, cradling a thermos of coffee. Jane watched and tried to make sense of the chaos on the field. This was more difficult than she ever could have imagined, especially since clouds of smoke and dust had begun to obscure parts of the field. On top of that, soldiers kept popping in and out of trenches. After a while, Jane had a hard time distinguishing their uniforms.

"Is that a French unit?" she asked Eloise, pointing at a cluster of men along the tree line on the opposite side of the field.

"I have no idea!" Eloise shouted back.

Suddenly, a grenade detonated close to the spectators. One of the village ladies let out a terrified shriek. Jane got up, intending to assure the woman that all was well when a pair of soldiers in German uniforms popped out from behind a tree and fired their weapons. Three American soldiers dropped to the ground. Two of them went still, but the third cried out in a pretense of pain. A medic and a chaplain rushed toward the men. Even over the battle din, Jane could hear the distinct sounds of children crying. She looked to where the students were seated and saw that a girl in the twins' class was visibly upset.

"This is no place for children!" yelled a man in the crowd.

The teachers had apparently come to the same conclusion. They were gesturing for the students to line up with their backs to the battlefield. Instead of obeying, Fitz and Hem were protesting. Jane watched in horrified embarrassment as they pointed at her. The teacher followed their gaze, shook her head, and motioned for the boys to fall in line.

Good woman, Jane thought.

A handful of adult spectators departed at the same time as the children, and though Jane wanted to join them, she thought it was more important to honor the efforts of the reenactors. After all, they were the ones running, jumping, ducking for cover, and dying all over the field. They were getting covered in muck and were undoubtedly hot and thirsty.

"We're going to make a killing at the pub tonight!" Betty exclaimed. "Every villager will want to outdo the next man in telling the story of today's events. I hope Bob is saving enough energy to change out a bunch of kegs."

"Can you see him?" Mabel asked.

Betty squinted. "A few minutes ago, he was standing near a mounted officer. The officer is riding Ajax, that stunning gray gelding."

Violet spotted the horse racing toward enemy lines. "There!" she cried. "They must be charging that bunker. Isn't that how they score points? By collecting enemy flags?"

The women watched, enthralled, as the small group ran straight into a volley of gunfire.

Jane tensed, momentarily forgetting that no bullets were flying through the air. Eloise had gone rigid, and Betty was clinging to Mrs. Pratt like a vine.

Suddenly, grenades exploded right in front of the line of soldiers. The soldier riding Ajax pulled on the horse's bridle, directing him away from the bunker. Jane clenched her fists, hoping that Ajax wouldn't panic and throw his rider. She trusted Sam's instincts when it came to his horses, but everything about this scene felt unpredictable. There was no telling how a horse would react to a loud explosion or to men popping out of trenches like overgrown meerkats.

"Ajax's rider has been shot!" Phoebe yelled. "Look!"

Straining to see through a cloud of dust, Jane

saw Ajax heading back to the orchard. His saddle was empty.

"I hope that was intentional," Betty said. She was on her feet now, her eyes scanning the field. "Oh, dear. I guess everyone in Bob's regiment or unit or whatever you call it is dead. None of them made it to the bunker."

Eloise frowned. "Wait. One of them got through. See the guy running away with the flag? The one with the bright red hair? Guess he lost his helmet in the fray."

"Isn't that your cooking partner, Jane?" Mrs. Pratt asked. "He's quite fast. Looks more like a track-and-field star than a history professor."

Jane had to agree. Michael Murphy was flying. As the women looked on, he leaped over a fallen tree, darted around a supply wagon, and returned to base camp to receive a triumphant pat on the back from Clarence Kelley.

Clarence signaled to a French soldier, a thin man in his twenties, and the man darted off. In no time at all, he'd caught Ajax by the bridle and was walking the horse to one of Sam's trailers.

By and by, Jane and her friends grew accustomed to the noise. The battle had its ebbs and peaks, but after two hours, the Allies had captured more flags than the Central Powers. To the relief of all the Cover Girls, the action began to wind down.

Sweeping her arm over the field, Mrs. Pratt

said, "I wonder if it felt like this to be a Roman citizen at a gladiator match. Entertainment equaled carnage. It's a relief to know that these corpses will rise again."

"Sounds more like *Dracula* than *Ben-Hur*," teased Phoebe.

Violet looked at Eloise. "Is *Ben-Hur* a novel? I've seen the movie, which was so-so. If there's a book, it's probably better."

"Repeat after me. The book is *always* better," Eloise said. She got to her feet and stretched. *"Ben-Hur: A Tale of the Christ* was written by Lew Wallace in the 1880s. I haven't read it either. After the books we read for tonight's discussion, I need a light read. I'll bring a list of recommendations with me."

"I can think of some," Mrs. Pratt offered. "I know several books that feature sexy, saucy gladiators."

"I thought you preferred your men in kilts," Mabel said.

Mrs. Pratt shrugged. "I'm not fussy. Kilts. Loincloths. I care more about their—"

"Depth of character." Jane winked at her. "Listen, ladies. We need energy to talk about characters tonight, so we'd better fortify ourselves with treats from Mrs. Hubbard's Victory Tea."

"Sounds good to me," said Betty. Taking one last look around the field, she added, "In the real battlefields, there weren't winners or losers. Only losers. Lost lives, lost loves, lost years. Even the earth is scarred by war."

Jane put her arm around Betty's shoulders. "I know how you feel. But we get to welcome our soldiers home. Every one of them. They might be a little tired or sore, but the only injuries they sustained today were to their pride."

"How long do they stay dead?" Mabel wanted to know.

Jane had no idea. "Until they're ready to live again, I suppose. Some are probably taking a well-deserved rest."

The women carried their chairs to a Storyton Hall pickup truck, their thoughts already turned to tea and pastries.

The men who'd fallen closest to the spectators saw their audience departing. They waited until the non-participants were out of sight before slowly getting to their feet. Over the next fifteen minutes or so, all the dead soldiers were heading back to the base camp.

Except one.

After indulging in another impressive tea spread, most of the reenactors went to their rooms. The day after tomorrow, the participants were invited to the Victory Banquet, which would feature food and music from postwar America.

There was a seemingly unending list of tasks

to complete for this event, and Jane checked as many as she could. She thought of Ram? Parrish as she worked, wondering how he w finding his new accommodations and if she been right to force his hand.

Jane wanted to ask the Fins about Parrish but before she knew it, the twins were hom from school. After wolfing down an afternoon snack, they asked Jane if they could play on the battlefield.

"Why not? I'll drive you over in a Gator," she said. "I want to be sure that all the weapons have been picked up."

Though the boys were disappointed that they were unlikely to find a grenade, helmet, canteen, or other military treasure, they dashed to the garage and hopped into a Gator. Jane was collecting the keys from a wall box when Sinclair appeared from the small room Sterling used as a lab.

"How is our special guest?" she quietly asked.

Sinclair waved at the twins before returning his gaze to Jane. "Where are you heading?"

"The battlefield. The boys had to miss some of the action because some of their classmates weren't as captivated by today's event as they were."

Sinclair nodded. "I can understand that. Even with the doors closed, the sounds of battle carried into the Henry James Library. These things are

not my cup of tea, but I believe Mr. Butterworth enjoyed himself immensely."

"Would you like to ride down to the field with us?" Jane asked.

"I would."

Sinclair climbed into the passenger seat and asked the boys about their day. Fitz and Hem tripped over each other to talk about their classmates' reactions to the reenactment. At one point, Hem mocked the little girl who'd burst into tears. After listening to her son's scoffing tone, Jane stopped the Gator. She turned around and glared daggers at Hem.

"Never tease someone for being afraid," she said. "We're all afraid at one time or another."

When Hem apologized, Jane told him that he should be apologizing to the girl, not to her.

The boys were somewhat subdued when they arrived at the destination but quickly perked up after climbing into one of the trenches.

"Can you tell me about Parrish now?" Jane asked Sinclair when the boys were out of earshot.

"Mr. Parrish is neither surprised nor perturbed by his change of scenery," Sinclair said. "Honestly, I find his composure unsettling."

Jane gazed across the field. Days ago, it been covered by long, gold-green grass. It was now almost unrecognizable. Depressions, shallow craters, trampled grass, boot prints, and scraps of debris had completely changed the landscape.

The sun winked off a piece of metal in the distance, and Jane pointed at it.

"Do you see that? I wonder if someone forgot their helmet."

She and Sinclair began walking toward the object.

"I don't know what to do about Parrish," Jane confessed, picking her way over a cluster of stones.

"I don't think there's anything more to be done but wait," Sinclair said. "I can find nothing pertinent on the man, and I've exhausted all of my sources. The obvious details are available for the finding—Social Security number, birth certificate, driver's license, tax records, real estate records, but that's all. I can't find a single photo, a family connection, or any other mark of his presence in cyberspace. It's as if he's successfully avoided leaving a footprint. He's nothing but the sum of a dozen documents."

Jane shook her head in amazement. "I didn't think it was possible to be invisible anymore."

They spoke in low murmurs until they came upon the mysterious metal object.

Jane was correct in her assumption that it was a helmet. She picked it up, remembering how she'd seen Michael Murphy without his.

Sinclair had wandered over to a nearby trench, and when he drew in a sharp breath, Jane knew that he'd found something else.

It was not another helmet.

It was a body.

Sinclair scrambled down into the trench. He touched the man's neck, feeling for a pulse.

When he looked back up at Jane, she knew that there was no pulse to be found.

The man lay in the trench with his face turned to the side. Dust and dirt covered his entire head. There was blood too. As Jane knelt by the edge of the trench, she saw the angry laceration just over the man's left temple. The blood had run down his cheek to mix with the dirt, hardening into a dark crust.

With extreme care, Sinclair rolled the man onto his back. He used a handkerchief to wipe the man's face. His movements blocked Jane's view, but she saw Sinclair's shoulders abruptly stiffen. It was clear that he'd identified the body.

In a frightened whisper, Jane asked, "Who is it?"

"Archie Banks," Sinclair said.

"No!" Jane cried. "No, no, no. How am I supposed to tell Butterworth that his cousin is dead?"

CHAPTER ELEVEN

Sinclair offered to stay with the body while Jane carted the twins back to Storyton Hall. With a potential murderer on the loose, she wasn't about to leave them unguarded. As Sterling wasn't needed to drive guests, he offered to watch the twins while they tossed a football on the great lawn. Jane headed for the garages.

When Butterworth exited the door leading to the basement room where Parrish was being held, Jane was momentarily paralyzed. Butterworth was such a formal, formidable man. He was her unflappable protector. How could she find the words to tell him about Archie? How could she hurt him so deeply?

"Miss Jane? What's wrong?"

There was no use delaying. Above all else, Butterworth appreciated directness and candor. Jane would give him both.

"I'm sorry to be the one to tell you this, but Archie is dead. Sinclair and I just found his body on the battlefield."

Butterworth's eyes widened a fraction, and the muscle in his jaw tensed. "Are you quite certain? By what means?"

How can he be so calm? Jane wondered.

"A head wound. I'm so very sorry."

Butterworth raised a single finger. "Miss Jane, your sympathy might be misplaced. I spoke with Archie not too long ago. Unless he was on his way to the field . . ." He frowned. "There's no sense our standing here, conjecturing. Would you take me to him, please?"

Jane gestured at the Gator, which she'd left parked just outside the garages, and Butterworth climbed into the passenger seat. It was a strange role reversal to be driving Storyton Hall's head butler over the grounds he knew so well. He'd been custodian to the estate for as long as Jane could remember. Like Sinclair, Butterworth was one of several men who'd helped raise her. They'd been her teachers, her confidants, and her family. But she was a grown woman now, and she wanted to give back to them. She wanted to be a shoulder to lean on. A friend. A surrogate daughter.

Some of them have real families, she reminded herself. *Families they never see because of the oath they took to protect my family and the treasures housed within Storyton Hall.*

"Would you fill me in on Parrish as we drive?" she asked Butterworth. She knew he wouldn't find the question insensitive but would welcome the distraction.

"If possible, the man was more complacent than usual."

Jane shot Butterworth a worried glance. "Could he have orchestrated Archie's death?"

206

Instead of replying, Butterworth said, "Tell me about the day's event. What details stand out? I spent most of my time watching the field from the starting position of the Central Powers. You had a midfield viewpoint."

"What struck me most was the noise," Jane said. "It was easy to believe that what we were seeing was real. Not a Great War battle, but a genuine conflict. I found the soldiers very convincing—even those pretending to die." Regretting this phrase, Jane hurried on. "Three things interrupted my complete immersion. Seeing Bob wave at Betty, hearing the children in the twins' class cry, and watching Ajax pitch his rider."

This detail caught Butterworth's attention. "Did you see the rider fall?"

Jane thought back on the scene. "No. Ajax just appeared from behind a big cloud of dust without a rider. A minute later, we saw Michael Murphy looking a little dazed. He was headed toward the orchard. His helmet was in his hand."

"Was Michael Murphy Ajax's rider?"

"I assume so."

Jane brought the Gator to a stop but didn't get out. "Thinking back on it, I can't say who rode Ajax. I thought it was Michael Murphy, but I didn't actually see him on horseback. In any case, Sam will know. Is this important?"

"Sam would never entrust his horse to a man

he didn't know," said Butterworth. "Therefore, I think it's important."

Jane didn't have time to mull this over because Butterworth alighted from the Gator and pointed at the field. "Please lead the way."

Sinclair was kneeling next to Archie's body so that his torso shaded the dead man's face. When he saw Butterworth, he slowly got to his feet and spread his hands. Butterworth responded to this wordless gesture of sympathy with the faintest of nods. He then knelt on the ground opposite his friend and stared at his cousin.

His eyes traveled from Archie's dirt-encrusted face, to his hands, and back to his face. Next, he removed a handkerchief from his pocket and cleaned Archie's cheek. Very gently, Butterworth took his cousin's chin in his hand and pivoted his face skyward.

"This man is not Archibald," Butterworth said, turning to Jane. "They bear a close resemblance, especially because they're both bald. They're also of a very similar build. However, this is not my cousin."

"Thank God," Jane said and instantly lowered her eyes in shame. "I don't want a stranger to be dead. I'm just relieved that you don't need to grieve."

Butterworth reached up and squeezed Jane's hand. The touch was brief but conveyed his gratitude. When he focused on the dead man again, he was all business.

208

"We should call the sheriff and Doc Lydgate. Mr. Sinclair, did you find anything of note at the scene?"

Sinclair shook his head. "I searched for his helmet as well as any clue as to what caused his head injury, but the field was cleaned up quite thoroughly. The efficiency of the groundskeepers makes this discovery all the more unusual. How was this man missed? Every sandbag and detonated grenade has been removed, but a body lies undetected? Something is off about this scenario."

"Do you think he was killed after the battle?" Jane asked.

"All I know is that we need to discover what happened here without delay," said Sinclair. "Luckily, this event was filmed from several angles. If we can identify this man, we can track his movements using the footage."

Jane gestured at the man's green wool coat. "He's an American. At least, he was today. All we need to do is ask the uniform rental people for the name of the man who neglected to turn in his uniform. They're probably looking for him as we speak."

Sinclair arched his brows. "Shall I place the call to the sheriff?"

With her gaze fixed on the dead man, Jane nodded. She knelt down, touched the soiled shoulder of his uniform coat, and whispered, "I want you to know that you look like a genuine Great War doughboy, and I'm sure you put your heart into today's battle. Rest in peace now."

After this farewell, Jane and Butterworth drove back to Storyton Hall to identify the unknown soldier.

"It's been a long time since my days as an Army doc, but I never thought I'd be examining a patient killed in the line of mock duty." Doc Lydgate rubbed the white whiskers of his beard and frowned. "Such a shame."

Jane handed him a cup of tea before passing a mug of black coffee to Sheriff Evans. "Any idea what caused his death?"

"I'd say we're looking at head trauma." Doc Lydgate dropped a lemon slice into his teacup. "The patient struck a rock or another unyielding object. I expect the coroner to find a fractured skull and bleeding to the brain. Not long after the initial blow, it would have been lights out for this gentleman. He wouldn't have felt pain after losing consciousness."

Sheriff Evans, an honest and intelligent lawman in his late fifties, touched his temple. "I was wondering if the fall into the trench killed him, but I saw nothing for him to hit his head on. The wood planks on the bottom couldn't have made that wound."

"No," the doc agreed. "I believe he sustained

the injury elsewhere and was disoriented by the time he came upon that trench. He probably toppled in, possibly exacerbating the damage caused by the original injury, and died shortly after."

The sheriff looked at Jane. "Mr. Sinclair, Deputy Phelps, and I searched a fairly wide circle around the body. We found no rock or other object marked with blood. Did the groundskeepers clean up man-made objects only or did they remove natural debris too?"

Jane shook her head. "I don't think so. They mostly filled in holes caused by grenades. Tomorrow, they'll use a Bobcat to fill in the trenches."

"Would you ask the crew about hard or sharp objects found near that trench? Maybe one of them will remember seeing something," the sheriff said.

"Right away."

Jane placed the call, and her head grounds-keeper promised to check with the crew and get back to her. She'd just hung up when there was a knock on the door.

It was Butterworth. "Pardon the interruption. We have identified the Rip Van Winkle."

Rip Van Winkle was code for the presence of a dead body in Storyton Hall's manor house or grounds. The term had first been coined after a guest suffered a fatal heart attack on the pickleball courts, and Jane had had to use it several times since. Storyton Hall wasn't the only resort to employ a code name for an expired guest. Jane had heard of several others during the hotelier conference.

"Death is a part of hotel life," another manager had said. "With a stream of people coming and going, it's bound to happen. Our job is to continue to treat the expired guest with respect."

Jane always focused on discretion. As did her staff. Which is why Butterworth closed her office door and waited for Jane to give him the signal to speak.

"The gentleman's name is Ray Pizzolato," Butterworth said. "He's a middle school history teacher known as Mr. Pizza to his students and coworkers alike. Mr. Pizzolato was thirty-four and a bachelor. He's from a small town in Tennessee. His passions were teaching and participating in reenactments. He was friendly with several of our current guests. These historians have attended many of the same events and describe Mr. Pizzolato as witty, fun-loving, and easygoing."

"Sounds like the perfect teacher. An affable man with a passion for his subject. What a shame," said Doc Lydgate.

Jane couldn't have agreed more.

Butterworth handed a piece of paper to Sheriff Evans. "Mr. Pizzolato listed his mother as his emergency contact. Her name and phone number are here. I don't envy you that phone call, Sheriff."

Butterworth left the room. As soon as he was gone, Sheriff Evans put down his coffee cup and donned his hat. "Ms. Steward, I'll give you an update when I have the coroner's report. For now, I'm viewing this case as death by misadventure. Though others might call it accidental, there are risks involved in these reenactments. It's why waivers are required. Mr. Pizzolato took a risk by participating, and unfortunately, the risk resulted in his death."

Doc Lydgate murmured in agreement.

"I'm leaving Deputy Phelps behind in case a guest has information to share," the sheriff said as he moved toward the door. He reached for the handle and hesitated. "You know, I thought about signing up for this event, but half of the department wanted to participate. With all the members of the Storyton Sheriff's Department on that field today, I feel confident someone would have noticed any funny business."

"I'm sure you're right," Jane said. Her words rang false to her ears, but neither the sheriff nor Doc Lydgate appeared to notice. After promising to touch base, both men left her office.

"Mr. Pizza," Jane mused aloud.

She spent several moments thinking of how much the dead man's family, students, coworkers, and friends would miss him. His loved ones would want answers. A mysterious head wound was not enough of an explanation to grant them closure. It certainly wasn't enough for Jane.

Reaching for her phone, she sent a group text telling the Fins to meet her in the William Faulkner Conference Room in thirty minutes. By then, she wanted them to have finished collecting footage from the battle. She planned to host her own Great War film screening so that she and the Fins could scrutinize every frame. They wouldn't be looking to be entertained. They'd be searching for a killer.

Jane hadn't expected Archie to join their meeting. She glanced at Butterworth, her mouth opening in protest, when Sinclair placed a hand on her arm.

"You need to hear what he has to say," he whispered.

With a tight smile, Jane invited Archie to take a seat.

"Ms. Steward," he began. "I have reason to believe that the body you found on the battlefield was supposed to be mine."

Jane stared at him in surprise. "Please explain."

Archie leaned forward, clearly eager to do just that. "When we lined up to rent our uniforms, I was right behind Mr. Pizzolato. He and I started talking. He was an engaging guy." A note of sadness entered Archie's voice. "When we got to the front of the line, the man distributing the uniforms commented on the resemblance between us. It was our baldness and our overall stature. Mr. Pizzolato had brown eyes to my blue, and his face was more angular. But from a distance, it wouldn't be easy to tell us apart."

"Were you registered as an American or a British soldier?" Jane asked.

"British," said Archie. "But the man distributing the uniforms messed up and gave my uniform to Mr. Pizzolato. Because everything was in a bag, I didn't realize what had happened until it was time to get dressed. I phoned Mr. Pizzolato's room. When he didn't answer, I went ahead and put on the American uniform."

Jane shot a quick glance at Butterworth to see what he made of this story. His expression was as inscrutable as ever. Turning back to Archie, she asked, "Didn't this create confusion for your American unit?"

"Things were fairly chaotic in that group, so I didn't explain the mix-up. I just jumped in. I spotted my British regiment right before the battle began. I noticed Mr. Pizzolato and we exchanged waves. He seemed to have been adopted by my brothers-in-arms."

"Naturally. They were British, after all," said Butterworth sotto voce.

"So we've gathered here to identify the person

215

who meant to kill *you?*" Jane studied Archie for a long moment. "For what reason? Because you're Butterworth's cousin?"

"Because I'm a Fin. Which means I'm your man for as long as I'm at Storyton Hall." Archie quickly undid the top three buttons of his shirt, revealing a small tattoo of an arrow over his heart. An arrow tattoo was the mark of a Fin.

"Do you have a Guardian back in New York?" Jane was unable to hide her astonishment.

Archie looked stricken. "I did. He passed away recently, leaving no heirs."

Jane scanned the faces of her Fins. Had they known about this other Guardian? Were there more places like Storyton Hall?

No doubt, Sinclair could tell that Archie's remark had piqued Jane's curiosity, for he pointed at the screen and said, "Miss Jane, shall we start watching the footage?"

Jane knew her attention was being misdirected, but she also knew that she had a duty to Mr. Pizzolato. She had failed Gerald Tucker. She would not fail to seek justice for one of her own guests. With a nod, she indicated that she was ready to look for a killer.

The footage had been provided by three historians who filmed reenactments rather than participating in them. Each videographer had a different vantage point. The first man followed the movements of the Allies. The second tracked those of the Central Powers. The third shot his footage from the middle of the battlefield.

Sterling loaded the Allied footage and Archie moved to the front of the room, ready to call for a pause should his regiment appear. However, they showed up only during the first ten minutes of filming. At this point, the various units were still getting organized. Neither side had started firing the gas guns.

Next, the group watched the footage shot by the cameraman following the Central Powers. After a while, all the noise, shouting, and movement became a blur to Jane.

Suddenly, Archie bolted out of his chair and asked Sterling to pause the video.

"There's Mr. Pizzolato." He moved to the screen and placed his index finger on a man standing in profile. "His left puttee is coming unraveled. He must not have wrapped it tightly before the battle started. I noticed it when we waved to each other, but I never had the chance to tell him."

Catching Jane's blank stare, he said, "A puttee is a length of cloth wrapped around the lower leg." He turned back to the screen. "Also, Mr. Pizzolato forgot to remove his watch. I guess he thought it wouldn't show under his uniform sleeve, but it's peeking out here. That neon yellow band draws the eye."

"Did you notice that watch when the two of you

and Mr. Pizzolato were in line for uniforms?" Sinclair asked.

Archie said that he had, and the group continued to watch Mr. Pizzolato, frame by frame. His face was shining, and there was no doubt that his final hours were happy ones.

Jane wondered where his once-animated body was now. On a metal slab? In a storage drawer? Was his face covered with a white sheet, or was he being examined under a harsh light?

Onscreen, Mr. Pizzolato veered off to the right while the camera stayed with a group of men running in the opposite direction. He never appeared again.

When the recording was done, Jane rubbed her temples. She needed a break.

She looked at Butterworth. "Could you order a tea tray before we watch the final footage? I could use a hit of caffeine and sugar."

"Certainly."

Instead of calling the kitchen, Butterworth left the room. He returned wheeling a trolley, which he parked next to Jane. After pouring her a cup of tea, he asked if he could make her a plate.

Jane chose a dill, Havarti, and turkey finger sandwich, a two-bite ham and chive quiche, and a pear and ginger scone. Mrs. Hubbard had thoughtfully sent bowls of apricot jam and clotted cream to accompany the scones, and Butterworth added dollops of each to Jane's plate.

After taking several sips of black tea and eating the finger sandwich, Jane felt more human. The men were also partaking of the teatime treats, though they skipped the scones and doubled down on the quiche and finger sandwiches.

When the final round of footage began, Jane recognized the cameraman's viewpoint, as she and the Cover Girls had been sitting nearby. Though he'd been closer to the action than the other spectators, he kept out of sight by filming between two tree trunks. His main focus was on the center of the field, but he happened to catch the second charge of soldiers on horseback. He recorded the moment when Ajax shied from the blast of a detonating grenade, pitching his rider forward. Lachlan reviewed this sequence in slow motion, and Archie gave a soft shout when the rider was captured seconds before hitting the ground.

"There's his watch again! Do you see it?"

"Yes. This raises a new question, however, which is how did Mr. Pizzolato end up on that horse?" Sinclair directed his question at Archie. "Sam vetted the riders weeks ago. He said they'd all be people he could trust. People he knew well."

Archie looked like he wanted to say something, but at the last moment, he changed his mind and simply shook his head. The silence was quickly followed by a buzz of conversation as the Fins came up with possible theories.

"We'll have to speak with Sam," Jane said, wondering what Archie might be holding back. "We need to find out how a stranger ended up on one of his horses."

The men agreed, and Lachlan continued playing the footage. Everyone in the conference room strained to see what had become of Mr. Pizzolato after his fall, but the detonated grenade created too much dust. Their view was completely obscured.

The cameraman panned away from the dust cloud, focusing on a group of German soldiers. The men charged in a rough line, shouting as they ran. They all faced forward, their gazes locked on some target straight ahead. Except for one man. The soldier on the far end was looking sharply to the right. It was as if he knew he was being filmed and had deliberately turned away.

"That gentleman isn't watching where he's going," said Butterworth.

Jane and the rest of the Fins nodded. They'd all noticed the same thing.

"Sterling, would you track down one of the German reenactors shown here and ask them to identify the camera-shy soldier?" Jane asked. "Until we have answers from them and from Sam, there isn't much more for us to do. We'll have to make an announcement to the guests, but I'll wait for the sheriff to confirm his ruling first. The groundskeepers have already gone over the field again and found nothing marked with blood. If a weapon was used on Mr. Pizzolato, it's gone."

Butterworth got to his feet and clasped his hands in front of his waist. "Considering our current circumstances, I believe one of us should stay in your home to keep watch over Masters Fitzgerald and Hemingway."

"Thank you, Butterworth. I'll have the boys spend the night with Uncle Aloysius and Aunt Octavia. If one of you would stay in the guest room next door, I'd sleep easier."

Sterling readily volunteered, and the meeting was officially over.

Before Archie could leave, Jane grabbed him by the arm. "Is there anything else you want to tell me? I felt like you were on the verge of saying something, but you held back."

Archie gave her a blank look. "No, sorry. If I can help, I will. But right now, I think you're doing everything that can be done."

Jane walked through the staff corridor feeling more than a little glum. She was holding a man prisoner with seemingly no purpose, a man had died during what should have been a celebratory historical reenactment, she had to worry about the safety of her family, and she had no one to lean on. Not in the way she wanted.

What she wanted was Edwin.

What harm could it do to see him?

And before she knew it, she was on her bike heading into the village. She exited Storyton Hall's property, zoomed by the pasture where the twins always stopped to feed an apple to the resident pony, and came upon the sharp bend in the road that had sent many a patient to Doc Lydgate.

Jane smiled as she recalled the latest verse added to the ever-changing ditty dedicated to the infamous bit of roadway. The twins were absurdly proud of the last two lines, which they'd thought of during their last rainy-day recess.

> Broken Arm Bend, Virginia's sharpest curve,
> It makes all the cars and bicycles swerve.
> If you don't watch out, and you don't
>   drive smart,
> You'll go *pffttt* just like a giant fart!

Jane's spirit lifted as she neared the village. She rode past Storyton Outfitters, rumbled over the wooden bridge traversing Storyton River, and finally slowed as Run for Cover came up on her left. Dismounting, Jane was pleased to see how many rental bikes were parked in the rack.

"Go, Eloise," she said to her friend's storefront. "Get those books out into the world."

Knowing the front door to Daily Bread would be locked because the café served breakfast and lunch only, Jane walked down the narrow alley separating Edwin's stone and brick cottage from his neighbor's. She knocked on the kitchen door, hoping Magnus, the manager, was in.

The door was opened, but not by Magnus.

"Edwin!" Jane threw her arms around him and buried her face in his shoulder.

Pulling her into the kitchen, Edwin shut the door with one hand and pressed Jane against him with the other. "Jane," he whispered. "Sweetheart."

He cupped her face in his hands and stared at her. Then, he kissed her. Hungrily. He held her so close that Jane could barely breathe. Still, she wanted to get even closer—to melt into him. She wanted to erase any divide between them. She didn't want to be separated by so much as a molecule of air.

"Wait," said Edwin, pushing Jane away a little. His voice was hoarse. "What about William?"

Jane traced Edwin's jawline. "I'm in love with you, Edwin. I want *you*."

Right or wrong, she spoke the truth. She couldn't deny her feelings, and she'd already missed too much time with the man she loved.

Edwin read the need in her eyes. It had been months since they'd touched each other the way they wanted to.

"Take me upstairs," Jane whispered.

Without a word, Edwin swept her into his arms. He stopped to kiss her on every step, so it took a long time to reach his second-floor living quarters. He kissed her forehead, her mouth, her cheek, and her neck.

By the time they reached his bedroom, Jane was nearly dizzy with desire.

Over the next hour, she forgot her worries. She forgot everything but Edwin. His body, his hands, his smile, his tender whispers. He became a sea that she willingly dove into, drowning in a tide of joy.

CHAPTER TWELVE

Jane tried not to think about Ray Pizzolato during her book-club meeting, but the video footage she'd seen of him kept replaying in her mind.

The Cover Girls had finished sharing their views on *The Long Engagement* and were ready for dessert and a discussion of *Maisie Dobbs*.

Eloise joined Jane in the kitchen with an offer to deliver decaf coffee to the rest of their friends. After serving Mabel and Mrs. Pratt, Eloise returned for Violet's and Betty's mugs. "Phoebe said that she's already over her coffee limit. A hazard of her profession, I guess."

When Jane responded with an automatic grin, Eloise touched her on the arm and said, "Hey. What's going on with you?"

Her friend's touch was a comfort. "Sinclair and I found a body on the battlefield this afternoon. There weren't supposed to be casualties. But a man died."

"Oh no!" Eloise cried. She lowered her voice. "How did it happen?"

"I'm not sure. Doc Lydgate thinks he hit his head on something and, in a state of confusion, stumbled into a trench. He was a history teacher from Tennessee. It's really sad."

Eloise gestured toward the living room. "Would it help to talk about it?"

Jane nodded. She always felt better after confiding in her friends. Not only were they excellent listeners, but they were also smart, loyal, and brave. When Jane couldn't solve a problem on her own, the Cover Girls helped her reach a solution. They asked astute questions, batted theories around, and made her laugh when she felt like crying.

Eloise delivered the last of the coffees, and Jane put a platter of cake slices on the table.

"Mrs. Hubbard insisted on making a wartime cake for our meeting tonight. This one is moistened with applesauce and frosted with buttercream," Jane said. "Would everyone like a piece?"

"Not me," said Mabel. "This gal is *not* a raisin fan, California or otherwise."

Jane popped up from the table again. "I almost forgot. Mrs. Hubbard also sent some Anzac biscuits—just in case some of us had an aversion to raisins."

"That woman is a gem," said Mrs. Pratt. "I read about those biscuits in a novel. Aren't they cookies made with oats and coconut?"

Jane, who'd just returned from the kitchen, smiled at her friend. "You never cease to amaze me. And you're right. These biscuits were shipped to soldiers. They were packed with as much nutritional value as the women could get into them. Oats, coconut, golden syrup, and butter were the main ingredients."

"Plus a hearty dose of love," added Betty.

Eloise waited until everyone had a slice of cake or a cookie before saying, "Ladies, as much as I enjoyed *Maisie Dobbs*, we need to talk about something else right now."

When she looked at Jane, the other Cover Girls did too.

"You've been pretty quiet tonight," Violet said to Jane in concern. "Is everything okay?"

Jane cradled her coffee cup, feeling the warmth of the ceramic spread across her palms. "I'm sorry. I wish I could focus on the fictional mystery, but I can't. Not when I have a real one to solve."

Mrs. Pratt, who'd been on the verge of biting into a cookie, abruptly closed her mouth. Her eyes shone with interest. "A murder mystery?"

"Not exactly." Jane described how she and Sinclair had discovered Mr. Pizzolato's body. "I expect the sheriff will stick to his ruling of death by misadventure, but two things bother me about Mr. Pizzolato's passing. The first is that I don't see how our groundskeepers missed finding him during their cleanup. The second is that we have no way of knowing what caused Mr. Pizzolato's head wound."

"Do you have reason to believe that his death was something other than an accident?" Phoebe asked, twisting one of her corkscrew curls around her index finger in agitation.

227

Jane couldn't tell her friends that Archie was a Fin. She couldn't tell them that he was Butterworth's cousin either. They needed to believe that Archie was just another historian.

"There's no reason to suspect foul play," said Jane. "Mr. Pizzolato was well liked by everyone. He was my guest, and I was responsible for his safety. I feel like I let him down. I won't be able to let that feeling go until I know what happened to him."

Betty tapped the cover of her *Maisie Dobbs* paperback. "One of my favorite quotes from this book was from Maisie's mentor, Dr. Maurice Blanche. He says, 'Truth walks towards us on the path of our questions.'"

Mrs. Pratt said that she'd underlined that quote as well. "Let's try to find the answers to Jane's two questions. Number one; why didn't the groundskeepers see Mr. Pizza?"

"Because he wasn't in the trench when they were cleaning the field," said Mabel. "Could he have been in the woods?"

Jane shrugged. "I guess so, though I don't see why."

Betty rolled her eyes. "That's because you're not a man. Men take great pleasure in answering nature's call *in* nature. I bet Mr. Pizzolato was injured on his way to hose down a tree trunk."

Several Cover Girls murmured in agreement.

"Betty's theory would also explain why there

was nothing left on the field that could have caused his head wound," Eloise added. "If he was hurt and passed out in the woods, he may have woken later, dazed and confused, and stumbled into that trench."

"Was the trench close to the woods?" Phoebe asked.

"Yes," said Jane. "We haven't searched that area yet, but we will tomorrow. Thanks, gals. What would I do without you?"

Eloise smiled. "You'll never know the answer to that question because we'll always be here for you." Gazing at the rest of the Cover Girls, she said, "Let's spend a little time with Maisie. After that, we need to vote on our next read."

"I'd love another clever heroine like Maisie without the sad backdrop of war," said Betty. "Even though I knew it was a novel—a work of fiction—I got very emotional reading it."

Jane understood. There had been so much conflict in her life recently. She'd give anything for a long stretch of peace. How many millions of people felt that way at the end of the Great War? Or at the end of any war? But peace never seemed to last. There was always another war waiting around the corner.

"Why don't we read a classic children's chapter book?" she suggested. "Something uplifting and heartwarming."

Eloise grinned. "I love that idea. And since

those books are usually shorter than our regular picks, we could read two or three."

Before the Cover Girls left that evening, they'd agreed their next book picks would be *The Phantom Tollbooth*, *Anne of Green Gables*, and *Island of the Blue Dolphins*.

Between her stolen hour with Edwin followed by her book-club meeting, Jane felt a renewed sense of hope.

However, when she walked by the twins' room and saw their empty beds, her heart sank again. What kind of life was she giving her sons? If they couldn't safely sleep in their own home, then something was very wrong.

Jane entered the room, sat on Hem's bed, and picked up the teddy bear he'd had since he was three. "I'll fix this," she whispered to the furry face. "I'll find a way to keep the monsters out."

Victory was the theme of the next two days. Today, the historians would attend a mock peace conference followed by a remembrance lunch. There would be an afternoon lecture on postwar America. Tomorrow held no scheduled activities, and the centennial celebration would wrap up with a Victory Gala in the Great Gatsby Ballroom.

The staff buzzed about, making preparations, but Jane had a hard time getting into the spirit of the victory theme. In a week's time, she'd seen two dead bodies, Gerald Tucker's and Mr. Pizzolato's. In her mind, there wasn't much to celebrate. She couldn't do anything to influence Tuck's case, and her investigation into Mr. Pizzolato's death had been stalled. It had been her plan to visit Sam yesterday, but according to his voicemail message, he'd driven to Maryland to look at a horse and wouldn't be back until today.

Until she could see him in person, Jane tried to focus on other work. But negative thoughts kept destroying her concentration. She remembered how she'd foolishly believed that she'd have an advantage over Parrish once she was back at Storyton Hall. That didn't prove to be the case and she felt just as she had at Biltmore—like she had no control over her circumstances.

Yesterday, she'd shared her feelings with Edwin, and he'd told her that she could take control by discovering what Parrish truly wanted. Why had he come to Storyton Hall? What rare book or unique material was he really after?

"If I had to guess, I'd say he's looking for something written by a Lost Generation author," Edwin had said. "Parrish collects their works with a fervor that goes beyond the norm. I believe he wanted Randall to search your secret library for books by a particular author or authors. I think the entire kidnapping scheme was set up to give Parrish's agents access to the library without his involvement. He's obviously tired of entrusting the job to his subordinates and has come to Storyton Hall to see that he finally gets what he wants."

Reflecting on this conversation now, Jane decided that Edwin was right. She couldn't wait around to see what horrible event would unfold next. She couldn't depend on her Fins to protect her family and Storyton Hall. *She* needed to take charge—to be the leader she'd failed to be since the twins were abducted. Fear of losing them had completely unbalanced her. She'd been deeply terrified and intensely angry, and this onslaught of emotions had made her weak.

"No more," she muttered as she entered Storyton Hall and strode down the lobby. Marching straight up to Butterworth, she said, "I'd like a word with your cousin. Please send him to my office."

If Butterworth was surprised by her request, he didn't show it.

Archie arrived within minutes. He knocked on Jane's door and waited until she invited him to sit in the guest chair opposite her desk.

"How did Mr. Pizzolato end up riding that horse when he wasn't listed as a vetted rider?"

"I've been asking myself the same thing," said Archie. "I was going to skip this morning's session, head up to Hilltop Stables, and talk to Sam in person. I wouldn't leave without telling you first."

Jane wasn't impressed by this show of respect. Archie might be related to Butterworth, but she didn't know him from Adam. Which meant she didn't trust him.

"Tell me how you know Sam," she said. "It's clear to me that you do. You almost told me in our meeting yesterday. You were on his list of vetted riders because he must know you. He must trust you. How is this possible?"

Looking resigned, Archie said, "I didn't say anything because I didn't want to embarrass Sam. I thought he could tell you this story himself, but I realize that this isn't the time to be sensitive."

Jane waved for him to continue.

"Sam and I attended a boarding school for troubled boys. In other words, for boys who'd been arrested, gotten involved with drugs or alcohol, or had other behavioral issues. Mine was fighting. I'd been kicked out of two schools before my parents sent me to Rollingwood. One of the school's behavioral modifications was having students learn to take care of various animals. Sam and I both fell in love with the horses."

Jane had never known that Sam had attended Rollingwood, but she understood why he might not talk about having been enrolled at a school for troubled boys.

"Have you two kept in touch since you were in school together?"

Archie shrugged. "The occasional email and Christmas card, which is probably why Mr. Pizzolato ended up on Ajax. I think Sam mistook him for me. I haven't actually connected with Sam since coming to Storyton. I want to find out if he recognizes me. That's why I wanted to see him in person."

"I'll drive you to Hilltop," said Jane. "Meet me in front of the garages in fifteen minutes. No one should see us leave. After all, you're supposed to be at a mock peace conference."

Instead of taking one of Storyton Hall's vintage Roll-Royce sedans, Jane chose the same pickup truck she and Lachlan had driven to Asheville. The road to Hilltop was riddled with potholes, and Jane didn't think Sterling would appreciate her damaging the undercarriage of a Phantom or throwing off the alignment of a Silver Cloud.

As soon as Archie was in the truck, Jane repeated the question she'd asked him in the conference room. Only this time, she rephrased it. "Why would someone want you dead because you're a Fin? And why you over one of my men?"

Archie looked out the window. "Butterworth doesn't want me to tell you my story. We had a big argument over the subject." He shot a quick glance at Jane. "I've heard about you my whole life, Ms. Steward. You're the apple of my cousin's eye. I know he rarely shows emotion.

But when he talks about you, there's music in his voice."

Though Jane was deeply touched, she didn't want to discuss her relationship with Butterworth. "That's nice of you to say, but—"

"I'm not trying to avoid your original question," Archie interrupted. "I'm sharing this because I think your Fins are protective to a fault. They may see themselves as father figures, but as your protectors, they should be completely transparent." He turned to Jane. "Do you think they are?"

Jane frowned. "What are you trying to tell me?"

"You're not the only Guardian. Just as your family were descendants of the original Templars and vowed to preserve knowledge, other families have made the same vow. There's only a handful left in the world, but they exist."

"Like your former employer?" Jane asked. "Why wasn't I told about these other Guardians? We should all be working together—helping each other. This secrecy is ridiculous."

Archie was quiet for a long moment. Reluctantly, he said, "The others do talk. In fact, they have an annual meeting. It's held at a different house each year."

Jane was floored. "I'd give a kidney to be invited! Why wasn't I?"

"Your exclusion stems from the guilt my uncle and Mr. Sinclair feel over your parents' death."

"My parents weren't even in this country when they died. I've combed through all the documents relating to their death. That plane crash was an accident."

Archie nodded. "Even so, my uncle and Mr. Sinclair believe that they'd failed your parents. I was just a kid when it happened, but I remember how my uncle changed. He was always serious, but he could laugh and tell jokes on occasion. After the accident, I think he stopped smiling altogether. His whole existence became focused on protecting you."

"But Uncle Aloysius was the Guardian at the time. Not me."

"You were groomed to take the mantle. And when you showed up at Storyton Hall, pregnant and newly widowed, Butterworth and the other Fins vowed to keep you safe."

Jane felt her anger rising. "By keeping secrets from me?"

"They acted out of fear. And out of love," Archie said. "They might have told you these things eventually, but when you expressed a desire to share Storyton Hall's collection with the world, they hesitated. Your Fins don't see eye to eye over this issue. Mr. Sinclair supports you. My cousin doesn't."

Jane turned off the main road and began to climb the winding lane to Hilltop Stables. "I talked my great-uncle into putting a single book on display. Because of that decision, a man died, and my sons were abducted. I'd like to be angry with Butterworth, but he was right. Displaying our treasures is dangerous."

"Does that mean that you'll keep them a secret forever?" Archie sounded disappointed.

"Do you know what I'd like?" Jane's voice was tight with emotion. "I'd like to give away the whole collection. To a museum. Or a university. What we have is amazing. Astounding. I love spending time in the secret library. I will never tire of looking at unpublished plays, alternate versions of famous novels, scandalous poetry, and political pamphlets. No one *else* can experience these wonders. Which is a crime. They belong to all readers."

Archie held up his hands. "I completely agree with you. So did my Guardian. He also wanted to donate his collection. After doing some research, he realized that most of his materials would end up sealed away in a subterranean vault. Do you know how much of the Library of Congress's collection is available for public view? They have 164 million items."

"It doesn't matter, because even if people can't hold a book in their hands, the contents have been digitized," Jane said. "The Library of Congress is a perfect example. Their treasures are accessible through digitization. They belong to everyone. *That's* what I want. For our collection to belong to everyone. Books were written to be read. Stories were created to be shared."

The truck crested the final rise, and Hilltop Stables came into view. Jane knew that she had to shift her focus, but it was incredibly hard after all she'd just learned.

Think of the man known as Mr. Pizza to his students. He deserves your full attention. He deserves justice.

Jane got out of the truck and hailed one of Sam's employees, an African American man named Deacon.

Deacon, who was in his mid-sixties and had close-cropped black hair threaded with gray, was leading a horse with a gleaming chestnut coat toward a vacant stall. Jane waited until the horse was settled inside before approaching Deacon.

"Ms. Steward! You here for a ride?" He gestured at the surrounding woods. "It's a beautiful day for it."

"It sure is, but I have a surprise for Sam. This is a longtime friend of his." She introduced Deacon to Archie.

Deacon warned Archie that his hands smelled like Jasmine—the horse, not the flower. Archie laughed and said, "Barnyard scent is my favorite perfume."

The remark won Deacon over. He and Archie chatted about Jasmine as Deacon led them toward the log cabin that served as Sam's office.

"Come back when you have more time," Deacon said to Jane as she entered the cabin. "And bring this fellow along." He pointed at Archie. "I bet he'd take to Jasmine like a duck to water."

Deacon walked away, whistling as he went.

Jane envied his contentment.

"You should hear him sing," said Sam from behind his desk. "The horses love his voice."

Sam was good looking in an all-American way. He was tall, broad-shouldered, and had brown hair streaked with blond. His eyes were a brilliant blue, and he had a dimpled chin. He'd been smitten with Eloise for as long as Jane could remember. He'd finally stopped flirting with Eloise when he realized that her heart belonged to Landon Lachlan.

Sam greeted Jane before turning to Archie.

"Archie?" he asked, clearly confused.

"In the flesh." Archie's face broke into a wide grin. "With a little less hair than when we last saw each other."

Sam got to his feet. He tried to smile but couldn't. "Wait. At Storyton Hall . . . I met this guy. I thought he was you. He . . . he *said* that he was you."

"When did this man introduce himself as Archie?" Jane asked.

"At the makeshift paddock," said Sam, his eyes locked on Archie. "You emailed that photo from

Yellowstone Park, remember? So I thought I knew what you looked like. Oh man, I feel like a total idiot."

"It's not your fault, Sammie. That guy could have been my twin." Archie moved forward and held out his hand. "It's great to see you. It's been way too long."

Sam came around from behind his desk, and the two men embraced.

Though Jane found the demonstration of affection heartwarming, she had to speak before they started reminiscing and forgot about her. "Sam? Did the other man say that his name was Archie Berry?"

"Now that you mention it, no. He never told me his name." Sam glanced at Archie. "I thought it was you, so I gave him a big bro hug—like I did just now—and said how awesome it was to see him. I told him that we'd catch up after the reenactment and that he'd be riding Ajax. I said that Ajax was like Titan, a horse we rode back in school. The guy made a comment about Titan being a handful, and we both laughed."

"At least my doppelgänger knew how to ride," said Archie.

"Ajax isn't for beginners. That's for sure."

Sam didn't see Archie's doppelgänger again. At some point during the battle, Ajax was caught by Duncan Hogg of the Pickled Pig Market and returned to the makeshift paddock.

"I was shocked when I saw Duncan leading Ajax," Sam said, looking at Archie. "I didn't think you'd leave a horse alone in the middle of all that noise and chaos. In fact, I wondered if you'd been hurt. After all the horses were back here, I called Storyton Hall and Mr. Butterworth said that you were fine. I figured I'd ask you what happened at the Victory party."

Jane hated to tell Sam the sad fate of Archie's double, but she had no choice. "The man who rode Ajax was a teacher from Tennessee. He was injured during the reenactment. He received a fatal head wound. I'm sorry to tell you this, Sam, but he died on the battlefield."

"That's awful! He seemed like a really nice guy." Suddenly, Sam's eyes widened in alarm. "Oh my god, Ajax threw him. Is that what killed him?"

"No, no," Jane said. "Mr. Pizzolato struck his head on something hard. He wasn't wearing a helmet, and the blow injured his brain. It wasn't Ajax's fault. Or yours."

Seeing that Sam was clearly distressed, Archie asked Jane if he could stay at Hilltop Stables for a little longer.

"Of course," Jane said. After thanking Sam for his help, she got in the pickup and headed back down the mountain. She'd barely parked the truck behind the garages when Sterling came out to the lot to meet her.

"Miss Jane, you'd better come with me."

Instantly alarmed, Jane demanded, "What is it?"

"I have something to show you. It's in my lab."

As she followed Sterling, Jane tried to suppress a strong feeling of foreboding.

In the lab, a jagged rock about the size of football sat on the counter. It was tawny in color, but Jane could see a darker splotch on one end. This russet-colored stain could be only one thing: blood.

"Mr. Lachlan brought this to me a few minutes ago," said Sterling. "We wanted you to see it, though we'll have to call the sheriff before we can know for sure that the blood is a match to Mr. Pizzolato's."

"Where was this found?"

"In the woods near the trench—exactly where you suggested we look."

Jane stared at the rock. "Is this a murder weapon?"

Sterling followed her glance. "It seems very unlikely that someone would trip, smash his head against a rock, and later stumble into a trench. Unlikely, but not impossible."

"We need to find out who that German soldier was—the one avoiding the camera. Maybe he saw Mr. Pizzolato going into the woods." She pointed at Sterling's phone. "You'd better call the sheriff. He'll want to see where Lachlan found this. I'm going to search for the German soldier I couldn't identify. I'm tired of questions without answers."

"The remembrance lunch started a few minutes ago. All the reenactment participants should be in the Madame Bovary Dining Room."

Jane was already moving toward the door when she said, "Which means a killer might be there too."

CHAPTER THIRTEEN

The Great War Memorial Luncheon was to be a solemn affair. It would begin with prayer followed by a moment of silent reflection. When this was over, Clarence Kelley, Michael Murphy, and Archie Banks would discuss Virginia's role in the war. While they spoke, the names of Virginians killed in action or by disease would appear on a large projector screen at the far end of the room.

When Jane popped her head in the Madame Bovary Dining Room, the waitstaff was serving the soup course.

"One hundred thousand men from the Old Dominion served in this war," Clarence said from his position behind a lectern. "Nearly four thousand died during the conflict."

Michael pointed at the image on a second projector screen. It was of a group of African Americans in uniform, posing in front of a row of tents. "Black Virginians made up thirty-nine percent of the draftees. Though they fought as bravely as any man, they returned home to the same inequality. We'd like to honor their memories now."

It was Archie's turn to speak next. "Most of the wartime organizations in Virginia were run by women. These women's groups raised funds to benefit soldiers and the Red Cross. The Knitting for Victory auction taking place after our meal will feature practical pieces, like those the ladies on the home front would have shipped to the soldiers, to items for the family, to unique pieces of fabric art donated by artists across the country. All proceeds will benefit the Great War Historical Society."

Clarence held up a striped scarf made of cornflower blue and sapphire yarn. "The knitting auction was my wife's idea, and I'd like to thank her for her hard work. Isabel, would you stand?"

A beaming Isabel received a round of applause. Clarence momentarily abandoned the lectern to drape the scarf around his wife's neck. After quickly kissing her cheek, he returned to his place.

As the BackStory officers continued to share interesting facts and photographs with the other historians, the names of those lost in the war steadily scrolled on the screen behind them. Jane hoped that each name was read by at least one person in the room. When her gaze landed on the name of a fallen soldier, she whispered, "Thomas V. Beale. Thank you for your service."

Clarence started talking about war as an industry, and Jane decided to take the opportunity to grab a bite to eat in the kitchens. She wanted to return in time for the auction and, if possible, bid on a few items. After all, Christmas was only a few months away.

Thoughts of Christmas gave her pause. What would it be like to have William here at Christmastime? If his memory didn't return, Jane would need to make some major decisions about his future. He'd need employment and a place to live.

Standing under a ball of mistletoe will be much more complicated, she thought.

"You're miles away," said Mrs. Hubbard, coming upon Jane staring at an untouched bowl of butternut squash bisque. "Is everything all right?"

Since Jane couldn't tell the beloved head cook about William or Edwin, she told her about the unexpected casualty during yesterday's reenactment.

"That's awful!" Mrs. Hubbard exclaimed. Despite the gleam in her eyes, which betrayed how thrilled she was to hear the gossip-worthy news, she was still genuinely sorry.

"The other historians don't know yet. They'll be informed after the luncheon," Jane said.

In the face of any tragedy, Mrs. Hubbard's natural inclination was to prepare food.

"That soup won't see you through," she chided, disappearing into the larger of the two kitchens. She returned with a plate of roast chicken, mashed sweet potatoes, and asparagus.

Jane thanked Mrs. Hubbard and ate half of the food. She covered the rest in plastic wrap to finish tomorrow and returned to the Madame Bovary just as the first auction item appeared on the screen.

"Forgive my lack of auctioneering skills and please raise your bid cards high so that my two spotters can see them," Clarence was saying when Jane entered. "If there are no questions, then let's spend some money!"

The first item was a women's cardigan with cranberry and cream color blocking. The bidding was intense right from the get-go. After several items were fought over tooth and nail, it became obvious that a friendly rivalry existed between some of the historians.

When a gentleman outbid his tablemate to win a multicolored alpaca cowl, another man shouted, "Go, Yalie!"

"Another lap blanket?" someone taunted when a bidder near the back of his room won a chunky afghan done in shades of gray. "You Vardians sure do like to lie around!"

The man who'd won the afghan grinned broadly and said, "Yes, sir. Harvard men are happy to support the cause. Let's see *you* put your money where your mouth is, Big Red!"

Big Red rose to the challenge and bid top dollar for the next item, a handsome Icelandic style wool sweater in beige with thin red stripes.

Jane decided not to interfere with the competition between the academics. She could buy similar items from La Grande Dame, supporting her friend and a local business at the same time.

The next lot elicited a roar of laughter. It was a pink sweater with a hood and a pair of bunny ears. To Jane's surprise, the historians bid more aggressively for the bunny sweater, the tacky Christmas vest, the shawl with green alien heads, the brown and mustard beach shorts, and the octopus hat with tentacles, than they'd bid on any of the previous items.

They were having a grand time, and Jane hated knowing that she was about to put a serious damper on their merriment.

The final item of the auction was a ski hat with an attached knit beard done in yellow yarn. When this was sold, Clarence praised his fellow historians for their generosity, and everyone clapped.

"Ladies and gentleman, please remain in your seats. Jane Steward, the manager of Storyton Hall, has an important announcement."

Clarence stepped away from the lectern.

Jane held out a red tissue paper poppy. " 'In Flanders fields the poppies blow,' " she began. "As you know, the red poppy became a symbol of the blood spilled in the war to end all wars. The poppy I hold is meant to honor a man who lost his life during yesterday's battle. It is with my deepest sympathy that I tell you of the passing of Mr. Ray Pizzolato." There was a collective gasp, and Jane hurried on. "Mr. Pizzolato met with an accident during the reenactment. He passed away from a head injury before he could receive medical attention. It's my hope that all who knew Mr. Pizzolato can draw comfort in knowing that he died doing what brought him the most joy."

At that point, Jane passed the mic to Archie. She'd spoken with him earlier about her plans to honor Ray Pizzolato, and he'd immediately offered to help.

"Mr. Pizzolato's parents are en route from Tennessee," he said. "They've been driving all night and won't have much to look forward to when they get here. The other officers and I would like to ask a favor. If you knew Mr. Pizzolato at all, would you write a few words about him? We have blank notecards on the table by the hostess podium. We'll collect the finished cards and put them in a book for Ray's parents."

Michael Murphy waited for the historians to turn and locate the table before saying, "I didn't know Ray Pizzolato, but I hear that he had a lust for life, a passion for teaching, and a deep love of history. We can honor his memory by emulating his traits. Tomorrow, during your free day, why not feed a falcon? Go kayaking on the Storyton River. Land a big fish. Hike one of the trails. Make it a day worth remembering."

After Archie moved away from the podium, the diners stayed seated. They seemed dazed. Unable to shift to their next activity. One man finally stood and headed for the table of blank notecards. His motion broke the spell and other historians soon followed him.

Jane stood in place, watching and waiting. She expected to field questions, and it wasn't long before three men approached her.

"Ms. Steward, this is terrible news," said one of the men. "We knew Ray from other reenactments. He was enthusiastic, but he was also a rule follower. Which is why we can't understand how he was killed. How did the accident occur?"

"There's only so much I can tell you," Jane said with genuine regret. "Mr. Pizzolato received a head injury at some point during the battle. We think he passed out in the woods, out of sight. It's possible that he was concussed and never regained his senses."

Jane didn't want these men picturing their acquaintance lying in the dirt while blood swelled inside his brain, so she offered them no additional details. Instead, she asked, "Did any of you see him during the battle?"

A slender man with curly brown hair nodded. "We fought together for an hour. Ray was having a ball. He was a young man in his prime, which is why this is such a shock."

"I've studied battlefield injuries in great

depth," said another man with pale skin and round glasses. "I'm not asking for details out of simple curiosity. Could you explain *how* Ray received a head wound? We use air-soft weapons and egg grenades."

"We're assuming he was thrown from his horse," said Jane. "By *we,* I'm referring to the office of the Medical Examiner. I wish I had more answers for you. I truly do. If you'd like to speak with the sheriff, I can give you his number."

The man with the curly hair took Sheriff Evans's information, and then Jane showed them the printout of the German officer she'd yet to identify. None of the men recognized him.

Jane watched them walk away. The curly-haired man patted the man with glasses on the back. The men were mourning the loss of a friend. They hadn't known Ray intimately, but they'd known him well enough to feel sorrow over his passing.

Who's next? A niggling voice whispered in Jane's mind, and she knew it was time to take control.

She found Butterworth in his customary position by the front door. "We've heard from Mr. and Mrs. Pizzolato," he said. "They're due to arrive around four."

"I doubt they'll want tea but offer it to them anyway. I'm taking mine on the terrace with Uncle Aloysius and Aunt Octavia, and I'd like Ramsey Parrish to be our guest. I want him

251

released. Immediately, please. He should freshen up before joining my family. Can Billy cover for you for a bit?"

"He's searching for a lost suitcase, but he should be back shortly."

Jane felt like she'd been struck by lightning. She suddenly knew why Parrish had come to Storyton Hall. She knew what he hoped to find in the secret library.

"The lost suitcase," she murmured. "Why didn't I see it before?"

Butterworth issued a sharp cough to keep Jane from dashing off. He clearly didn't want to act on her orders without an explanation.

"Is this course of action wise?" he asked.

"Here's how I see things," Jane said, her eyes flashing. "I can continue letting Parrish push pawns on his chessboard until another person dies, or I can totally change the game. He expected to be taken captive. He planned to have Archie killed. He thought the death of a Fin would give him leverage. We have no idea who the next intended victim is, but I'm sure there is one. My only move is to turn his plan upside-down."

"An interesting strategy," Butterworth said. "And one with many risks."

Jane smiled. "Luckily, I have the Fins. And Edwin. And the Cover Girls. It's time for all of this *Tinker, Tailor, Soldier, Spy* nonsense to come to an end. I'm going upstairs to speak with my great-uncle. Please see to Mr. Parrish."

If Ramsey Parrish was pleased to be sitting on the back terrace on a glorious fall afternoon, he didn't show it.

After introducing him to Uncle Aloysius and Aunt Octavia, Jane offered to pour his tea. "It's not the blend you're used to, but I hope you find it satisfactory. Sugar?"

Parrish accepted his tea along with a zucchini and bacon mini quiche, a ham and mustard finger sandwich, and a caramelized banana macaroon. He passed on the French onion mini muffins, the turkey and cheddar biscuit, and the buttermilk scones with apple butter.

Jane let her guest sample his tea before saying, "Mr. Parrish, as you've probably guessed, I'm not going to fulfill all of your requests. However, I'm willing to help you gain possession of the materials you want most. If they're related to a Lost Generation author, now is the time to tell me. I'm discussing this in front of my family because we'll all work together to get you what you want. Afterward, you can leave our home in peace."

During Jane's speech, Parrish had worn that smug half-smile she found so irritating. He turned from her to gaze out over the great lawn. "You would hand over one of your treasures? Just like that?"

"To restore harmony to Storyton Hall? Yes, I would." Watching him closely, Jane added, "Are you searching for Ernest Hemingway's lost suitcase?"

Parrish's smile slipped. "How did you come to that conclusion?"

"You zealously collect the works of Lost Generation authors. You especially admire authors who've served in the military. You've either quoted or praised Ernest Hemingway multiple times in my presence. The contents of the lost suitcase are extremely valuable. Irreplaceable. And to a collector like you, incredibly desirable. To you, the contents of that suitcase would be worth killing for."

A glimmer appeared in Parrish's eyes. It was a glimmer Jane recognized. It shone from the eyes of all bibliophiles when they talked about a book they loved. A book that had moved them. Changed them. Forever imprinted itself on their memory.

"Do you have it?" The question betrayed Parrish's desire.

Jane shook her head. "Our Hemingway materials are on display in the Henry James Library. I looked in other places for anything he might have written but found nothing. However, my great-uncle has his father's papers in his study. Cyril Steward was a consummate traveler. If the lost suitcase were entrusted to him, the clue of its whereabouts would be hidden in those papers."

"Excuse me," said Aunt Octavia. She sounded annoyed. "I was resting when you spoke with Aloysius, which means I can't follow this conversation at all. What is significant about a suitcase?"

Jane held out her hand, palm up, toward Parrish, inviting him to explain.

"In 1922, Ernest Hemingway was a journalist," Parrish began. "During his coverage of a peace treaty in Switzerland, he met a magazine editor who expressed an interest in reading his fiction. Hemingway wired his wife, Hadley, and asked her to bring his work from Paris to Switzerland by train. For some absurd reason, Hadley packed everything Hemingway had written up to that point—both originals and carbon copies—into a suitcase."

Aunt Octavia stared at Parrish in astonishment. "There was nothing left behind? All of Hemingway's eggs were in one basket?"

"Everything was in that suitcase," said Parrish.

Leaning forward, Aunt Octavia whispered, "What happened to it?"

For a moment, Jane could almost believe that Ramsey Parrish wasn't her enemy. As he settled into a storyteller's posture, relaxing his shoulders and the hard set of his jaw, he became transformed. His passion for this author was almost palpable.

"Hadley's story is that she left the suitcase on the platform for a minute while she nipped into a shop to buy water." Parrish's tone was laced with disgust. "When she returned, the suitcase was gone. No one witnessed the theft. Perhaps it was an innocent mix-up. There was nothing about the suitcase that made it seem valuable. It was hardly a Louis Vuitton trunk—just a well-used case."

"That poor woman," said Aunt Octavia. "That mistake probably haunted her for the rest of her life."

"It did," Jane said. "I listened to one of Hadley's last interviews when I was in college. When asked about the stolen suitcase, her confident voice wavered. Even though Hemingway went on to write new material, she doesn't think he ever forgave her for losing those early works."

Parrish's face clouded over. "She didn't deserve forgiveness. Despite her claims that she was distraught over her colossal mistake, I believe she deliberately left that suitcase on the platform. Another person was meant to take it. It remains a mystery as to whom, but the bigger mystery involves the contents. When the suitcase was stolen, Hemingway's first novel had not yet been published. However, after he became a household name, one would expect those early works to emerge—to be put up for sale in a legitimate forum or on the black market."

For once, Jane wasn't interested in Mrs.

Hubbard's tempting treats. Her focus was entirely on Parrish. "If the suitcase was intentionally taken, then someone was determined to possess its contents. Hemingway claimed that it contained his juvenilia—coming-of-age stories—but was he working on something else? What was in that case?"

"I have my suspicions," said Parrish cagily. "What I would very much like, Ms. Steward, is to see the contents for myself."

Jane sipped her tea, glancing at Uncle Aloysius and Aunt Octavia over the rim of her cup. They both responded with slight nods. "If Hemingway's lost work is at Storyton Hall, you may have it. If we can find these papers, I will give them to you. If you acquire them, will you promise to stop persecuting my family?"

Parrish weighed his answer for a long time. "My order will disapprove if I return with so little when such an abundance of riches is housed in these walls." He looked at the mountains, and a wistful expression crossed his face. "However, I've been searching for Hemingway's missing work my entire adult life. It has been my grail quest. If you can deliver his missing material to me, you will have earned your peace."

"How did you come to the conclusion that Storyton Hall held Hemingway's papers?" asked Uncle Aloysius. "We've never run across them."

"A letter from your father to my grandfather

contains an unusual reference to Hemingway."

Jane looked at Parrish in amazement. "Cyril and your grandfather were friends?"

"Friendly," Parrish corrected.

Uncle Aloysius got to his feet and held out his hand to Parrish. "Shall we also be friendly in the name of our shared goal?"

Ramsey Parrish stood. With great solemnity, he took Uncle Aloysius's outstretched hand.

"Jane, Mr. Parrish and I will be cloistered in my library, sorting through my father's papers," said Uncle Aloysius. "This is just the sort of treasure hunt I enjoy. Word clues. Literary references. Voices echoing through the ages."

Uncle Aloysius touched the back of Aunt Octavia's chair, ready to pull it out for her. However, she made no move to rise. "I don't understand why Cyril would hide these papers where only he could find them. Still, I'd like to read whatever you find. It's not every day that undiscovered works by one of America's greatest authors are pulled out of a hole in the wall or from under the floorboards. Above all else, we are readers. You wouldn't deny us this chance to read these literary gems, would you, Mr. Parrish." This was spoken as a statement, not a question.

For the first time since Jane had met Parrish, he smiled with genuine warmth. "I wouldn't dream of depriving you."

Uncle Aloysius led Parrish away while Jane and

Aunt Octavia lingered at the table until the twins joined them. The boys spoke of their school day, talking over each other about recess, the monster-sized spider discovered in the girls' restroom, and their spelling test.

"I have a surprise for you two," Jane said when she could get a word in.

Hem reached for another scone. "What is it?"

Jane pulled the plate away. "One is enough. Besides, you'll want to be extra hungry for dinner. It's being cooked by your favorite chef."

"Mr. Alcott?" the twins asked in unison.

Jane nodded, and the boys cheered. Edwin always included the twins in meal prep. The three of them had a wonderful time. They made a huge mess, but it was worth it.

After tea, Jane waited until the twins had finished their homework and were relaxing in front of the TV before changing into exercise clothes and heading down to the mews.

Lachlan was in the middle of a falconry lesson. William was serving as his assistant. Jane stood at the back of the crowd as Lachlan raised the arm upon which Freyja, a Cooper's hawk, was perched. After sending Freyja on two short flights, Lachlan lined up the guests. William slipped a leather glove on a woman's left arm, and the Cooper's hawk hopped from Lachlan's limb to the woman's.

"Don't be nervous," William said as the hawk settled on the woman's forearm.

"I'm trying," she said with an anxious laugh. "I just can't take my eyes off her beak. Or those talons!"

William smiled kindly at her. "Don't worry, they can't get through the glove."

Seeing that the woman was still uncomfortable, William put a glove on the next person in line, and the bird was transferred.

Jane waited until the lesson was almost done before waving William over.

"Want to take a walk? I thought I could tell you a few more things about your life."

William happily accepted, and Jane led him to her favorite hiking trail—the Walden—that wound through the hills behind Storyton Hall.

For the first part of their hike, they were too absorbed by the beauty of the woods to speak. Sunbeams slanted through the trees, burnishing the leaves a soft copper color. The air smelled of pine tree sap and damp soil.

William was the first to break the silence. "How long will I be staying?"

"As long as you'd like," Jane said. "Is there anywhere else you want to go?"

He didn't answer right away, but when he did, there was an undertone of sadness in his voice. "I'd like to see where I grew up. And where I went to college. I want to visit all the places I lived before the accident. That might help me fill in the blanks."

Parrish's grail quest is Hemingway's lost suitcase, Jane thought. *William has a quest too. To find his lost memories.*

Jane wanted him to succeed. "I think we could arrange that. For today, why don't I tell you about the time you got into a full-blown argument with your history professor? You were a freshman, and he was a famous scholar who'd written dozens of books on the Middle Ages. You challenged one of his theories, and the two of you went at it."

William soaked in every word of her story, his eyes shining with amusement as he listened to the details he desperately wanted to remember.

"Did we have lots of classes together?" he asked.

"Not really. I was an English major. You were a history major. You loved all of your history classes and practically lived in the library. You also worked there part-time on evenings and weekends."

Jane went on to describe William's dorm rooms, his roommates, the posters he'd hung on his walls, and the music he liked best. Nothing sparked a memory, and by the time their hike was done, Jane felt more than a little dejected.

William thanked her for trying and begged her not to give up on him. Hearing this, she was tempted to wrap him in a fierce hug. But she couldn't touch him. She had no idea how touching him might impact the scars that had calcified over her heart—scars created by his loss. She might not love this man, but she'd loved the man he used to be. Every time she was close to him, it was like being with a living ghost.

She left him at the mews with the promise to talk again soon.

Returning to her house, she saw the light shining through the kitchen window.

Inside, Edwin stood in front of the stove, sautéing chicken in one pan while boiling water in another. The twins were trimming string beans. The room was filled with steam and the clanking of utensils. Edwin's deep voice interwove with the boys' higher voices. To Jane, it was a beautiful sound.

Following a dinner of chicken piccata, buttered noodles, and roasted green beans, the four of them played several rounds of Parcheesi. The twins were then packed off to bed. Jane tucked them in and warned them not to read by flashlight because it was a school night. She went back downstairs, poured two glasses of wine, and carried them into the living room. Snuggling close to Edwin on the sofa, she told him about her hike with William.

"I feel so guilty. Like I'm cheating on him, even though he doesn't know me," Jane confessed, her eyes filling with tears. "This is so hard, Edwin. I've waited all this time to be with you, and now that you're here, it feels like I'm doing something wrong."

"Sweetheart." Edwin squeezed her hand. "Until it becomes easier, we can be together like this. We can have dinners, fiercely competitive board games, and wine time. We can flop down and read on rainy Sunday afternoons. We can take horseback rides or run errands together. I don't care what we do, as long as I'm with you."

"Will you escort me to the Victory Gala tomorrow night?"

Edwin raised her hand to his lips. "I wouldn't miss it for all the books in the British Library."

Jane arched her brows. "How many do they have?"

"Twenty-five million."

Jane sighed. "That must be heaven."

"No." Edwin clinked the rim of his wineglass against hers. "This is."

CHAPTER FOURTEEN

On the final morning of the conference, Michael Murphy was scheduled to give a lecture on the non-human cost of the Great War. The afternoon was left open for the historians to enjoy the reading rooms or available activities at Storyton Hall, to stroll through the village or sign up for a fishing or canoeing trip with Storyton Outfitters.

Jane ran into Michael by the lobby coffee urns.

"I heard you can expect a full house for your talk," she said, gesturing for him to fill his cup first. "I guess people *do* want to listen to you even though you're not talking about art theft."

Michael laughed. "Don't give me too much credit. This audience is far more forgiving than my students."

"Well, if you impart a quarter of the information that you, Mr. Kelley, and Mr. Banks shared during yesterday's lunch, then everyone in the Shakespeare Theater is in for a treat."

Noting that Michael's neck had gone red, Jane realized that she should make it clear that she wasn't being flirtatious. Stirring cream into her coffee, she asked, "Did you buy anything in yesterday's auction?"

"A scarf. It's thick and super soft."

"A gift for your fiancée?"

Michael's neck turned a brighter shade of red. "The scarves weren't really Robin's style, so I got it for myself."

Though Michael was pouring a sugar packet into his coffee as he spoke, he turned his body slightly away from Jane's, his right foot pointing down the hall. His body language indicated his desire to escape this conversation.

"You supported the cause at any rate." Jane began to move away from the table. "Good luck with your talk."

Jane had planned to check off items on her to-do list, but she was too distracted by her interaction with Michael to go to her office. Instead, she went to see Sinclair.

The head librarian was on the fifth rung of the wheeled ladder, dusting a shelf housing folk and fairy tales. It had always been one of Jane's favorite sections of the Henry James library.

"Housekeeping?"

Sinclair looked down at her. "The shelves don't really need dusting. Still, the task lets my mind wander, and I have a reason for it to wander in this particular section."

Naturally, Jane was interested in Sinclair's remark. However, she wanted to ask him about Michael Murphy first.

"During one of my first classes on interpreting body language, Butterworth told me to pay attention to feet. People use their feet to indicate open or closed positions, or to make it clear that they'd like to get away from you."

Sinclair looked down at his feet, which were encased in black loafers polished to a high shine. "Do mine say that I'm paying attention?"

"Yes. They're lined up and facing forward," said Jane. "As were Michael's. Until I brought up his fiancée. He didn't mention her name when we were cooking together. Today, he did. I think he regretted it and wanted to end the conversation as quickly as possible. What do we know about Mr. Murphy's personal life?"

"Let me return to terra firma, and we'll see what I have in my office."

Sinclair had done more digging on the BackStory officers than the rest of the historians because the officers had organized the entire centennial event. This meant Michael Murphy's folder was thicker than most.

Leafing through papers in the folder, Sinclair frowned. "I found no trace of a significant other. None of Mr. Murphy's social media posts reference a partner. No one else is on his lease, bills, or bank accounts."

"Can we check under his list of known associates for someone named Robin?"

Retrieving the list, Sinclair scanned the names. He looked at Jane. "No Robin. But I trust your instincts. I'm going to call the supervisor of Mr. Murphy's apartment building. If our ginger-haired guest is engaged, the super will know."

Sinclair had barely finished spinning a yarn about being an agent of the Census Bureau searching for clarification regarding the permanent residents of Mr. Murphy's apartment when the super interrupted.

"I only got one name on the lease. If Michael and Robin are getting hitched, I say good for them. It ain't against the law no more. Am I right?"

Jane now knew why Michael avoided discussing his love life. Robin was a man. He was a fiancé, not a fiancée.

After Sinclair ended the call, Jane said, "Why would Michael hide his relationship? I doubt he's the only gay professor at his university."

"There must be another reason." Sinclair began to review the material in Michael's folder from the beginning.

Jane felt a sudden chill. "He could be Parrish's man. He's a professor who also has time to travel. Look at how much leave he got for this centennial tour. Even if he's in league with Parrish, he might want to keep his relationship a secret. Otherwise, he couldn't protect Robin."

Though Sinclair made a noise, he didn't look up from the stack of papers.

Jane waited patiently for as long as she could. However, her mental to-do list kept growing. It was time to move on.

"This will take a few more phone calls," Sinclair eventually said. "Before I start, I want to explain why I was dusting the folk and fairy-tale section. Mr. Parrish and your great-uncle believe they found a clue in Master Cyril's journal yesterday evening. The entry makes reference to Mr. Parrish's grandfather and to Champ with a capital C."

"What does that mean?"

Sinclair set Michael's file aside. "Champ was one of Hemingway's many nicknames. Master Cyril's entry seems deliberately confusing. He was in Africa when it was written, and I've been wondering if it makes reference to an African folktale."

"Do you know many African folktales?"

"Only a few. After looking in the library, I realized that most of our books on this subject are in the Beatrix Potter Playroom. Our other African books are in the Safari Room."

Jane decided that she needed to read this diary entry for herself. As she made to leave, she asked, "What country was Cyril visiting when he wrote that entry?"

"South Africa."

Jane thought of the books she'd read in the setting. Titles like *Ancestral Voices* by Etienne van Heerden, Alan Paton's *Cry, the Beloved Country*, and *The Covenant* by James Michener ran through her mind. The last title tickled something in her memory, and Jane took the staff stairs two at a time until she reached her great-aunt and great-uncle's apartments.

After letting herself in, Jane walked into the living room and froze. Aunt Octavia was on the sofa. Muffet Cat was snoozing on her lap. And a guest sat in the sofa opposite Aunt Octavia's.

"Hello, Nandi." Jane smiled at the postmistress of Storyton before turning to her great-aunt. "You must have read my mind."

Nandi grinned. "Why? Were you going to invite me for a social visit too? I only get one lunch break per day. I'm a government employee—not the lady of the manor."

"You're a stellar postmistress and Storyton's expert on African folktales," said Aunt Octavia. "I've heard the story of Anansi the spider dozens of times while waiting in line. I enjoy it, but not as much as your tales about leopards. Muffet Cat listens very attentively when I repeat them to him."

Muffet Cat gave Aunt Octavia a look of pure adoration. As a reward, she pulled a treat from the pocket of her hibiscus print dress and fed it to him. She then looked at Jane and said, "I was hoping Nandi might help us make sense of the strange line from Cyril's diary. It mentions a place called the Castle."

Nandi frowned. "My ancestors didn't exactly live in castles."

Jane knew that Nandi was part Zulu and part British and that she was named after Shaka Zulu's warrior mother. She was very proud of her heritage and spoke of the Zulu whenever she had the opportunity.

"I thought it might be a modern name for something far older," said Aunt Octavia.

Nandi suddenly brightened. "It could be a reference to Giant's Castle."

"Is that a building?" Jane asked.

"No, it's a mountain in KwaZulu-Natal. In South Africa," said Nandi in a dreamy voice. "It's very beautiful. Tall, rugged, and mighty. Even more wonderful is what exists *inside* Giant's Castle."

Jane sat down next to Aunt Octavia. Nandi's reverent tone was hypnotizing. "Which is?"

"Rock art by my ancestors. The San." Nandi's dark eyes sparkled as she spoke of the caves and the images painted on the cave walls. Many of the paintings had been there for nearly four hundred years. Others had been there for thousands.

"They sound magical," said Jane. "Have you seen them in person?"

Nandi wore a faraway expression. "Yes. And magical is the right word to describe them. You see, to my ancestors, animals were much more than food. Man and beast shared a special connection. My people believed that every animal had a spirit. The animals also had gifts to give to man. Or to take away from him." She glanced at the mantel clock and spread her hands in a show of disappointment. "I would love to talk to you about this all day, but I need to get back."

"Could we call you at work if we have more questions?" Aunt Octavia asked.

"Sure. Even better, Jane could ride to the village with her bike basket filled to the brim with Mrs. Hubbard's cookies."

With a booming laugh, Nandi showed herself out.

Jane pointed down the hall. "Is Uncle Aloysius in his study?"

"No. He and Mr. Parrish are in the Safari Room. They're searching the African books for answers."

"What was the line from the diary? Do you remember it exactly as it was written?"

Aunt Octavia snorted in affront. "I may be old, but my mental faculties are still intact, thank you very much."

Catching sight of Muffet Cat's glare, Jane quickly apologized.

Mollified, Aunt Octavia recited the line. " 'Our victory near the Castle ensures that he will remain the Champ.' "

"I think I'll do a little online research on Giant's Castle," Jane mused aloud. "Any message for Uncle Aloysius if I see him later?"

Aunt Octavia seemed vexed. "No message.

271

Just look out for him, Jane. He's like a little boy in a sandbox, digging for pennies. To him, the treasure isn't as important as the actual digging. I have a feeling his partner doesn't share his sentiment."

"I'm not sure if Parrish is capable of happiness," Jane said and left the apartment.

In her office, she sat at her computer and ran a search for Giant's Castle. Though she found several fascinating facts about the mountain, none seemed to apply to the cryptic line in Cyril's diary. Next, she read about the region's rock art. To her, the collection in Game Pass Shelter at Kamberg was the most compelling. As she scanned images of the paintings, she was amazed by how vibrant the colors were after so many years. She was also captivated by the movement the paintings conveyed. The antelopes looked ready to leap off the wall.

Eventually, she came across an article on symbolism and shamanism, which explained the meaning of the images on the wall.

When she finished the article, she sat back in her chair and thought about Hemingway's African hunting trips. Cyril had also hunted in Africa. Had Parrish's grandfather as well? Was hunting the common tie among these men?

Turning back to her computer, she searched for info on Hemingway's hunting excursions. Jane wasn't squeamish, but she disliked seeing images of the animals Hemingway had killed. Their dead eyes stared at the camera in doleful accusation. It was the same look Jane saw whenever she entered the Isak Dinesen Safari Room. As she thought about those mounted heads, she wondered if Cyril Steward and Ernest Hemingway had pursued the same game.

Did they meet in Africa?

The notion wasn't outside the realm of possibility. Ernest Hemingway respected other men who shared his interests, which were primarily boxing, hunting, mountaineering, flying airplanes, fishing, and drinking. According to Uncle Aloysius, Cyril enjoyed all of these activities.

Jane decided to share what she'd discovered with Uncle Aloysius and Ramsey Parrish. She caught the two men on their way to lunch in the Rudyard Kipling Café.

"Why don't you join us?" her great-uncle said. "We can fill you in."

Jane agreed, and the three of them found a table facing the Anne of Green Gables Gazebo. Jane ordered tossed salad with grilled shrimp. Uncle Aloysius and Parrish went with a soup and sandwich combo.

Stealing a glance at Parrish, Jane reminded herself that he was dangerous and turned to her great-uncle. "Before you fill me in, can you tell me if Cyril ever met Ernest Hemingway? On a hunting expedition, perhaps?"

Uncle Aloysius shook his head. "There's no indication of such a meeting. The mention of Champ is the only thing we've found that *might* refer to Hemingway. Like you, we thought it possible that they met on safari. There's no written or photographic evidence of this, however."

"Mr. Parrish, we don't know your grandfather," said Jane. "Maybe he's the key. Could you tell us about him?"

Parrish gave a little shrug as if to say he'd provide a few details, but that was all. "An outdoorsman and a scholar, I consider him to have been a kindred spirit of Hemingway's. He excelled at nearly every sport, served in two wars, and was a global traveler. He loved food, drink, and literature. His short marriage produced one son."

"Was he in South Africa at the same time as Cyril Steward?" Jane asked.

"He was. However, his diary doesn't mention an encounter."

The waiter arrived with their drinks, which gave Jane the chance to think of another question. "And the letter from Cyril to your grandfather?"

"Nothing but politeness and platitudes. What led me to Storyton Hall in search of the lost suitcase was the following two lines, 'It eases my mind to know that the case will be safe in your home. In another life, we might have worked together with much success.' "

Jane stared at Parrish. "They *were* in league. At least, for this particular mission. It proves that our families can collaborate—that enmity can be put aside for the greater good."

The waiter delivered their food and moved on to take drink orders from a neighboring table. Following him with her eyes, Jane saw Clarence and Isabel Kelley dining with Archie.

"I sent you the list of the books I read," Clarence said to Archie. "What was your favorite?"

Though Jane was close enough to hear Archie's reply, she didn't listen. Instead, she put her hand on her fork and froze.

"A book list," she murmured.

Uncle Aloysius raised his brows. "Pardon?"

"I need to look at an image on my phone," Jane said to Parrish. "A letter written from William Cecil to your father."

Parrish, who'd just started on his soup, put down his spoon. "Is it dated?"

"I'll pop in the ladies' room to look," said Jane. "It wouldn't do for the manager of Storyton Hall to break the technology rules by using my cell phone in a public space."

Jane hurried to the restroom and locked herself in a stall. She pulled up her phone's camera roll and found the image of the letter from William Cecil to Cyril Steward. It seemed like weeks ago that Sinclair had shown this to her in the secret library.

As Jane reread the short missive, she found nothing of interest. It was a cordial letter sent from the master of one great house to another. Mr. Cecil had also included a list of the books he'd recently read. He didn't go into specifics about the titles. He simply listed them, which was rather odd.

After committing the titles to memory, Jane returned to the table.

"The letter is from January 2, 1923," she began without preamble. "When was Hemingway's suitcase lost?"

"The end of December 1922," said Parrish.

Jane's pulse quickened. "The four book titles William Cecil listed are *Lost Illusions*, *Stories of the Railway*, *The Casebook of Sherlock Holmes*, and *Ivanhoe*."

Uncle Aloysius glanced at Jane and Parrish. "*Lost Illusions* by Honoré de Balzac was set in Paris. The book's hero was a poet."

"So we have a writer in Paris. Next, we have a book about trains," said Jane. She could sense them homing in on a significant clue—the thing that would lead them to Hemingway's missing work.

"The reference to Sherlock Holmes is likely twofold." Parrish said. "First and foremost, the stories are all mysteries. Secondly, the word *case* is in the title."

Jane's face broke into a smile. "It has to be

a reference to the lost suitcase. What about *Ivanhoe*? It's been a long time since I read that book."

"It contains numerous references to the Knights Templar." Uncle Aloysius looked at Parrish. "Because your order stole the suitcase, didn't they?"

Parrish didn't bother trying to refute the remark. "My grandfather, to be specific. However, he didn't return to England with its contents as instructed. He continued his travels and, not long after his African trip, met with a fatal accident climbing the Alps."

Jane nearly choked on a piece of grilled shrimp. "Can't you see? There are *too* many deaths in our families. The way things have been done is wrong. *Seriously* wrong."

Uncle Aloysius put a hand over hers. "This is not the time, my dear."

"George Vanderbilt was once a Guardian," Parrish said, ignoring Jane's outburst. "After his death, his collection was moved from Biltmore to one of his homes in New York. A cousin became the new Guardian. Mr. Cecil knew Vanderbilt's secret, and because he was an honorable man, he kept it to himself. He was later recruited to join Mr. Alcott's faction."

Jane focused on Parrish. "How soon after your grandfather wrote that letter to Cyril did he have his *accident?*"

"A week after it was postmarked."

Jane sucked in a breath. "The two men must have met. Your grandfather gave Cyril the contents of the lost suitcase, and Cyril hid those papers somewhere in Storyton Hall. For whatever reason, they saw eye-to-eye on the need to hide Hemingway's work. You need to share your theory on the contents of that suitcase, Mr. Parrish. We're missing something. So tell us, what had to be hidden?"

Parrish scanned the room. Historians occupied every table. They were all eating and chatting. No one was even looking their way.

"I believe that war is the key," said Parrish. "Hemingway was a war hero. He was a war correspondent. My guess is that he'd written something the United States government would disapprove of. It's just a theory."

Because Parrish had shared his nugget of information, Jane decided to reward him with one of her own. "I have a theory too. I believe your grandfather and Cyril met at Giant's Castle in South Africa. Afterward, Cyril flew home and hid the papers. Your grandfather continued his travels."

A greedy gleam surfaced in Parrish's eyes. "Giant's Castle. Of course." He turned to Uncle Aloysius. "The clue to Hemingway's work must be somewhere in the Safari Room. Not in a book, though. We've searched every book. Where else could a man hide a roll of papers?"

Jane had never heard such emotion in Parrish's voice, but his excitement was contagious. Uncle Aloysius swallowed the last bite of his sandwich, gulped down some tea, and told Jane to stop by the Safari Room when she could.

As much as Jane wanted to poke around her ancestral home in search of a literary treasure, she had too much to do to help the staff prepare for the Victory Gala. The historians had booked nearly every room in Storyton Hall, and she wanted their final event to be memorable.

She took a quick peek in the Great Gatsby ballroom and saw that six men had mounted high ladders to string a huge net holding red, white, and blue balloons to the ceiling. The decorations were simple. There were balloons, paper flowers, and crepe streamers. The tables surrounding the dance floor were covered with white cloths and patriotic bunting. The same bunting hung from the long tables where the kitchen staff would set out punch bowls, water pitchers, and colorful cocktails.

Other than centerpieces of roses, mixed greens, and small American flags, there were no other decorations. Jane found the end result amazingly festive. She could almost hear the band playing and see couples gliding across the dance floor.

Suddenly, she felt a presence behind her and swung around.

"Sorry, I didn't mean to startle you," said

Michael Murphy. "I was just sticking my head in. I'm supposed to take pictures for the club newsletter."

"I'm glad you're here," Jane said. "There's something I want to say to you."

Michael, who'd been surveying the room with approval, looked at Jane. "Oh?"

Jane nodded. "I figured out that you're one of Parrish's creatures. Frankly, I was surprised to learn this because I believe you truly care about Robin. Why would you put his life in danger by aligning yourself with Parrish?"

Michael arranged his face into a mask of confusion, but Jane raised her hand. "Don't bother lying. We've spoken with the super of your building."

There was a long pause as Michael decided how to handle Jane's accusation. Finally, he moved his hand over his beard and said, "Parrish knows about Robin. That's why I have to do exactly as he asks. I don't enjoy answering to that British Beelzebub, but I have to do what he wants to protect the man I love."

Jane shook her head. "I could understand dying for love, but murdering for it? That's not exactly noble. Do you think Robin would approve of your being a killer?"

Michael stared at her in horror. "I've never hurt anyone. My role is to observe and report. That's all. I had nothing to do with Ray's death."

"Do you steal materials for Parrish? Is your university library missing a few rare books?"

Michael took a step closer, and Jane tensed. She was ready to defend herself if need be. "You have to keep my secret. Please. For Robin's sake. I'm leaving tomorrow. Just let me go."

"Who killed Ray?" Jane demanded.

"I don't know. And even if I did, I couldn't tell you."

Jane's anger, which was never far from the surface as of late, surged through her veins. She thought the force of it must make her glow a bright red. "What about the people who loved Ray? Do they matter less than Robin? What about the lovers and family and friends of all of the people Parrish has had killed? I was at Biltmore for less than seventy-two hours, and during that time, a kind old man died. What if he was someone's Robin? How can you be so selfish?"

"Because there's no way out!" Michael's voice was a desperate whisper. "I joined the order before I met Robin. I thought the Templars were the gallant knights from the books I'd read as a boy. I had no idea how wrong I was until it was too late. By then, I'd fallen for Robin. Men in our order aren't supposed to have relationships. We're supposed to be lone wolves. But the heart is a willful organ. Mine insisted on loving Robin, no matter what the cost."

"*My* heart is willful too. And my *children's*

lives were put at risk a few weeks ago. Did you know that your order sanctions the kidnapping of children?"

Michael had the decency to be mortified. "No . . . I . . ." He glanced around the room once more. "I want out, believe me, but I can't get out."

"I'll help you," Jane said. "I have something Parrish wants very badly. Before I give it to him, I'll make your freedom part of the bargain."

"Why?" Michael almost touched her arm but thought better of it and lowered his hand. "Why would you help me after I just admitted to spying on you?"

"If you stay in New York and live happily ever after with Robin, then you're one less threat I have to worry about," Jane said. "And despite my better judgment, I like you. You make a mean apricot charlotte."

Michael managed a small smile. "How do you foresee this going down?"

Jane waved him over to one of the tables. "Have a seat. We have lots to talk about."

The attendees of the Victory Gala had been asked to dress their best. Period costume was optional but encouraged. At the time of the 1918 armistice, ladies' fashion had not yet evolved into the flapper style of the 1920s. Jane wore her flapper dress anyway. It allowed for free movement, and she felt beautiful in it. Mabel, who'd made the dress two years ago, had outdone herself with the detail work. The dress included a formfitting bodice embellished with gold sequins giving way to a skirt of pink fringe. Since the skirt nearly touched the floor, Jane could wear ballet flats instead of heels. It also had two pockets, which meant Jane had a place to store her phone and a small folding knife.

Leaving Sinclair at her house with the twins, Jane walked across the great lawn. The evening air seemed charged with a strange energy, and Jane pulled her shawl tighter around her shoulders. If Edwin were here, he'd draw her in close, comforting her with his touch.

However, Jane had asked him to meet her in the lobby when it was time to be seated. There was something she needed to do before dinner. And she had to do it alone.

The Isak Dinesen Safari Room was empty. Lamps cast a soft light on the leather reading chairs and sofas, and a fire burned in the hearth. Jane paused for a moment to take in the scent of woodsmoke and pipe tobacco. Of all Storyton's reading rooms, this was the most masculine. Its wood paneling, dark furniture, and mounted heads sent most of the female guests in search of cozier corners. However, Jane had always liked the exotic feel of the space. She liked the leopard-print pillows and faux zebra-hide rug, the African drums and masks. And though she disliked both the elephant tusks flanking the fireplace and the animal-head trophies, Uncle Aloysius left them intact as proof of his relatives' folly. He'd also hung framed letters of thanks from various animal-conservation groups as evidence that the Stewards had changed their ways.

Jane walked past the gun case, the glass armoire of Africa weapons, and the bookshelves. She continued on to the farthest corner of the room. She then stopped to gaze up at a mounted antelope head.

Unlike the other heads, this one was missing the plaque listing its name, the date, and the place where it had been brought down. Jane stared into the animal's glass eyes and scanned the length of its dark horns. It was an eland. She'd read about the animals that morning while researching San rock art. The eland was a major food source for the San people and had always been treated with the utmost respect.

In a room like this, with its impressive elephant tusks and massive buffalo heads, the eland was easily overlooked. Jane had overlooked it for years. She'd never been curious about it at all. She'd never wondered why it didn't have a plaque like the other trophies, or why it had been stuck in this shadowy corner.

"You came home with Cyril Steward, didn't you? We thought you were just another hunting prize, but you're so much more." Jane carefully removed the head from the wall and pried it off its wooden base. "I'm sorry to have to do this," she said to those doleful black eyes. They stared back at her until she turned the head around, nose pressed against the carpet.

Holding the head by the left horn, Jane took out her knife and plunged it through the piece of felt stretched across the back of the eland's neck. She repeated the motion again. And once more. When the tear in the fabric was big enough, she thrust her hand into the opening.

Inside the cavity, her fingertips brushed against treasure.

A treasure made of paper.

CHAPTER FIFTEEN

Jane felt like the heroine of a mythical tale. After everything she'd been through, she'd found the prize.

Pulling the tight roll of papers out of the opening, she realized that some people wouldn't consider Hemingway's lost writing the least bit valuable. But to book lovers, it was more precious than a mountain of diamonds.

Jane removed the rubber band encircling the papers, and they sprang open. Carefully flattening them with both hands, her eyes latched onto the first sentence of the top page.

" 'Nick Adams was in the boat with his father,' " she read aloud. " 'His father rowed while Nick watched the sun rise through the trees.' "

She paused to take in the enormity of this moment. In her hands was an original, undiscovered work by Ernest Hemingway. Nick Adams was one of Hemingway's first characters, and many literary critics believed Nick's stories were a reflection of Hemingway's own coming-of-age experiences.

"The published stories came from a later draft," she said to the papers. "You're the originals."

The roll contained typewritten pages, carbon copies, and handwritten pages. Seeing the cursive letters that had flowed directly from Ernest

Hemingway's pen was overwhelming. Jane was so moved that tears beaded her eyes.

"You found them," came a voice from the center of the room.

Jane looked up to find Parrish standing on the faux zebra rug. With the fireplace behind him, he was little more than a dark silhouette, but Jane could see the feverish glint of his eyes.

Parrish started walking toward Jane. "Give them to me."

His movements were predatory, and Jane heard his unspoken threat.

"I will," she said, getting to her feet as fast as she could in her dress. "I just want to see what's here. I already read through this pile"—she held out a thin stack—"so you can take a look at that. I'll be done with the rest in a moment."

Parrish snatched the proffered papers from her hand. Gone was the genteel calm. Gone was the emotionless veneer. Parrish's true nature was on full display. His avarice. His ruthlessness.

He's my enemy, Jane thought. *That will never change.*

While Parrish was preoccupied with the papers, Jane reached into her pocket and pressed the call button on her phone. She then pulled out her folded knife. She opened it behind her back, revealing the short but deadly blade.

Parrish was oblivious to all but the thin sheaf of papers Jane had given him. He drank in the words, his face radiant with triumph. His fingers were trembling, and the soft rustle of pages echoed the crackle of the fire.

If Jane liked Parrish even the tiniest bit, she would have enjoyed seeing how much pleasure this discovery gave him. He was a bibliophile. But more than that, he was a collector. He would keep Hemingway's words to himself. He would never share this treasure with the world.

Jane glanced down at the top page of the stack she'd held back from Parrish. It wasn't a piece of fiction but an article. Hemingway had been a war correspondent at the time he'd written it, and its contents would have shocked the readers of the *Toronto Star* and many Americans as well.

Hemingway had always claimed that he moved to Paris to be in the middle of the literary scene— not because he was disenchanted with America. He declared himself to be a staunch patriot. However, this article made it clear that his experience with war, including his injury, had changed him. He criticized the treatment of veterans and described the terrible effect war had on civilians. He also wrote that while war was meant to bring justice and restore order, he saw no proof of that. The more he knew of war, the more he witnessed injustice and chaos. The article was a brutally honest piece that would have no doubt created an uproar had it been published.

"What did you just read?" Parrish asked.

"An article," said Jane. "You were right. He wrote a controversial piece on war." She passed over the article while holding back the remainder of the pages. "Why Hemingway?"

Without glancing away from the paper in his hands, Parrish said, "What?"

"You're British. There were Lost Generation writers from England. Why not collect Aldous Huxley? And why did your grandfather and Cyril Steward feel the need to hide Hemingway's article?"

Parrish smirked. "You can't understand the effect the Great War had on my country. The loss of life. Of income. Of security. My family lost our house and factory in a German airship raid. That day, we lost everything. Our home, our collection of priceless art and books." He shook the pages. "Something like this might discourage men from enlisting in the next war. Where would that have left England? What was needed were headlines shouting "Halt the Hun" and "Back the Empire." Not this lily-livered 'war is hard' nonsense. The soldiers in my family—the men who'd seen all the things Hemingway saw—they *had* to sign up for the next war. If not them, they had to send their sons. We couldn't have them cowering in their closets. Hemingway's duty was to paint military men as heroes. He did that better than anyone. That's why I collect his work. That's why this had to stay secret."

Parrish was right about her lack of experience with war. Jane hadn't lost a family member to war. She hadn't spent terrifying nights huddled in a bomb shelter. And she hadn't watched an air raid turn her home into a pile of rubble.

"Hemingway once said that the first draft of anything is shit." Jane pointed at the pages in Parrish's hands. "The loss of that suitcase didn't break him. He kept writing. He held on to the ideas from these pages and rewrote them. He went on to write his first novel. He wrote dozens of other articles."

"Do you have a point, Ms. Steward?" Parrish's voice was a contemptuous growl.

Jane considered covering Parrish's smug face with the eland head, but she mastered her annoyance and said, "Hemingway didn't write any of this for you. He wanted his writing to be read. Hide the article if you must. But the rest of his work? It's unconscionable to lock it away."

Parrish responded by holding out his hand and crooking his fingers in a "gimme" gesture.

"If I give these to you, you will leave my family alone for the rest of your days." Jane gave Parrish a hard stare. "And you will also release Michael Murphy from your order."

"He has proven to be such a disappointment." Parrish narrowed his eyes. "Give me the papers. *Now.*"

Jane didn't flinch. "This is just the beginning

for you, isn't it? One Storyton Hall treasure will never be enough. I'll never be rid of you."

"If you don't hand them over, you'll die. It's quite simple, really."

Setting the papers down on a side table, Jane brandished her knife. "I don't think so."

Parrish flicked his eyes at her weapon before pulling a pistol from the inside pocket of his suit coat. "Haven't you heard the line, don't bring a knife to a gunfight?"

"Looks like she brought both," said the man standing behind Parrish.

Parrish swung around to find Michael Murphy aiming a revolver at his chest.

Jane could have used the distraction to plunge her knife into Parrish's side. She could have driven her blade right between his ribs. Except she wasn't Parrish. She was not a killer. Despite everything Parrish had done—orchestrating the abduction of her sons, imprisoning Edwin, and ordering the deaths of multiple people, she couldn't hurt him. Instead, she scooped up some of the white paper that had been stuffed inside the eland head and shoved it into her pocket. She had another plan to stop her enemy.

Parrish chuckled. "I'm surrounded by weaklings. Shall I panic now or later?"

"I *will* shoot you," Michael said with icy calm. "I'd gladly go to prison as long as Robin is safe."

"He'll never be safe," Parrish scoffed. "His fate

is sealed. As is yours. Put that gun down. This isn't one of your silly reenactments." Turning his back on Michael, he advanced on Jane. "Give me those pages."

Jane drew herself to her full height. "No."

Pushing past her would-be assailant, she took cover behind the side of a mammoth bookcase pressed against the back wall. She heard the blast of gunfire and let out a cry as a bullet tore through the wood an inch from her face. Suddenly, the doors to the room burst open, and the Fins rushed in. Butterworth, Sterling, and Lachlan leaped behind pieces of furniture while shouting at Parrish to freeze.

Jane crept along the wall, intent on making it to the fireplace.

"The game is up, sir," Butterworth said to Parrish. "Lower your weapon."

Parrish complied. Even though she was now on the other side of the room, Jane could see his face. He didn't look the least bit defeated. In fact, he still wore that maddeningly smug smile.

"My business with Ms. Steward isn't over. Storyton Hall will never know peace until I have all of Hemingway's papers."

"Oh, our business is definitely over!" Jane called to him. "Do you know why? Because we value human life more than these." She shook the pages in her hand. "Friends. Family. They're more precious than Hemingway's undiscovered work."

Jane crumpled the top page into a ball. What she threw on top of the blazing fire was paper from the eland head, but Parris wouldn't know that.

"No!" he bellowed and lunged forward, his face contorted with rage.

Butterworth and Sterling moved to intercept him. Suddenly, they stiffened mid-stride. With grunts of surprise, they dropped to the ground like stones. Seconds later, Michael followed suit.

"That's how it's done!" cried Nandi from the doorway and shook her blowgun in triumph. Next to her, a man dressed all in black with a baseball cap pulled low over his brow reloaded his blowgun and fired a dart at Lachlan. He missed, and the dart struck the side of a leather chair. Springing forward, he reloaded again.

Jane stared at the two figures.

"William? Nandi?" she muttered, too flabbergasted to manage anything else.

Parrish began making his way to her side of the room. The movement shook Jane out of her trance. She showed Parrish another balled-up another sheet of paper. Again, it was from the eland head. Again, Parrish believed it was a page of Hemingway's writing.

"Don't!" Parrish commanded.

"I'll throw in the whole stack if you don't stay where you are!" she warned. "If burning our literary treasures takes Storyton Hall off of your order's radar, then I'll build the biggest bonfire you've ever seen!"

Jane tossed the wadded page into the fireplace. It landed on a log and was immediately swaddled in flame.

"Burn one more page, and I will kill you and everyone you love." Parrish's body was practically humming with rage. He raised his pistol again, and his dark, furious gaze bored into Jane.

She darted a glance at William. He gazed back at her with a blank expression.

"He doesn't know you," said Parrish. "I wasn't lying when I said that he'd sustained brain damage. After his accident, he was a clean slate. The perfect soldier. Fit, strong, obedient, and lacking emotion. Unfortunately, his training damaged an already damaged brain. He developed chronic traumatic encephalopathy. In other words, he has an incurable brain disease. He's been degenerating rapidly over the past few months and is plagued by tremors and micro seizures. That's why I decided to show him to you. I wanted him to complete this final mission before he died."

"You turned him into a murderer!" Jane spat. "William killed Tuck, didn't he? And Ray. But he's not the monster in this room. You are."

Parrish moved his shoulders in the ghost of a shrug. "He would kill you too if I commanded it.

He's an emotionless drone who's of no more use to me. Why not let a dying man take the blame for my decisions? It's incredibly convenient. But my patience has come to an end. Put the papers on the ground and keep your hands where I can see them. Do it now, or I will shoot you."

There was a scuffle by the doorway. Nandi let out a small cry and was yanked from the room into the hallway.

Parrish looked at William. "Find out what's happening."

"William!" Jane cried before he could leave the room. "You're my husband. We met in college. In one of the library reading rooms. I was supposed to join a study group, but I went into the wrong room. You and I ended up studying together. We both bombed our test because we talked and laughed more than we studied."

Parrish told William to go, but he didn't listen. His eyes were locked on Jane.

"The twin boys you met at the mews? Those are your sons, William. You're a father. I was pregnant when you drove off that bridge." Jane spoke as fast as she could. She knew she couldn't suddenly make William feel. His brain was clearly too damaged for that. But a small part of her hoped that the truth might make him question Parrish's authority.

"My sons?" William asked. Something like wonder crossed his face.

"William!" Parrish barked. "You will find out what happened to Nandi or I will send you back to the facility."

William rushed out of the room.

"You've been using him this whole time," Jane said. She felt utterly defeated. "You made him your slave."

"More like a trained dog. If only you were half as obedient." He gestured at her to lower the pages to the floor.

Jane ran through several scenarios in her head, but none were prudent in the face of Parrish's gun. Her Fins were paralyzed by the same darts they'd used to incapacitate Parrish, and her martial-arts skills were of no use at this distance.

I need to lure him closer and try to kick the gun out of his hand.

It was a maneuver Sinclair had made her practice again and again. Believing it to be her last option, Jane did as Parrish asked. She put down Hemingway's papers.

"You're a tiresome woman," Parrish said, carelessly stepping over Butterworth's outstretched arm.

"Spoken by a man who knows nothing about women. My Jane is exceptional in every way," came a clear, strong voice from the doorway.

"Edwin!" Jane was overjoyed to see him.

He wasn't alone either. Archie was by his side, and both men were armed.

Edwin looked at Jane. "Let him take the papers and go. It's either that or we kill him. There isn't a third option."

After a moment of hesitation, Jane gathered up the papers. She looked at the fire and considered how much anguish she could cause Parrish by burning Hemingway's work. However, she remembered her college English classes, the books she'd read, and the hours she'd spent researching Ernest Hemingway, F. Scott Fitzgerald, and many of the same authors Parrish admired. She thought of the day her sons were born, and of how the friendship between Hemingway and Fitzgerald had influenced her to name her twins after the two writers.

Turning away from the fire, she walked over to Parrish. As he reached out to take the papers, he flashed that smug smile of his. Rage pulsed through Jane, and she slapped Parrish's cheek. Hard.

"That's for abducting my sons and destroying my husband's life," she seethed. "Hemingway would have despised you. He would have called you a fascist and a coward. You aren't worthy of touching his work. Those papers are all you'll ever take from Storyton Hall. Take them and never return."

Before Parrish could respond, Edwin gestured at the hall. "You'll be leaving without William or Nandi, so don't bother waiting for them."

Parrish threw one last venomous glance at Jane before exiting the room.

When he was gone, Jane felt like she could breathe again. She rushed to Butterworth and dropped to the floor beside him.

"Don't worry," she told him. "We'll put you on the sofa."

After she repeated this assurance to Sterling, Lachlan, and Michael Murphy, Edwin and Archie moved each man. With their paralyzed limbs, they sat like slumped ragdolls.

"We're locking the door behind us," Jane told the sorry-looking group. "I'll be back to check on you as soon as I can." To Edwin, she said, "Where are William and Nandi?"

"Nandi's in a conference room," said Edwin. "Tied and gagged. We should find William and be sure Parrish is truly gone before we deal with her."

Jane had a terrifying vision of Parrish heading to her house.

My boys!

"Archie, will you stay with Nandi? I need to make sure my sons are safe."

She and Edwin rushed past the guests lining up for dinner. Pulling out her phone, Jane dialed Sinclair's number and almost sobbed in relief when he picked up on the first ring.

"Miss Jane? Is everything all right?" he asked.

His calm voice was an instant balm. The twins were okay. "Parrish might be headed your way."

As she and Edwin hurried across the lawn, Jane gave Sinclair the short version of the evening's events. By the time she reached her garden gate, Sinclair was caught up.

All was well at her house. The boys were in pajamas, and a board game was set up on the kitchen table.

Hem smiled when he saw her. "Mom! You're early. Wanna play Monopoly with us?"

Fitz picked up a game piece and showed it to Edwin. "You can be the dog if you want."

Jane was touched by this offer, seeing as the Scottie was Fitz's favorite.

"We can't play, guys," she said. "I just wanted to say good night."

"It's not our bedtime yet," Hem protested, and Sinclair assured both boys that he planned to take all their money and property long before then.

"Challenge accepted," Fitz said.

Jane mouthed a "thank you" to Sinclair, and she and Edwin left.

"Let's take a Gator to the guest parking lot," she said once they were outside.

They'd barely rounded the corner of the garage when she pointed at a pair of receding taillights. "There he goes! William's in the passenger seat! But that isn't Parrish's car."

"No," said Edwin. "It's yours."

They watched the Rolls-Royce Phantom race toward the front gates.

"Sterling *is not* going to be happy about this. I can't even report the theft. What would I say? That a deranged Templar stole one of our vintage cars?" Jane laughed. It was a half-crazed, weary laugh without a trace of humor.

"Come on, sweetheart. You need a drink."

Edwin took her hand as they headed for the terrace entrance of Storyton Hall.

Night had fallen. A crisp breeze sent dry leaves tumbling over the grass, and the air was much sharper than it had been during the day. Few stars burned in a dark sky. The moon looked like a smudge of chalk dust.

"How did you know about William?" Jane asked.

"Ever since I left Storyton Hall, I've been watching him," said Edwin. "He maintained his cover almost perfectly, but he made one mistake. He left the mews during the reenactment."

A knot formed in Jane's stomach. "To kill Archie. Only he killed Ray instead. It crossed my mind that William might be a killer, but since he was with Lachlan while the reenactment occurred, I dismissed the possibility." She glanced at Edwin. "Did you witness the murder?"

"No." Edwin lowered his gaze. "I saw William in the woods on the opposite side of the field from where you and the other spectators were sitting. I caught a glimpse before he vanished again. I suspected he was up to something."

300

Edwin stopped and looked at Jane. "I should have followed him more closely, but I didn't want to reveal myself until I had concrete evidence that your husband was working for Parrish. He's your *husband,* and the last thing I wanted to do was falsely accuse him. I didn't want to hurt you. But if I hadn't been so careful, I might have kept an innocent man from dying."

"Mr. Pizzolato's death is not your fault, Edwin. *I'm* responsible for my guests. His parents are here tonight. While everyone else is celebrating, they're grieving the loss of their son. And I have no comfort to offer them." Tears pooled in Jane's eyes. She let them fall, unchecked. "How many lives has Parrish destroyed in the name of his maniacal collecting? And I just let him go. And what about William? He's dying, but he's still dangerous."

Edwin wiped Jane's cheek with the pad of his thumb. "Parrish's order won't be pleased with how things ended here. He'll play a hefty price for disappointing them."

Jane shook her head. "And then there's Nandi. I can't believe she's in league with these zealots. I've known her for years! She drove to Storyton Hall to hand-deliver that postcard from you, though I still don't understand how you got that card out during your imprisonment."

"Parrish made me write those postcards," Edwin said. "They were meant to deceive you

301

and Eloise into believing I was out of the country. Thankfully, you didn't fall for it."

Wrapping her fingers around the door handle, Jane whispered, "How will I ever make things right? The death at Biltmore. The death here. Nandi. Parrish and William driving off, free as two birds. It's too much for one person to manage."

Edwin put his arm around her shoulders. "We'll sort it out. Together."

Jane leaned into Edwin's chest. He put his other arm around her and held her for a long moment.

Eventually, Jane asked Edwin to bring Nandi to the Safari Room. She took the staff corridor to the reading room, where she found the Fins exactly how she'd left them.

Nandi was brought in, bound and gagged. Her dark eyes shimmered with anger. Muffled shouts came from behind her gag, and when Edwin removed it, she spat curses at Jane.

"If you can't calm down, I'll duct tape your mouth shut," Jane threatened when she could get a word in. Nandi tossed out another insult before mercifully going quiet.

"Were you against me all along?" Jane asked. "Or is this betrayal recent?"

Nandi gestured around the room. "I was never against you. I'm against *this!* I remember the first time I saw this room. How could I feel anything but rage? These aren't souvenirs to be hung on your walls or stuck in your cabinets. They're sacred relics! The masks, drums, necklaces, and baskets. The weapons. This is my people's history, pilfered by your ancestor and put on display for your family and your *guests!*"

Jane saw the room through Nandi's eyes and reddened with shame. "You're absolutely right. The animal-head trophies have always made me sad and embarrassed, but I never stopped to consider the cultural items. I never looked around and had the sense to realize that religious objects shouldn't be used as decoration. Nandi? Will you help me return these items to your people? Will you help me fix this?"

Nandi gaped at her. "Are you for real? I helped the bad guy, remember? And now you expect me to believe that you'll do what should have been done decades ago? After I used a blowgun on your people?" She snorted. "I am *not* that gullible."

"You know me, Nandi." Jane used her knife to cut the other woman's bonds. "And I know you. You're a good woman. No one could tell stories the way you do if you weren't. We can move past this night. We can learn from it. Both of us. Please, my friend. Help me."

Nandi covered her mouth with her hands as if trying to hold back a sob. "I am *so* sorry. I got caught up in righteous anger. But that's not how you solve problems. It only creates new ones. I know better than that." She took both of Jane's hands in hers. "Can you forgive me?

In reply, Jane hugged the other woman. After promising to talk more about returning the artifacts, she let Nandi go.

With one assailant out of the way, it was time for Jane to consider what to do about William. William, her husband. William, the father of her sons. William, the killer.

Though Jane was in the same room as Edwin and the Fins, she felt completely alone. There wasn't a person alive who could know what she was going through at this moment. No one could understand how she was being pulled apart. Loyalty warred with justice. Memory fought with anger. Her wedding vows threatened her reason. When she considered reporting William to the authorities, she was as paralyzed as her Fins.

Jane looked at Edwin. "Would you ask Aunt Octavia and Uncle Aloysius to join us? I have something to say, and I need them to hear it."

Edwin shot her a worried glance but left the room without a word.

While she waited for her family, Jane called Sinclair and asked him to have Ned, Butterworth's assistant, take over guarding the boys. Sinclair promised to arrive without delay. He appeared ten minutes later carrying a handful of loaded syringes.

"Mr. Sterling wisely created a serum to

counteract the effects of the poison," he said. "It was easy to find in such an organized lab."

At that moment, Aunt Octavia entered the reading room. She took one look at the slumped Fins and screamed. Uncle Aloysius turned chalk-white and leaned on the wall for support. Jane explained what had happened as quickly as she could, but it took several minutes and several sips of whiskey before her great-aunt and great-uncle recovered their strength.

Their reactions reinforced Jane's decision. Aunt Octavia and Uncle Aloysius were too old to deal with this kind of strife. Their golden years shouldn't be filled with imminent threats and murder investigations. Their days should be peaceful, with worries limited to which book to read next, which fishing fly to use, or which of Mrs. Hubbard's pastries to eat.

And I should be able to go out to dinner without my sons requiring a bodyguard, Jane thought as Sinclair ministered to Michael Murphy, Butterworth, Sterling, and Lachlan.

"The reversal isn't immediate," he told the room at large. "They'll regain speech first, and that shouldn't take long."

Jane moved to the middle of the room so that everyone could see her. As if he'd caught wind of a special meeting, Muffet Cat sauntered in through a crack in the doorway. He trotted over to Aunt Octavia and jumped onto her lap.

She stroked his fur and cooed at him, clearly comforted by his presence.

"I've come to a decision—one that I won't be talked out of," Jane began. Muffet Cat stared at her through hooded lids, but she ignored him. "When I agreed to be Guardian, I had no idea how dangerous the role would be. If I continue to allow my family and friends to be threatened, then I am not only a fool, but I'm also an unfit mother and a despicable friend. Before I was Guardian, I didn't have to lie. I didn't have to spend my precious free time training to fight enemies. I've done everything I was asked without knowing the whole truth about my position. As a collective, you asked me to step into this role. Yet none of you were transparent about what I would face. You also neglected to mention the allies I might have gained had I known they existed."

Uncle Aloysius opened his mouth to speak, but Jane put up her hand to stop him. "None of that matters now. An innocent man was killed this week. Because of our secret. He wasn't the first, and he won't be the last. I refuse to dishonor him or his family by covering up his murder. Our secret isn't worth a lie of that magnitude. Some of our books are dangerous. I've seen horrible books touting the benefits of eugenics, ethnic cleansing, slavery, and more. But those books aren't nearly as dangerous as the people who want to own them. Which is why I'm going to ask Sheriff Evans to come see me. I plan to tell him everything. And I mean *everything*."

Aunt Octavia and Uncle Aloysius exchanged anxious glances. Sinclair's eyes were shining with pride. Sterling blinked once, which Jane took as a sign of agreement. Lachlan didn't respond while Butterworth gargled something unintelligible and Edwin nodded in support. Jane didn't look at Michael Murphy. She wasn't interested in his opinion.

"The sheriff is a good man," she said. "We can't be above the law. If we believe we are, then we're no better than Parrish and his people."

"Will the sheriff believe you, my girl?" asked Uncle Aloysius.

Jane managed a tired smile. "He will. Because I'm going to show him what we've been protecting."

"That is *not* how things have been done." Aunt Octavia couldn't hide her disapproval. "Are you truly planning to break with centuries of tradition?"

Jane knelt down in front of her great-aunt and said, "T. S. Eliot once asked, 'Do I dare disturb the universe?' I used to think I didn't dare, but I've changed. I'm about to disturb our universe in a big way. It'll be okay, though. You have my word as Guardian of Storyton Hall and as the girl you raised."

From the comfort of Aunt Octavia's lap, Muffet Cat began to purr.

CHAPTER SIXTEEN

There was no need to call Sheriff Evans. He was already at Storyton Hall meeting with Ray Pizzolato's parents. Aunt Octavia called the kitchens and requested that two trolleys of food be delivered to the Safari Room.

"We'll bring them in," she said to the member of the kitchen staff on the other end of the line. "No need to tie anyone up on a busy night."

Jane wasn't sure she could eat anything in the reading room—not after all that had transpired there—but she managed a few bites of pasta.

Aunt Octavia's appetite was as robust as ever, and Muffet Cat was delighted to be fed choice morsels from her plate.

While half of the room's occupants ate, Michael Murphy and the Fins began to regain control of their bodies. Butterworth, the largest of the men, was the first to sit upright.

"That was most undignified," he grumbled.

Jane had asked Billy the bellhop to intercept the sheriff before he had the chance to leave Storyton Hall, and she'd just finished picking at her dinner when Billy sent her a text message.

"I need to do this alone," she announced. "I'll come back when I'm done."

"Good luck," Edwin whispered and squeezed Jane's hand.

Jane gestured at one of the food trolleys before looking at Sinclair. "Please be sure Archie gets something to eat. I don't know what we would have done without him."

"I'll leave that to Mr. Butterworth," said Sinclair. "I'd like to walk with you for a minute if that's all right."

Together, Jane and the man who'd been like a father to her left the room.

"I hope you're not going to try to talk me out of this," Jane warned. "I've made up my mind."

"I'm quite familiar with your stubborn side," said Sinclair fondly. "I know when you're not going to budge. This is clearly one of those times. And I have no intention of talking you out of anything. In fact, I agree with you. The role of Guardian must be redefined. I want you to live a fulfilling life, Miss Jane. I don't want your days to be riddled with fear and worry. No man would want that for his daughter, and I'll always think of you as my daughter."

Jane smiled at him. "Thank you, Sinclair. But I don't think all the Fins support my decision."

"We chose this life. You didn't. You were destined for this role from birth, so why not mold it to suit you?"

"I feel like I'm choosing between the wishes of Uncle Aloysius and Aunt Octavia and the welfare

309

of my sons," Jane said. "I don't want to be pulled apart by my responsibilities, and I don't want to hurt anyone. But our family secret is literally killing people."

Sinclair nodded gravely. "What's right is not always popular. I'm in your corner, Miss Jane. Now and always."

They found Sheriff Evans pacing in the lobby. Music and laughter floated out of the Great Gatsby Ballroom. The grim look on the sheriff's face was incongruent with the sounds of revelry.

Jane asked the sheriff if he could spare a few moments.

"I'm on duty, but sure," he said.

"I'd prefer a quieter setting, so if you wouldn't mind following me upstairs, I'd appreciate it."

Leaving Sinclair to take Butterworth's customary position at the front door, Jane led the sheriff to her great-aunt and great-uncle's apartments and asked him to have a seat in the living room.

Jane sat on the sofa facing him. "How are Mr. and Mrs. Pizzolato?"

"Distraught. Exhausted. Confused."

"How did they respond to the ruling of death by misadventure?"

The sheriff glanced around the room, clearly wondering why he was there. "They're having a hard time accepting it, as most people would. I didn't want to get into the details from the ME's report, but small rock fragments were found in the wound to the head, supporting the theory that Mr. Pizzolato struck his head against a rock."

Or a rock was struck against his head, Jane thought.

"I'm not trying to be nosy," she said. "I'm asking because I don't think it was an accident. I believe Mr. Pizzolato was murdered. The worst part is that he wasn't the intended victim."

The sheriff removed his hat and placed it on the sofa cushion. He ran his hands through his salt-and-pepper hair and sighed. "I'm not following you, Ms. Steward."

"Sheriff, we've known each other for years. You've been to Storyton Hall multiple times to investigate crimes. I've been honest with you during those investigations. But only to a point."

At this, Evans arched his brows.

"I've been forced to tell you half-truths. I never interfered with the course of justice, but I'd like you to understand why I had to act this way. I'd like to show you something, Sheriff. Because I trust you. And because I need your help."

The sheriff stared at her. "I still don't understand."

Jane removed her watch, turned it over, and showed Evans how she could press two buttons on the case to release a hidden key.

"There's a room above us," she said. "It can only be accessed with this key. The room has always been here, but few people know of its existence. It contains a treasure beyond imagining, Sheriff. I see it as the Eighth Wonder of the World. And I'd like to show it to you."

Without waiting for the sheriff to respond, Jane hurried into Aunt Octavia's closet, pushed the shoe rack away from the air vent, and pulled the vent cover off the wall. Instead of ductwork, she faced a keyhole and a lever. By turning her key and the lever at the same time, she released the lock to the china cupboard in the living room. Hearing the soft creak of hinges, she knew that it had swung away from the wall, very likely startling the sheriff.

He was on his feet, his body tensed in a defense posture when she returned to the living room. "What's going on, Ms. Steward?" he barked.

"This is the entrance to a secret library," Jane replied. "If you're willing to follow me up the narrow staircase on the other side of this wall, I can show you why Storyton Hall has been the setting for a host of crimes."

The sheriff donned his hat and gestured at the dark cavity behind the cupboard. "After you."

Jane grabbed one of the battery-powered lanterns stored just inside the opening and turned it on. The faint light illuminated the twisting staircase leading up to the turret. When Jane and the sheriff reached the top, Jane unlocked the metal door and pushed it open.

She knew that when Evans entered the room, he wouldn't understand the significance of the drawers and cabinets. It looked more like a bank vault than a library.

"Not exactly a Wonder of the World in appearance," she said in a hushed voice. "It's what's inside that counts."

Opening a drawer marked SHAKESPEARE, Jane removed an unfinished play read only by the Bard and a handful of people.

"This is a tragedy written by William Shakespeare. Because it contained more social criticism than any of his previous works, Shakespeare's benefactor bought it from the playwright and gave it to my ancestor for safekeeping. It was never seen again."

She returned the play to its drawer and showed Evans a Gutenberg Bible next. After that, she unfurled an Egyptian scroll thought to have been lost when the Library of Alexandria was destroyed. She continued producing treasure after treasure until the sheriff asked her to stop.

"Why aren't these things in a museum? Or the Library of Congress?" He picked up a pair of white gloves that Jane kept in a box near the door.

Jane told him what she'd been told by Uncle Aloysius. She explained that some of the material was considered harmful at the time it had been written. Other items were entrusted to the Stewards because they had been custodians of rare and precious books for centuries.

"This is the real reason you've had to investigate violent crimes at Storyton Hall," she said, gesturing around the room. "Certain people will do anything to discover the location of this library. They'd like to help themselves to its contents. Mr. Pizzolato was killed by people like this. I never knew of their existence until my great-uncle showed me this library. Shortly after he did, there was a murder in the Mystery Suite."

"Can we go down now?" the sheriff asked. "I think I need to sit for a minute."

Jane led Evans back to the living room and poured him a finger's worth of her great-uncle's whiskey.

"For medicinal purposes," she said, offering him the crystal tumbler.

The sheriff silently sipped his whiskey. He stared at the rug and seemed to be lost in thought.

Finally, he asked Jane to tell him more about her role and the strife it created. Jane started with the abduction of the twins. When she got to the part about their kidnapper's connection to the Templars, Evans drained the rest of his whiskey.

Jane poured him another splash and continued talking. She felt surprisingly calm. Sharing her secret with the sheriff lifted a great weight from her shoulders. She would no longer need to omit certain truths or lie to him. She could be completely transparent.

When she was done with her long and complicated story, Jane sat quietly and waited for the sheriff's reaction.

"This is a remarkable tale, Ms. Steward," he said. Setting his glass aside, he tented his hands and studied her. "What proof do you have that your back-from-the-dead husband killed Mr. Pizzolato?"

"Ramsey Parrish admitted it."

Jane sensed that the sheriff needed more facts before he'd accept what she just told him.

"The same Ramsey Parrish who drove off in one of your cars with your husband in the passenger seat?"

"Yes, he—"

The sheriff raised a finger. "Hold that thought, I have an incoming call and I'm still on duty." Putting his phone to his ear, he said, "Evans here."

He listened attentively, his expression betraying his concern.

"Broken Arm Bend? Tell Phelps I'll be there in five."

He stood up. "There's been an accident. Fire and EMS are already on the scene. I need to go." He began moving to the door. "The car involved is yours."

Parrish! Jane thought, trailing the sheriff out of the apartment and down the staff stairs.

"We'll talk more about Mr. Pizzolato and . . .

everything else another time." At the door to the lobby, he stopped and turned. "For what it's worth, I appreciate your candor. I always felt like you were holding something back when we spoke, so it's good to know that I haven't completely lost my edge."

"I doubt you ever will," said Jane.

She didn't see the sheriff out but hurried back to the Safari Room. Uncle Aloysius, Aunt Octavia, and the Fins were gathered around the eland head. Michael Murphy and Edwin were gone.

Jane walked up to Sterling and tugged on his arm. "Parrish didn't get far. He and William crashed at Broken Arm Bend."

"I guess Storyton refused to let them escape," Aunt Octavia declared very softly.

Sterling, who'd been out in the garages, strode into the room and told Jane that the key cabinet had been forced open.

"This was inside."

It was a slip of paper containing a single line of messy cursive.

I'll take the wheel.

It was signed by William.

Jane looked at Sterling. "Do you think he caused the accident?"

"That's the conclusion I came to."

Jane shook her head in dismay. "I didn't want that. I didn't want him to make that sacrifice."

"Let's not assume the worst," Sterling said. "We'll take one of the trucks to the scene. William might have tampered with other cars in our fleet to prevent us from following him. No one drives a Rolls until I examine every car."

Sterling drove at a conservative pace on the gravel driveway but immediately picked up speed after hitting the main road. Multiple emergency vehicles were parked along Broken Arm Bend. Their light bars lit up the night with an eerie red glow. Shadows danced on the asphalt, and the trees seemed to loom as tall and thick as giants. Jane opened her car door to a chorus of shouts and the smell of smoke.

"This isn't good," whispered Sterling.

Jane was thinking about William. Was he alive? Was Parrish? And what of Hemingway's work? Imagining the pages turning black inside Parrish's bag, Jane hurried toward the emergency vehicles.

"Parrish tried to brake," said Sterling as they moved. "He pumped them. Then, he pressed down on the brake pedal with all his strength. If I were a betting man, I'd say the brakes completely failed. And these tire tracks?" He pointed at dark skid marks on the asphalt. "Here's where the wheel was jerked to the right—forcing the car right over the edge. That must have been William's doing."

Jane still had his note in her hand. Her fingers

were curled around it so tightly that her nails bit into the skin of her palm.

"Why would the car catch fire?" she asked, searching for an indication of survivors.

Sterling looked at the column of smoke rising into the night sky. "Probably a fuel leak." He lowered his gaze and murmured. "A vintage Rolls isn't exactly known for its safety rating. No airbags. No antilock brakes. We can only hope those men survived the crash."

Not long after, four paramedics hoisted a stretcher over the edge of the embankment. The patient was already zipped into a body bag.

Jane's heart felt as heavy as an anchor when another bagged body followed several minutes later.

"Oh, William," Jane whispered. She felt numb. She didn't think anyone would mourn Parrish's loss, but she would grieve for William all over again. Shielding her eyes against the strobe flash of the light bars, she searched for the sheriff. "I want to see what happened with Hemingway's papers," she told Sterling in a flat voice. "It would be miraculous if they were intact, but I could use a miracle right now."

As she approached the nearest sheriff's department cruiser, Deputy Phelps intercepted her.

"I'm sorry, Ms. Steward. You can't get any closer. It isn't safe. There's not much to see now. The victims have been cleared from the wreckage, and your car is totaled."

"Is it still on fire?" she asked.

Phelps shook his head. "They're just saturating the surrounding area as a precaution."

Jane glanced from the smoke to where Sheriff Evans was standing. After catching her eye, he wrapped up his conversation with the paramedics and headed over to her.

"Mr. Parrish is dead." He put a hand under Jane's elbow in case she needed support and added, "As is your husband."

"He tried to make amends," Jane said, offering the crumpled slip of paper to the sheriff. She didn't say anything else. A hard lump had formed in her throat, blocking her words. She wasn't sure she could express her feelings anyway. Mixed with a fresh pang of loss was a glimmer of pride and relief. Though the man she'd once loved had died long ago, this version of William had reached down and found something more than Parrish had instilled in him. He'd found a desire to do the right thing. Perhaps, he'd wanted to protect Jane and his sons.

I believe his sacrifice was for us, she thought, her eyes filling with tears. *He made sure Parrish would never hurt us again. It's what the man I married would have done. His last act didn't belong to Parrish. It belonged to William. My husband.*

Guessing that Jane and the sheriff needed privacy, Phelps gave them some space.

Sheriff Evans handed Jane a tissue. "Are you all right?"

Jane wiped her eyes. Instead of answering his question, she said, "Parrish stole a stack of valuable papers from Storyton Hall. They were written by Ernest Hemingway. Is there any chance they survived the fire?"

The sheriff was genuinely aggrieved. "I'm sorry, Ms. Steward, but the car is a blackened shell. Whatever was inside is gone."

"As are the two men responsible for Ray Pizzolato's death," said Jane.

She and Sheriff Evans watched the ambulance pull away.

"Justice has been served. But not in the way I prefer," the sheriff said. The fire chief hailed him, and Sheriff Evans indicated that he'd be right over. "Get some rest, Ms. Steward. We'll talk in the morning."

Jane stood by the side of the road, a lone figure blending in with the shadows, as the first responders finished working the scene. She gazed at the sky again, noticing the dense cloud of smoke hovering over the bridge traversing the river. William and Broken Arm Bend had stopped Parrish from entering the village of Storyton. They'd also sent a piece of literary history up in flames. Jane hoped Hemingway's words would live a little longer in the drifting smoke—that they would drift down the chimneys of the nearby houses and permeate people's dreams. Jane thought Hemingway would approve of this sort of ending.

Later, Jane and her Fins convened in the Daphne du Maurier Morning Room.

"So much for coming clean to Sheriff Evans," Jane said. Someone had poured her a glass of whiskey and soda, but she'd opted for coffee instead. "It didn't do us much good, did it?"

Sterling shrugged. "I think it did. Now, he'll know why the brake lines on the Rolls Parrish drove were tampered with. William punctured the lines in all the cars parked in the front row of the garage bays because he knew Parrish would steal one of them. Both men were doomed the moment they got in the car. William wasn't taking any chances."

No one in the room liked Ramsey Parrish. However, they could all imagine the acute terror he must have experienced as he tried to keep the Rolls from crashing through the guardrail and plummeting in a fatal nosedive.

Jane didn't think William was afraid. He knew he was dying, and he'd chosen how he would leave this world. Jane wanted to believe that he'd be filled with peace in those final seconds.

"Why didn't William tamper with the brakes in Parrish's car?" Lachlan asked Sterling.

"Parrish's car was boxed in by other cars in the valet lot. William knew this. He knew Parrish would be forced to take one of our cars." Sterling pointed at the slip of paper in the middle of the coffee table. "He planned to take Parrish over the edge at the sharpest bend."

Sinclair looked at Jane. "It was a noble act."

The group went quiet for a moment. The only sound was the soft ticking of the mantel clock. Eventually, Butterworth stood up to refresh empty tea or coffee cups.

"What would you like to do, Miss Jane?" he asked as he refilled Lachlan's cup. "We cannot possibly understand how difficult this experience has been for you. We will do anything in our power to ease your pain."

Jane rewarded him with a small smile. "Thank you. Knowing I have the support of everyone in this room makes this night bearable. Yes, it *is* painful. I would like to lay William to rest in the family plot. He belongs in Storyton. I'll see to the arrangements as soon as Sheriff Evans allows it."

"The men responsible for the deaths of Mr. Tucker and Mr. Pizzolato are gone. The sheriff is now privy to Storyton Hall's greatest secret. And the historians check out in the morning." Sinclair stared at a curl of steam rising from his teacup. "What else can we do to restore order?"

Jane poured cream into her coffee. She watched the swirls of white meld with the deep brown.

She gazed at the liquid chaos for several seconds before using her spoon to mix them together, creating a different hue altogether.

"I don't want to restore order," she said. "I want to create a new one."

The next morning, Jane stood in the lobby and said good-bye to the historians.

Jane saw Mrs. Pratt's cooking partner, Roger, heading their way. With a stab of guilt, she realized that she'd ruined Mrs. Pratt's chances with the charismatic historian by asking Betty to separate them at The Cheshire Cat.

"Mr. Bachman, thank you for coming," she said. "I hope you'll visit us again in the near future. My friend, Eugenia, would be especially pleased if you did."

Roger, who'd been looking rather downcast, immediately brightened. "Do you think so? She's a fascinating woman! I thought we were hitting it off quite well when she suddenly . . ." he trailed off, too embarrassed to continue.

"Mr. Bachman, I know for a fact that you *were* hitting it off. If you have time to spare before your train leaves, Eugenia might be able to meet you at The Canvas Creamery for a cup of coffee."

Roger dropped his duffel bag with a thud. "For her, I have all the time in the world."

Jane ducked into the staff corridor to make the call.

"He wants to see me?" Mrs. Pratt cried. "But I'm a mess! My hair! My makeup! What will he think of me?"

"I believe he already thinks the world of you. And Eugenia?"

Mrs. Pratt had already started talking about her appearance again. Finally, she said, "Yes?"

"After you're done with your coffee, don't forget to show Roger the Book Babes."

Mrs. Pratt giggled like a young girl. "Brilliant idea. There's nothing like racy art to get a man in the mood. I'd better run. I need at least ten minutes to apply my war paint."

And with that, Mrs. Pratt was gone.

Back in the lobby, Jane nodded at Roger, and he was out the door like a shot.

Butterworth watched him go. " 'To see a young couple loving each other is no wonder; but to see an old couple loving each other is the best sight of all.' "

Jane gave Butterworth a playful nudge. "You're a romantic. Who would have guessed?"

"Those are William Thackeray's words, not mine," said Butterworth stiffly. However, there was a faint twinkle of amusement in his eyes.

Jane returned to her office to review the architect's plans for the second phase of the Walt Whitman Spa. She'd barely begun to make notes when she received a phone call from Sheriff Evans.

"Your car has been recovered. It's completely totaled and everything inside was turned to ash. Neither occupant was wearing a seatbelt at the time of the accident. Both men were thrown from the car. A Biltmore employee drove up early this morning to identify the bodies."

Broken Arm Bend has claimed two more victims, Jane thought. Aloud, she told the sheriff of her plans to bury William with the rest of the Stewards.

"You're free to make those arrangements," he said. After a brief pause, he continued. "I've been thinking about your library. Quite a bit, actually. It's hard not to. I have no right to tell you what to do, but maybe you'd be willing to listen to someone who's a little longer in the tooth."

"I'd be glad to hear what you have to say."

The sheriff cleared his throat, and Jane sensed that he was choosing his words with care. "If I were you, I'd empty that library. Donate or sell the whole collection. Either get rid of it or hire professional security guards. You're in a high-risk situation, and I'd hate to see anything happen to you or your family. Let those things go, Ms. Steward. For your own good."

"I couldn't agree more." Jane thanked the sheriff and hung up.

She worked for another two hours before heading up to see Uncle Aloysius and Aunt Octavia. In a firm but gentle tone, she outlined her plan.

"Can't you wait until I'm dead?" Uncle Aloysius asked. "It's hard to accept this sort of upheaval at my age."

Muffet Cat, who'd been sitting next to Aunt Octavia on the sofa, issued a plaintive meow.

Aunt Octavia stroked the cat's fur. "You see, even Muffet Cat disapproves."

"We'll start with baby steps," Jane said. "And I want you both to be involved in the process. When you get a taste of what happens when we share our treasures, I think you'll come around to my way of thinking."

Aunt Octavia snorted and reached for a sugar-free candy.

"Which is why I'm going to use the speaker-phone when I call a woman at the Folger Shakespeare Library. I sent her images of our Shakespeare collection, and she's very eager to authenticate them. She understands our need for anonymity too."

Before Uncle Aloysius or Aunt Octavia could protest, Jane put her phone in the middle of the coffee table and placed the call. A woman answered. "Elizabeth Martin, may I help you?"

"This is Jane Steward. We spoke earlier about a donation. Did you receive the images?"

"I sure did!" Elizabeth exclaimed. "I'm trying to contain my excitement, but I can't really hide it. I'm *very* eager to see your collection in person. If you're ready to entrust it to me, I'd like to pick it up over the weekend. You're not too far from D.C., and there's nothing more beautiful than an autumnal drive on the Blue Ridge Parkway."

Jane glanced at her great-aunt and great-uncle before saying, "That would be just fine. And Elizabeth? I know you can't authenticate our collection at this time, but how would you feel if all the items I mentioned were actually written by the Bard?"

"How would I feel?" Elizabeth repeated. "Forget about me. How would readers all over the world feel?" She let loose a laugh. "I don't have the words to tell you how absolutely wondrous such a find would be. Ben Jonson said that Shakespeare was not of an age, but for all time. Century after century, he continues to be relevant. He continues to move us, to make us question, to make us laugh and cry. He forces us to think. To feel. What more could we ask of any writer?"

Aunt Octavia pulled a tissue from her pocket and dabbed her eyes.

After completing her call, Jane looked at her aunt and uncle. "You see? If we take our motto, the one emblazed on our front gates and embossed on every room-key fob—*their stories are our stories*—and reverse it, then we'll finally be getting things right."

"Our stories are their stories," said Uncle Aloysius. "By Jove, I think I like it."

CHAPTER SEVENTEEN

With the departure of the historians, life in Storyton resumed its natural rhythm.

The following weekend, Jane met with Elizabeth from the Folger Shakespeare Library and was delighted to deliver the Bard's writing into the older woman's capable hands. Even Uncle Aloysius and Aunt Octavia enjoyed the donation experience, which strengthened Jane's conviction that her decision was the right one.

Despite this small triumph, Jane did not feel at peace. After a tumultuous summer, she'd had a dramatic autumn, and these months had left her forever changed. For starters, she'd lost her trust in people. Both her family and her Fins had kept secrets from her. Edwin's entire life was defined by secrecy. She was sick and tired of deception.

One night, Edwin joined Jane and the boys for dinner at their house. When the meal was done, Jane asked him to walk in the garden with her before he went home.

"I'd love nothing more than to stroll around dying plants on a cold evening," he said with a smile.

The twins, who were watching *The Dark Crystal*, sat in front of the TV in a hypnotic trance. They were so engaged that they'd forgotten about the bowl of popcorn Jane had put on the coffee table. Knowing she wouldn't be gone long, Jane told them she'd be in the walled garden if they needed her. After receiving grunts of acknowledgment, she and Edwin left the house.

The night air was brisk, and Jane was glad she'd brought the shawl Mabel had gotten her to wear at a dinner with a pre-Raphaelite theme. The shawl reminded Jane of that bittersweet dinner and of another guest who'd been killed at Storyton Hall. She wore it because it was a beautiful thing and because she never wanted to forget that guest. Like Ray Pizzolato, Bart had been a good man. Like Ray, he'd been the hapless victim of another man's twisted soul. Jane would always think of Bart when she wore this shawl, and she'd remember Ray any time someone talked about a devoted educator.

"What's on your mind?" Edwin asked, reaching for Jane's hand.

"I've been mulling over all the changes I'm planning to make," she said.

Edwin stopped and looked at her. "Am I one of them?"

"In a way," Jane said. "When the twins were taken, I learned what real terror is. Terror isn't a monster from a scary movie. It isn't the fear of dying. Not when you're a parent, anyway. Terror is the fear of harm coming to your child. I can handle worry. I can handle stress. Hardship. But I never want to experience that terror again. I never want to think that I've let my boys get so close to the fire that they could be seriously burned. You, my love, are a kind of fire."

"Because of what I am." There was no inflection in Edwin's voice. He already knew the answer.

"Yes. And I'd never ask you to change." Jane continued walking, her hand still in Edwin's. "That won't solve our problem. You took an oath. Being a Templar is your calling. If I demanded that you give up that part of your life, you'd grow to resent me. I love you," she squeezed his hand to emphasize her point. "You know that. But we need to redefine what we are."

Edwin promised that he would be whatever she needed him to be.

"I want you just as you are," Jane said with feeling. "And I want to be with you. For the rest of my days. However, I don't want to involve the boys in our relationship. I don't want them to start seeing you as a father figure. You and I can be together, but the four of us can't. Do you understand why?"

Shooting a glance at Edwin, Jane saw that she'd wounded him. The hurt was etched all over his face. Even in the dark, with only the moonlight illuminating his strong jaw and chiseled cheekbones, Jane could see the pain shining in his eyes.

"As long as I don't lose you, I'll do whatever you ask," he said. "But I'll miss being with the boys. I liked feeling that I belonged with all of you. I love the warmth of your kitchen, the noisy chatter and endless energy those boys have. It makes my day to listen to their stories or to get one of their spontaneous hugs. I also love watching you with them. You're an amazing mother, and I'll miss seeing you in that role."

Having felt less-than-stellar as a parent lately, Jane thanked him for the compliment. "Fitz and Hem are my priority. I have to put them first. Before you, before Storyton Hall, before everyone and everything else. That's what good mothers do."

Edwin said that he understood, and they walked in silence until they reached the garden. They sat on the wall, in almost the exact spot where Edwin had first told Jane that he loved her. Perhaps remembering that moment, Edwin put his arm around her waist. She leaned into him, resting her head on his shoulder.

"I'd rather lose you to Fitz and Hem than to another man," he said very quietly. "Your husband, for example."

"Even though William came back into my life, he wasn't my husband anymore. That William died the night his car went off into that frigid lake," Jane said. "I will always love the man I once knew, just as I will always feel grief over what became of him. So yes, William will always occupy space in my heart. But you're not losing me, Edwin. I don't want us to end. I just want us to change what we are. Doesn't Rumi say that lovers don't meet— that they're in each other all along?" She touched Edwin's chest. "I'm at home in this heart."

Edwin grabbed her hand and raised it to his lips. He planted a kiss on her palm and then curled his hand protectively around hers. They sat like this for several minutes. Theirs was a peaceful silence, but Jane felt that the air around them was heavy with unspoken words, so she decided to lighten the mood. "In any case, it'll be nice to go out on dates like a normal couple."

Edwin laughed at this. "Has anything ever been normal when it comes to us?" He put his finger under Jane's chin, forcing her to look at him. "In this new version of me and you, do I still get to kiss you?"

"As often as possible," Jane whispered. "And I'm feeling a little cold, so could you hold me a bit tighter?"

"I think I can manage that." Edwin wrapped Jane in his arms and kissed her.

In no time at all, she forgot about everything but the warmth of his lips.

William was laid to rest on the last Wednesday in September.

The autumn sunshine lit the landscape with

a soft, golden glow, and the mountains rising around Storyton Valley were ablaze with color. The air smelled of cut grass and woodsmoke, and as Jane stood in the cemetery, she thought of how much the William she'd known would have loved a day like this.

Jane had hired a minister from a nearby town instead of using the local pastor because there was no way she could explain why she was burying her husband for the second time. And though she worried that an outsider wouldn't be as good as the pastor she and her family had known for years, he led the graveside service with a quiet sincerity that Jane found most comforting.

She also found comfort in the knowledge that William was joining the Stewards in their family plot. With this simple act, Jane had given her husband what he'd wanted most in life. A family. Like her, William was orphaned at a young age. This commonality was one of the things that had drawn them together when they'd first met. Jane remembered how William envied his friends their family holidays, vacations, photographs, and traditions.

"We'll make our own family," Jane had once promised him.

Now, as she gazed at his coffin, she felt incredibly relieved that she'd told him that he had a wife and two sons. William had died knowing that he was part of a family. And unlike the first time she'd arranged a funeral for him, Jane could say good-bye without wondering what had become of his body. He was here. This time, she could lay him to rest knowing that she had a place to go should she want to talk to him.

The minister opened his Bible and began to read, and Jane let the words of Scripture flow over her. In between readings, she closed her eyes and raised up a silent prayer for William. Then, she prayed for her sons.

When it was her turn to speak, she told William that she'd decided to express her feelings through the poetry of T. S. Eliot, which was far more eloquent than anything she could come up with.

> What might have been and what has been
> Point to one end, which is always present.
> Footfalls echo in the memory
> Down the passage which we did not take
> Toward the door we never opened
> Into the rose-garden.

The small mourning party, which included Eloise, the Fins, Uncle Aloysius and Aunt Octavia, took turns placing a rose on William's coffin. They'd all selected roses of different hues, and Jane smiled over how well they complemented the colors on the piece of construction paper she added.

The drawing, done by the twins when they

were six, had been done in crayon. The scene was of their house and included the front garden. Oversized bees and butterflies perched on wobbly blooms, and three stick figures stood off to one side. The stick figure with the long pinkish-yellow hair and the triangular skirt was Jane. The two smaller figures were Fitz and Hem.

"You have a family. That means you'll never be forgotten," Jane whispered to William. "Until we meet again . . ."

After a brief nod to the minister, she turned away. Eloise slipped an arm through Jane's and the two friends slowly walked toward the cars parked along the curb outside the front gates.

"Will you ever tell the boys that he's here?" Eloise asked.

Since Jane had already given this some thought, the answer came easily. "When they're older, I'll tell them everything. I've learned how secrecy can tear people apart, so I'm going to try to be as open with my sons as I can, even if I think the truth might hurt them. They can handle a little hurt."

"Yeah, they can," said Eloise. "Because they take after their mom. I know her pretty well, and she's one tough cookie."

Jane gave her a grateful smile. "What about you? Are you adjusting to Edwin's double life?"

Eloise shrugged. "I'm not a fan of what he does, but I do feel like the wall that's been between us for years is coming down, brick by brick. Now, when we talk, he has much more to say. I think it's been a huge relief for him to be able to share things with me."

She paused at a gravestone where someone had placed a trio of American flags in an urn in lieu of flowers. Jane saw that the grave belonged to a World War Two veteran.

"Are you thinking about Landon?" she asked.

"Yes," said Eloise. "I hope he'll get the help he needs. I don't know how you found a specialized center for people suffering from PTSD, but it's the best thing you could have done for him. Though we're all haunted by something from our past, some of us carry more ghosts around than others. Landon needs help letting go of his ghosts."

Jane glanced around the peaceful cemetery. The minister had left, as had Uncle Aloysius, Aunt Octavia, and the Fins. That afternoon, Archie and Lachlan would be traveling to New York. After accompanying Lachlan to the in-house treatment center, Archie would return to work. Lachlan would likely spend several weeks working on his issues and would take a train back to Virginia when he and his doctors felt he was ready.

"They say time heals all wounds," one of these doctors had told Jane over the phone. "But you have to find them first. With some of our military men and women, that's the hardest part. They have to fight against their training, against seeming weak, and against a powerful feeling that they're betraying their fallen brothers and sisters in arms by talking about them. That's why group therapy is so important here. When Mr. Lachlan hears other vets share their story—when he realizes that he's among friends—he'll eventually come around. Once he puts his pain into words, we can help him face it."

Eloise released her hold on Jane's waist and looked at her. The concern was plain on her lovely face. "Lachlan will be okay. But what about you? These last few months have been so hard on you, Jane."

Jane recalled a line a written by P. D. James. Of all the quotes she'd read about healing, it was this one that struck her as being the most accurate. "A wise mystery novelist once wrote that while time didn't heal, it anesthetized. I believe that. I believe that, in time, the pain I've felt over these last few months will lose its intensity. I have so much to look forward to, and that will help me recover too."

"Tell me about those things—the ones you're looking forward to," Eloise said as the two friends continued walking.

"The boys and I always have a ball with Halloween. And I have lots of ideas about winter spa packages to celebrate the opening of the Walt Whitman Spa. Also, I want to have a Willie Wonka–type candy festival around Valentine's

Day so that families can enjoy the holiday together. Did you know that Storyton Hall will be hosting a huge group of children's book authors and illustrators that weekend? I'm thinking that the Storyton players can put on a performance and Mrs. Hubbard can run a chocolate dessert competition."

Jane grinned when she saw her own excitement mirrored in Eloise's eyes.

"There's more," she went on. "Weeks ago, I posted the news about our Golden Bookmark contest on our website. You wouldn't believe the number of responses we got, but after picking a winner at random, I was able to invite a family of four to stay with us for a long weekend this winter. We'll have to get together with the Cover Girls and make plans for this family. I want them to have the time of their lives."

Settling into a Rolls-Royce Phantom equipped with a new set of brakes, the two women were so focused on the future that they left the cemetery behind without noticing.

At the next Cover Girls meeting, Jane took her friends on a tour of the Walt Whitman Spa, such that it was at this point in its construction.

Sweeping her arm over the foundation, Jane said, "This area will be the rooms where clients will receive facials, massages, or body treatments like a wrap or scrub."

"Can you scrub away cellulite?" joked Betty. "Or a decade or two of wrinkles?"

"You'll have to ask Tammy," said Jane, referring to the spa manager. "No matter what, you're bound to leave the spa feeling rejuvenated. We're offering a line of organic skincare for purchase, and our guests can relax between services in lounges near a large wall fountain. They can read in a comfy robe while sipping citrus-infused water. Tammy suggested we have a smoothie bar, but I don't want people to be subjected to the whine of a commercial blender. I want them to feel absolute peace."

Mabel sighed. "Hurry up and get this thing built! This girl needs some pampering!"

"Me too," said Violet. "I can't wait to try that lavender-mint anti-inflammatory foot massage. Lavender's my favorite scent. And not just because it's purple. After being on my feet all day at the salon, the thought of having my tootsies bathed in lavender-scented water is pure bliss."

Eloise waved her hand in dismissal. "You can have your lavender. The smell reminds me of my grandmother's closet. I'm going for that hydrating facial. Tammy told me that she'll be using strawberries, marshmallow, chamomile, and rue to draw out imperfections and refresh the skin until it glows. I'll walk out of that treatment room looking good enough to eat!"

"Landon Lachlan won't be able to resist you,"

teased Jane. "I saw you practicing on the archery range. He'll be really impressed to hear that you're working hard while he's away."

"I admit it. I'm trying to be a teacher's pet," Eloise said, blushing prettily. "I think Landon is already making strides in being more open and talkative. We actually spent an hour on the phone last night. Before this, the longest we've talked on the phone has been fifteen minutes."

Jane was delighted to hear about Lachlan's progress. She turned to Mrs. Pratt next. "What about you? How was your coffee date with Roger?"

"A lady never tells," was Mrs. Pratt's coy reply.

"But a little bird does," said Phoebe. "And *this* bird would say that Roger came to Storyton to celebrate a historical event and left dreaming about far less academic pursuits."

She wriggled her brows suggestively, and all the Cover Girls laughed.

"I wish Anna could be here. She would have loved to fantasize about a future spa day," said Violet. "I guess we'll just have to wait and see if she'll ever have time to rejoin our happy group."

"Speaking of happy, where are we having our book discussion?" Betty asked.

Jane smiled. "Considering our latest read was set in a bookshop, I thought we should be surrounded by books."

After leading her friends to the Daphne du

Maurier Morning Room, Jane told them to get comfy. She then poured glasses of Biltmore Moscato and distributed them. In honor of the British setting of their novel, Jane had baked a jam roly-poly as well as a sticky toffee pudding for dessert.

"This book is exactly what I needed after reading two wartime novels in a row," said Mabel, holding up her copy of *Love in a Bookshop.*

Eloise licked a drop of pudding from her finger. "I've always said that the right book will find you at the right time. I'm sure that none of you are surprised to hear that I felt like this novel was written just for me. A single woman running a bookshop in a small village. A woman who tries to be successful, find a decent man to date, and serve her community. Remind you of anyone?"

"It sure does." Mrs. Pratt smiled at Eloise. "Remember the line about the bookshop being the kind of place that stole time? That's how I feel about Run for Cover. I lose hours every time I go inside, but they're never wasted hours. Those hours are well spent."

Eloise returned Mrs. Pratt's smile.

"I loved the bookstore, and all the titles mentioned, but what I really appreciated was that every character was flawed," said Phoebe.

Violet pointed at her roly-poly. "And the characters ate. I love it when fictional people eat delicious food. After reading the descriptions of the lamb roast or the scene with all the wedding treats, I was ready to book a hotel room in a village that doesn't even exist, though I wish it did."

Her friend murmured in agreement. Everyone had similar dreams about journeying to a quaint village in the English countryside.

"I liked that the author created a complex young mother character. I could identify with her desire to have a successful career while being an amazing mom too." Jane touched her heart. "I struggle with that balancing act all the time."

The Cover Girls continued discussing the most memorable scenes. They frequently interrupted each other, talked over each other, and laughed.

When the wine was gone, they wrapped up as they usually did and took turns sharing their favorite quotes.

Jane didn't need to read hers because Betty had picked the same one. Signaling for her friend to go ahead, Jane listened as Betty said, " 'There's a book for everyone, even if they don't think there is. A book that reaches in and grabs your soul.' "

"That's so true," Eloise said.

After all the women had read their chosen quote, Mabel declared that it was time to call it a night. They carried their plates and glasses to the kitchen and left through the loading-dock door. Before Eloise could get away, Jane grabbed her arm and whispered, "Can you stay for a few minutes? There's something I want to show you. It's a book. A very special book."

"Who could resist that kind of invitation?" Eloise whispered back.

Jane took Eloise to the Henry James Library. She unlocked the doors and asked her best friend to sit in a reading chair. Jane then picked up the metal box from Sinclair's desk and carried it to the side table next to Eloise's chair.

"It's hard for me to remember a time when we weren't best friends," Jane began. "You've always stood by me, and I trust you completely. After all I've learned these past few months, I trust almost no one. But I've never had a single doubt about you. Because we have an unbreakable bond, and because of your love of books—particularly *Jane Eyre*—I wanted you to see this."

Jane removed a manuscript from inside the metal box and gently placed it on Eloise's lap.

"Go on. Untie the ribbon."

Eloise shot Jane a curious look and pulled at the ribbon. The silk fabric had once been white but was now yellowed with age. The ribbon fell away, revealing the manuscript's title.

"*Jane of Thornfield Hall*," Eloise read. She glanced at Jane, her eyes dancing with merriment. She assumed Jane was playing a joke on her. "What is this?"

"You might find this hard to believe, but it's the sequel to *Jane Eyre*. Though Charlotte Brontë died before she could complete it, there's still enough there to make a compelling story. I thought you'd like to read it."

Eloise grinned. "Is this a prank? Because if so, it's a good one. Look at this handwriting. And these first few lines—they take me right to Thornfield Hall. If I didn't know better, I'd say it was the same voice as *Jane Eyre*. The same narrative style."

"That's because it was written by Charlotte Brontë from 1854 to 1855. She died in March, sadly leaving the ending for us to decide."

Eloise gaped. "You're serious, aren't you? This is the *original* copy of the sequel to my favorite book ever?" At Jane's nod, Eloise stared at the manuscript again. "Where did you get it?"

"That's the crazy part. Storyton Hall has a whole library of treasures just like this. A hidden library. The collection has been kept in the dark for decades because some of the books were once considered dangerous or inflammatory. Others were kept secret at their owner's request for personal reasons that can't possibly matter anymore. I want to bring all of these books from the dark into the light. I want people to read them. And I could use your help in making this dream a reality. It's going to be a major undertaking."

"Well, I just happen to have some extra time on

my hands. With Lachlan gone until who knows when, I could use the distraction. Sure, I could keep working on my archery—" she suddenly stopped and grabbed hold of Jane's arm. "Wait. Did you say a *whole library* of books like this?"

Jane laughed. It was fun watching the realization spread across her best friend's face.

"I have so many questions, Jane. So. Many. Questions."

Pointing at the manuscript, Jane asked, "Would you like to see more books in our special collection?"

"Are you kidding? I'd kill to see them!" Eloise cried.

Jane let her friend see the anguish in her eyes. "That's just it. People will kill to find them. Which is exactly why I want to donate or sell our treasures. I love books, Eloise. You know I do. But I love my family and friends more. Which is why I need your help."

Eloise took Jane's hand. "I won't pretend to understand what you're asking of me, but whatever it is, I'll do it. I've always been, and will always be, your partner in crime."

"It's time to hang up your hat, Dr. Watson. We're going to be book heroes instead. We're going to send hundreds of long-hidden stories out into the world—"

"Where they belong," Eloise finished for her.

EPILOGUE

Eloise took Jane's request to heart.

Every afternoon, after she closed Run for Cover, she hopped on her bike and rode to Storyton Hall. Despite having worked at her bookshop for hours, Eloise was always eager to help Jane contact museums, pack books for shipment, or try to put a number value on the latest treasures laid out on a reading table in the Henry James Library.

"I thought I'd be tired, pulling all these double shifts," she told Jane as they wrapped up a stack of materials earmarked for an upcoming Sotheby's Books & Manuscripts auction. "But the second I see what you have waiting, I get a fresh burst of energy."

Jane understood exactly what she meant. "I know. I'm never too tired to work on this project. Cleaning the twins' bathroom, on the other hand . . ."

The two friends laughed.

"This is the first time you've mentioned selling material from the secret library," Eloise said and opened the cover of the top book on the stack. "You've already given away a fortune in rare books, and I'm glad that you're actually going to make money from some of these."

Seeing that her friend was examining the

frontispiece of the old book with an expression of distaste, Jane knew that Eloise had come across an engraving of a slave auction. The book, a slim, innocuous-looking volume, was filled with suggestions on purchasing and owning slaves. It was an abhorrent read. Jane had made it through three chapters before deciding she'd had enough.

"I could have given this to a museum," she told Eloise. "But this is one of several books I wish we'd never owned. I don't want to be connected to it, and I'm hoping that by taking the money from its sale and doing something positive with it, I'll feel better about its existence."

Eloise gestured at the books they still needed to wrap.

"These should bring a pretty penny. What will you do with the money?"

"I plan to donate to several literary organizations." Jane carefully wrapped a book in white tissue paper. "I'm also going to use some of the money to update our heating and air-conditioning systems. It's long overdue, and I can't afford such a major expense. All of our extra funds are devoted to the spa project. If there's any left after that, I'd love to repair the folly and bring the orchards back to life."

"I like that idea," said Eloise, holding up the offensive book. "This dead tree could create living trees."

The two women prepared the books for

shipment. After each book was wrapped in tissue, it was then cushioned in white kraft paper and several layers of Bubble Wrap.

"Isn't Sotheby's expecting you to provide documentation on everything you send?" Eloise asked when they were done.

"I have letters from the original owners to accompany a few. The letters are valuable documents themselves and will undoubtedly be sold as separate lots. As for the rest?" Jane shrugged. "Sotheby's has experts to determine authenticity. I'm not worried about being unable to provide provenance for every book. Imagine how ashamed you'd be to learn that a relative of yours had owned, or, God forbid, written, that book about the slave trade?"

"We can't erase the past. We can only strive to improve the future," Eloise said. She rested her hands on the shipping box. "Listen to me, waxing philosophical. I should shut up, so I can get back to *Jane of Thornfield Hall*. You're so mean—refusing to let me take it home. Especially after all I do for you."

Though Jane knew Eloise was teasing, she felt compelled to respond. "You know how valuable that original manuscript is. It has to stay at Storyton Hall until I figure out what to do with it. And you know that I can't copy it. That would be wrong too."

"Just promise that you won't give it to the

Brontë Parsonage Museum until I'm finished reading it, okay?"

Eloise looked so aggrieved that Jane had to laugh. "I'd never do that to you. In fact, I thought I'd show it to the rest of the Cover Girls at our next meeting."

"You mean, at your birthday meeting?"

Jane waved this off. "I'd rather Jane Austen be the center of attention."

Eloise rolled her eyes. "Every year, we read an Austen novel for your birthday meeting. I love these books, you know I do, but one of these years, you should do something different. Surprise us."

"I like Austen novels," Jane protested. "I find them comforting. Besides, it's like reading a new book every time I revisit them. Not because they've changed since I last read the story, but because I have."

Eloise shot her an amused glance. "You're the one who talked about making big changes. I'm just reminding you of your goals."

"I'll do something for my fortieth," Jane said.

"But that's years away!" Eloise protested.

"Not very many." She pointed at the shipping box. "Anyway, this is far more important than a birthday. This is my plans becoming a reality. This is the end to secrecy. It's the best gift I could ever give to myself, to everyone in Storyton Hall, and to readers all over the world. In fact, I think this might be my most exciting birthday yet."

Jane received Edwin's invitation to a private dinner by mail. Though the envelope bore Edwin's elegant cursive and a postage stamp had been neatly affixed to the corner, Nandi hand-delivered the missive.

The two women had been meeting on a regular basis to reverse Cyril Steward's cultural appropriation. However, returning the African artifacts he'd put on display in the Isak Dinesen Safari Room wasn't a simple endeavor. In addition to the emails she sent and the phone calls she made, Jane had to fill out countless forms and jump through dozens of bureaucratic hoops.

"Why is it so hard to do the right thing?" she'd shouted in frustration one day after another call with a customs official had been abruptly disconnected.

Nandi had laughed and clapped her on the back. "Because it just is. And I know I could be in a jail cell if you'd wanted me there, so I shouldn't be laughing, but your face turns all kinds of red when you're mad."

Knowing this was true, Jane had laughed too.

When Nandi showed up at Storyton Hall two days before their next scheduled meeting, Jane had a flashback to the time the postmistress had delivered a postcard from Edwin. A postcard he'd been forced to write. The memory reminded Jane of how she'd almost lost her boys. And Edwin too.

"Don't worry," Nandi had said, seeing the expression in Jane's eyes. As she pressed the envelope into Jane's hand, she gave her a comforting squeeze. "This one should make you happy. I happen to know what it says. You have a good time, you hear? You deserve a night out. We women forget to take care of ourselves. You take a break from all your worries and just enjoy yourself."

In her office, Jane had read the invitation. Edwin had planned an intimate birthday celebration for two at Daily Bread. Noting the suggestion that the recommended dress called for cocktail attire, Jane smiled. Edwin was making it clear that this wasn't to be an ordinary dinner.

That Friday night, Jane was waiting in the lobby per Edwin's instructions.

At seven o'clock on the button, Butterworth cleared his throat and said, "Mr. Alcott has arrived, Miss Jane."

He opened the massive oak door and wished Jane a pleasant evening. She was so stunned by what saw in front of Storyton Hall that she nearly forgot to say thank you. Butterworth gave her an indulgent nod of understanding. After all, it wasn't every day that someone appeared driving a horse-drawn carriage.

"What do you think?" Edwin asked, nimbly jumping down from the carriage. "Sam hooked me up. He's been training Sonny here to pull carriages and hopes to teach several of his horses to pull sleighs." He put his hand on the horse's shoulder. "Wintertime is pretty slow at Hilltop Stables, and Sam has decided to perk up his income by offering horse-drawn sleigh rides. I wouldn't be surprised if he doesn't call you to talk about adding these to Storyton Hall's list of winter activities."

Still astounded, Jane pointed at the carriage. "This is straight out of *Mansfield Park*. Where on earth did you get it?"

"A museum curator friend owed me a favor. The carriage is on loan for tonight only. I have to return it tomorrow. We're on the clock, just like Cinderella. Only I'm not taking you to a ball. We're having a nice, quiet dinner for two."

Edwin gave Sonny an affectionate pat and then performed a rakish bow for Jane's benefit. He was dressed in a formal suit, complete with gloves. His tie was the color of ripe persimmons. Jane didn't think she'd ever found him so dashing, and she longed to kiss him. Instead, she settled for accepting his outstretched hand. Jane was thankful that her dress, which was dark garnet, with a formfitting bodice and loose skirt, allowed her to climb into the carriage with relative ease.

Once she was settled on the seat, Edwin held the reins in one hand and pulled her closer with the other.

"You're more beautiful than the stars."

And then he kissed her.

The kiss took her breath away. And Jane would have gone right on kissing Edwin had Sonny not shifted slightly, causing the carriage to rock a bit.

Jane and Edwin broke apart with a laugh.

Edwin took the reins in both hands and waved at Butterworth, who had been pretending not to watch from his position at the front door. Butterworth dipped his chin in acknowledgment, but not before Jane saw the smile tugging at the corners of his mouth.

Edwin let Sonny walk at a leisurely pace. After the carriage rumbled over the bridge and they entered Storyton Village, the locals came to a dead stop to gawk and wave. Jane waved back, feeling like royalty.

When he reached the café, Edwin helped Jane down and asked her to go inside while he released Sonny from his harness and led him around back.

"I want to make sure he has water and a snack. I'll join you in a few minutes."

Jane pushed open the door to the café and had barely stepped into the dining room when the silent space exploded with cries of "Surprise!"

Reeling backward in shock, Jane blinked hard.

For a long moment, she felt like a deer in the middle of the road. She couldn't do anything but stand and stare.

Finally, the dimmed house lights were turned up

to their full brightness and Jane saw the familiar faces of her friends beaming at her in delight. All the Cover Girls, including Anna, were standing among the tables. Every woman was dressed to the nines. Violet had obviously done their hair. Delicate sprays of baby's breath were clipped to elaborate braids, buns, or twists.

The café had been transformed too. The interior typically featured British colonial furniture with Indian and African accents. Tonight, the antique maps on the walls had been replaced with framed watercolor paintings of Jane Austen book covers. Black-and-white banners decorated with Jane Austen silhouettes hung from the ceiling. Thousands of tea candles burned on the tables, the hostess stand, and in the lounge area. The centerpiece on each café table was a posy of tea roses in a shiny silver vase. A florist stake poked out from the middle of the roses. Attached to the stake was small flag bearing a line from an Austen novel.

Jane caught a quick glimpse of a cut-glass punch bowl with matching glasses and rows of champagne flutes on a buffet table before Eloise enfolded her in an embrace.

"Happy Birthday!" she softly exclaimed. "Were you surprised?"

"Completely," said Jane. "I thought Edwin was cooking me dinner. I expected the whole place to be empty, so when you all yelled, I nearly had a heart attack."

Eloise gestured at the other Cover Girls. "Edwin is cooking. For all of us." She nudged Jane in the side. "Sorry to fool you into thinking you were having an intimate dinner, but he can have you to himself later. Right now, you belong to us."

One by one, Jane received hugs from her friends.

Someone put a champagne flute in her hand, and Eloise got the party started with a toast. "In *Northanger Abbey*, Austen writes, 'There is nothing I would not do for those who are really my friends.' That line reminds me of our Jane. To the most generous, most beautiful, and most loyal of friends. To Jane!"

"To Jane!" echoed the rest of the Cover Girls.

After the toast, Edwin appeared with a white napkin draped over his arm. The women fell quiet in anticipation of his announcement.

"Ladies, you'll find mini quiche, pigeon pie, Bath buns, asparagus on toast, breadless cucumber sandwiches, and spring rolls with edible flowers on the buffet. In addition to champagne, we have a traditional punch such as Mr. Weston might have served in *Emma*. It is made with a mysterious spirit called arrack. This spirit is blended with lemon, water, sugar, and spices. The orange peel is mostly decorative. As a note of caution, I want to tell you that this is the headiest punch I've ever tasted."

Taking this as a dare, the Cover Girls practically tripped over each other to fill their glasses.

The women drank punch, sampled the appetizers, and paired off to take the Jane Austen trivia challenge Eloise had created. Jane's partner was Mrs. Pratt, and she correctly identified which character spoke the quote in question until Jane got down to the last question.

"A character from *Pride and Prejudice* said, 'I do not cough for my own amusement.' Who was it?"

Mrs. Pratt's brows knit in concentration. "One of those giggly, insipid, younger Bennett girls, no doubt. But which one?"

Jane was impressed. "Wow. I wouldn't have gotten that close, and I've read this book a dozen times."

"Let me finish my punch. Maybe the alcohol will bring me some clarity."

Jane laughed. "I don't think that's how alcohol works."

As Mrs. Pratt drank and thought, and then refilled her cup and drank and thought some more, Jane glanced around the room, soaking in the sight of her friends. She saw pink cheeks and smiles on every face. As she looked from Mrs. Pratt, to Mabel and Betsy, to Anna and Violet, to Phoebe and Eloise, she was almost overwhelmed by love for these women.

In the Cover Girls, she'd found a group of

like-minded ladies who shared her affection for books. However, she'd also found a group of funny, smart, reliable, hard-working women who enriched her life on a daily basis. Whether she saw them at their weekly meeting or someplace in the village, they all brought their own kind of sunshine into Jane's world.

"Don't get upset," said Mrs. Pratt, suddenly sounding alarmed. "I'll stop stalling and guess Lizzy."

Jane wiped away a tear and laughed again. "I'm not upset. I'm just counting my blessings. And sorry, but it's not Lizzy. It's Kitty."

"Ugh! Kitty!" Mrs. Pratt sounded so put out that Jane offered to refill her punch glass.

"I should be refilling yours instead. You're the birthday girl," she said, snatching Jane's empty cup out of her hand with a mischievous smile.

Edwin and Magnus, the café manager, cleared the appetizer buffet and laid it with the dinner items. Once again, Edwin moved to the center of the room to announce the dishes. "Ladies, for your Jane Steward Loves Jane Austen Supper, we have a roasted loin of pork with onions, poached salmon, glazed carrots, spinach salad, and an assortment of savory tartlets. Magnus will be pouring Madeira to accompany your meal. It has notes of caramel and hazelnut. If you prefer something else, please let him know. We have a variety of other beverages."

After performing a stiff bow that made the women giggle, Edwin pressed a button near the light switch and harp music floated out of the wall-mounted speakers. He then returned to the kitchen.

"What a catch," said Violet and she lined up with Jane to serve herself from the buffet's bounty.

"He's not half-bad," Jane joked, but her heart swelled when she thought of all Edwin had done to make this night special.

I'll show him my gratitude when we're alone, she thought.

Later, when it was time to blow out the candles rimming the edge of the two-tiered Jane Austen book cover cake Mrs. Hubbard had made her, Jane wondered what to wish for.

As she looked at the faces of her friends, and to where Edwin stood near the kitchen doors, she couldn't think of anything she needed. She'd been through a terrible ordeal, but it was over now. She had Uncle Aloysius, Aunt Octavia, and Fitz and Hem. She had the Fins, who were more family than protectors. And she'd found love with Edwin.

On top of all this, she had these amazing women. She also lived in the most wonderful place in the world. She was able to meet new readers and bibliophiles on a daily basis. Every day, she could share her home and the books within its walls with people who understood the value of the written word. Hers might be a world of turmoil and strife, but it was also a world of beauty and books.

"Well, Jane," Eloise prompted. "Make a wish."

After burying William, what Jane had wanted most was to move forward. She'd wanted to smile and to laugh. To focus on the future. Tonight, Eloise and the Cover Girls had given her what she most needed. A shining, perfect moment to celebrate the end of a dark time and the beginning of brighter days.

"It's already come true," Jane said. "Thanks to everyone in this room."

She blew out the candles.

Mrs. Pratt pretended to pout. "If that's true, then you probably won't want your presents."

Jane turned to see a stack of gift-wrapped packages that could only be one thing. Books. A stack of lovely, lovely books.

"Oh, I definitely want those," Jane said, and the little café filled with laughter.

ABOUT THE AUTHOR

ELLERY ADAMS has written over thirty mystery novels and can't imagine spending a day away from the keyboard. Ms. Adams, a native New Yorker, has had a lifelong love affair with stories, food, rescue animals, and large bodies of water. When not working on her next novel, she bakes, gardens, spoils her three cats, and spends far too much time on Pinterest. She lives with her husband and two children (aka the Trolls) in Chapel Hill, North Carolina. For more information, please visit www.elleryadamsmysteries.com.

Center Point Large Print
600 Brooks Road / PO Box 1
Thorndike, ME 04986-0001 USA

(207) 568-3717

US & Canada:
1 800 929-9108
www.centerpointlargeprint.com